Evelyn Abbott, Thomas Kerchever Arnold

A Practical Introduction to Greek Prose Composition

Evelyn Abbott, Thomas Kerchever Arnold

A Practical Introduction to Greek Prose Composition

ISBN/EAN: 9783337367275

Printed in Europe, USA, Canada, Australia, Japan

Cover: Foto ©Andreas Hilbeck / pixelio.de

More available books at **www.hansebooks.com**

A PRACTICAL INTRODUCTION

TO

GREEK PROSE COMPOSITION

BY

THOMAS KERCHEVER ARNOLD, M.A.

NEW EDITION, Edited and Revised

BY

EVELYN ABBOTT, M.A., LL.D.

FELLOW AND TUTOR OF BALLIOL COLLEGE, OXFORD

RIVINGTONS
WATERLOO PLACE, LONDON
1890

PREFACE

THOSE who are familiar with Mr. T. Kerchever Arnold's "Introduction to Greek Prose Composition" will find in this revised version of the book much that is familiar and something that is new. I have endeavoured to keep everything that seemed of value, and often I have adhered to the words of the explanations because I wished to preserve, so far as possible, the continuity of the book. But I have added illustrations, altered the order of the sections, and indeed re-arranged the matter of the sections themselves, wherever I thought that, by doing so, I could gain in clearness or simplicity; I have also rewritten, almost entirely, the sentences in the exercises. The precise arrangement which is best for teaching is a difficult question, and I do not suppose that the order in which I have placed the sections will be accepted by every one. But with the help of the vocabulary and the references it is quite possible to do the exercises in a different order from that given, or to omit any which do not appear to be needed. The lists of accents, irregular verbs, &c., which Mr. Arnold prefixed to his book, I have omitted, because all that is required on these matters can be obtained from the Greek Accidence; and I have also omitted the references to grammars now no longer in general use among scholars, the list of particles, and the questions on syntax at the end of the exercises. The table of idioms is retained, with alterations, and references to it are given in the exercises—though I would strongly recommend the student to learn this table by heart, and so render reference unnecessary. The vocabulary is, I believe, nearly complete,* and the index of matters will serve as an independent table of references, whenever those given in the text are insufficient.

The book is merely an "Introduction." It aims at teaching and illustrating the more elementary constructions of Greek grammar. But any one who works through it will find himself familiar with a great part of the constructions with which he is confronted in his reading, and till the latter part of the course at school this is as much, perhaps, as it is worth while to teach of Greek Composition. The finer applications of the prepositions and the particles, the exact use of the vocabulary, can hardly be gained in any other way than by constant and idiomatic—not merely correct—translation from Greek into English. Yet in the sections on ἔχω and ποιοῦμαι, &c. (§§ 59, 60), I have endeavoured to point out one way, at least, in which the Greek mode of expression differs from the English. To pursue the subject further and examine even the most striking differences in the two vocabularies —*e. g.* the use of abstract words, the advantage and disadvantage of gender in nouns—would have largely increased the size of the book, and carried it beyond the

---

* Synonymous expressions are not always represented; *e. g. to be afraid* is = *to fear*, and therefore not introduced in the vocabulary.

object with which it was originally composed and has now been revised.

It is with some misgiving that I send to the press a revised version of a book so well known and long tried as this. I am conscious that I may have spoiled where I have sought to improve, that in attempting to give what I believe to be the true account of some constructions, I may have used language less precise than that of the old explanations. A well-worn formula has, moreover, many advantages against a new one; we know its limits, we do not demand for it a universal application when we have long learned to take it with due modifications; we often use it as an indicator of knowledge which has gathered round it in our own minds—as the symbol in a *memoria technica*. New explanations, on the other hand, give us trouble; they set us in fresh grooves, where for a time it is not possible to run smoothly, even if we do not get off the road altogether. In regard to any changes I have made of this kind, I can only say that throughout my task I have kept before me a deep sense of the great services which for many years past Mr. Arnold's book has rendered to the student of Greek composition.

EVELYN ABBOTT

BALLIOL COLLEGE
OXFORD

TABLE OF CONTENTS

The figures in the Exercises above the line refer to the Table of Idioms at page 123.

The Article

§ 1. *The Definite and Indefinite Article.*

(1) The English 'definite article,' *the*, is translated into Greek by ὁ, ἡ, τό (Primer of Greek Accidence, 34).

The horse, ὁ ἵππος. *the woman,* ἡ γυνή. *the slave,* τὸ ἀνδράποδον. *the men came out from the city,* οἱ ἄνδρες ἐξῆλθον ἐκ τῆς πόλεως.

Obs. i.—The Greeks often use the definite article where we omit it, e. g. *the beauty of virtue,* τὸ κάλλος τῆς ἀρετῆς (§ 5 (2)); *this city,* ἥδε ἡ πόλις (§ 6); and with proper names, ὁ Σωκράτης, *Socrates* (as a famous man, § 4), &c.

Obs. ii.—The article may be separated from the substantive to which it belongs, e. g. instead of τὸ κάλλος τῆς ἀρετῆς, we can say, τὸ τῆς ἀρετῆς κάλλος. Similarly, αἱ τῆς πόλεως ὁδοί, *the streets of the city;* αἱ εἰς τὴν πόλιν φέρουσαι ὁδοί, *the streets (roads) leading into the city* (§ 9 (2)).

Obs. iii.—The forms ὁ, ἡ, οἱ, αἱ are *atona* (Prim. 30).

(2) The English indefinite article, '*a*,' is not expressed in Greek; *a man* is ἀνήρ, *a horse,* ἵππος. But when a particular person or thing is meant, though not named—in other words, wherever we might substitute *a certain* for *a*—the pronoun τις, *a certain one* (Prim. 96), should be used.

A certain man, ἄνθρωπός τις; *a certain slave came,* δοῦλός τις ἦλθεν.

Obs. i.—τις is *enclitic* (Prim. 29).

Obs. ii.—With names signifying the nation to which a man belongs, ἀνήρ is sometimes used, e. g. ἀνὴρ Φοῖνιξ, *a Phœnician;* and in like manner with the names of professions. e. g. ἀνὴρ μάντις, *a prophet.*

B

EXERCISE 1.

VOCABULARY.—*beautiful*, καλός. *to bring*, ἄγειν. *camp*, στρατόπεδον. *cow*, βοῦς, ἡ. *to happen to be*, τυγχάνειν ὤν (§ 35 (2)). *to have*, ἔχειν. *at home*, οἴκοι, ἔνδον. *horse*, ἵππος, ὁ. *house*, οἰκία. *in*, εἰς, with acc. (= into), ἐν, with dat. (of rest in a place). *Lydian*, Λυδός. *man*, ἀνήρ, ἄνθρωπος. *many*, πολύς, pl. πολλοί, αἱ, ἁ (Prim. 66). *to mount*, ἀναβαίνειν. *to pasture*, νέμεσθαι. *to present oneself, to be present*, παρεῖναι. *to ride away*, ἀπελαύνειν. *to send for*, μεταπέμπεσθαι. *servant*, παῖς, ὁ. *village*, κώμη. *who, which*, ὅς, ἥ, ὅ.

Obs. i.—Where in English we use the preposition *with* to denote *possession, accompaniment*, the Greeks often use the participles of the verbs ἔχω, *I have*; ἄγω, *I bring*, or *lead*; e. g. ἦλθεν ὁ δοῦλος ἔχων γράμματα, *the slave came with a letter*.

Obs. ii.—ἀνήρ is a man as opposed to a woman; ἄνθρωπος is a 'person;' hence the plural of ἄνθρωπος is used for '*people*,' '*persons*.'

1. He had a horse. 2. He had a beautiful horse. 3. A Lydian came bringing a beautiful horse. 4. He happened to be[49] in the village. 5. The men came bringing the horses. 6. The beautiful horses of the Lydians are brought. 7. Some (*certain*) men presented themselves in (εἰς) the camp *with* (= *bringing*) beautiful horses. 8. In (ἐν) the villages were many cows *at pasture* (= *pasturing*). 9. The men are in the house. 10. The king is at home. 11. The king sent for a horse. 12. The servant brought the horse. 13. The king *mounted and* (*having mounted*) rode away (**34**, (2) *b*). 14. He came to a village in which were many people.

§ 2. *Subject and Predicate.*

The article is often used to distinguish the subject of a sentence from the complement.

βασιλεὺς ἐγένετο ὁ πτωχός, *the beggar became a king.*

Hence when the substantive has the article, and the adjective has not, the latter is a predicate.

ἡ γυνὴ καλή, *the woman is beautiful* (Syntax, 56 ff.)[a]

---

[a] 'But 'when one part of a thing is to be distinguished from another part of the same' (Clyde, Syntax, § 9, Obs. 3), the predicative form is used for the attributive: ἔσχατον τὸ ὄρος, *the end of the mountain;* ἐπ' ἄκροις τοῖς ποσίν, *on tip-toes*, and the like.

These are quite simple instances, but the same rule holds good in less obvious constructions.

ὁ κύων τὴν οὐρὰν μακρὰν ἔχει, *the dog has a long tail.*

Here μακράν is the predicate because the assertion is that the tail of the dog is long.

ἥδετο ἐπὶ πλουσίοις τοῖς πολίταις, *he rejoiced at the wealth of the citizens (at the citizens (being) wealthy).*

Here the fact that the citizens are wealthy is the cause of joy, hence πλουσίοις is a predicate.

Obs. i.—To express, for instance, that a person ' has a very beautiful head,' or ' very beautiful hands,' the Greeks said : ' has *the* head very beautiful,' ' has *the* hands very beautiful.' In other words, they assumed that the person had a head and hands, and stated (predicated) that they were beautiful.

Obs. ii.—Commit carefully to memory the difference between—

ἡ καλὴ γυνή, or ἡ γυνὴ ἡ καλή, *the beautiful woman.* } and {	καλὴ ἡ γυνή, or ἡ γυνὴ καλή, *the woman (is) beautiful.*	

Exercise 2.

Vocabulary.—*also,* καί. *art,* τέχνη. *citizen,* πολίτης. *to come,* ἰέναι (for aorist use ἐλθεῖν). *in the evening.* ἑσπέριος. *few,* ὀλίγοι. *fleeting (short),* βραχύς. *to go away,* ἀπιέναι (for aorist use ἀπελθεῖν). *good,* ἀγαθός. *how,* ὡς. *just,* δίκαιος. *long,* μακρός. *memory,* μνήμη. *in great numbers* (= *many*), πολύς, πολλοί. *to perish,* ἀπόλλυσθαι. *prone to fall,* οὐκ ἀσφαλής (lit. *not secure*). *quick (swift),* ταχύς. *on the third day,* τριταῖος. *time,* χρόνος.

1. The men are few. 2. 'Art is long and time is fleeting.' 3. The citizens went away *in great numbers.* 4. The citizens came *on the third day.* 5. The just are also good. 6. The memory of the good perishes *quickly.* 7. How *quickly* perishes the memory of the good ! 8. The swift are prone to fall. 9. They came *in the evening.* 10. The men came with (*bringing*) the horses *on the third day.*

2. Use μέν—δέ, § 11 *a*, Obs. 3, &c. Use the adjective. Adverbs and adverbial phrases in English are often rendered by adjectives in Greek.

VOCABULARY.—*bring down*, κατάγειν. *brown*, ξουθός. *to conquer, overthrow*, νικᾶν. *crocodile*, κροκόδειλος. *to be delighted at*, ἥδεσθαι ἐπί, with dat. *to be distressed at*, ἄχθεσθαι ἐπί, with dat. *eagle*, ἀετός. *enemy*, πολέμιος. *exceedingly*, use superlative of adjective, e. g. *exceedingly beautiful*, κάλλιστος. *eye*, ὀφθαλμός. *feather*, πτερόν. *friend*, φίλος. *general*, στρατηγός. *golden*, χρύσεος. *head*, κεφαλή. *king*, βασιλεύς (Prim. 41). *large*, μέγας. *nightingale*, ἀηδών, ἡ. *Pactolus*, Πακτωλός. *poor*, πτωχός. *to be prosperous*, εὐτυχεῖν. *to retire*, ἀποχωρεῖν. *sand*, ψάμμος, ἡ. *to be slain (to perish)*, ἀπόλλυσθαι. *small*, μικρός. *soldier*, στρατιώτης. *statue*, ἀνδριάς, ὁ. *sweet*, ἡδύς. *to be unfortunate*, δυστυχεῖν. *voice*, φωνή. *wicked*, κακός. *wing*, πτέρυξ, υγος, ἡ.

1. The eagle has large wings[4]. 2. The crocodile has small eyes[4]. 3. The poverty of the citizens grieved the king[4]. 4. The overthrow of the enemy delighted the king. 5. In distress at the slaughter of his soldiers, the general retired. 6. The head of the statue is exceedingly beautiful. 7. The good are pleased at the prosperity of their friends[4]. 8. The voice of the nightingale is sweet. 9. The feathers of the nightingale are brown. 10. The Pactolus brings down sands of gold. 11. The wicked rejoice at the misfortunes of the good.

3. Say : The king was grieved at the citizens (*being*) poor. 4. The king was delighted at the enemy being overthrown (*participle*). 5. Being distressed at his [9] soldiers being slain. 6. The statue has the head exceedingly beautiful. 7. At their friends being prosperous. 8. Has the voice sweet. 11. At the good being unfortunate.

§ 3. *The Article used to denote a Class.*

Whenever it is intended to express a class, or any individual who represents that class, the noun, whether singular or plural, takes the article, as οἱ πλούσιοι, *the wealthy*; τὰ κακά, *evil things, what is evil*; αἱ καλαὶ γυναῖκες, *beautiful women*; ὁ κύων, *the dog* (as a type of the class). (Syntax, 55.)

☞ Observe especially the use of the article with ἄλλος, *other;*
πολύς, *many (much);* πᾶς, *all.*

ἄλλοι, *others.*	οἱ ἄλλοι, *the rest.*
πολλοί, *many.*	οἱ πολλοί, *the many, the multitude.*
πᾶς, *all, every.*	ὁ πᾶς, *the whole.*[a]

Exercise 4.

Vocabulary.—*affairs,* πράγματα.   *all,* πᾶς (Prim. 60).
always, ἀεί.   *bad,* κακός.   *city, state,* πόλις, ἡ (Prim. 40).
full, πλήρης.   *to govern,* ἄρχειν, with gen.   *honour,* τιμή.   *to
honour,* τιμᾶν.   *to manage,* πράττειν.   *not,* οὐ.   *obedient-to-law,*
νόμιμος.   *old, old man,* γέρων.   *to pursue,* διώκειν.   *rich,* πλούσιος.   *tumult,* θόρυβος.   *wise,* σοφός.   *worthy of,* ἄξιος, with gen.

1. Rich men are not always worthy of honour.   2. Good
men[5] are honoured in every land.   3. The old are wise.   4.
Honour the old.   5. The just are those who are[5] obedient to
law (*are the obedient-to-law*).   6. Ever pursue what is good.
7. Those who manage the affairs of the state[15] are wise (*those
managing*).   8. He was slain in pursuit of (*pursuing*) the
enemy.   9. Bad men are enemies of the state.   10. The rest[5]
went away.   11. The multitude govern the city.   12. All the
city[5] was full of tumult.

§ 4. *The Article with Proper Names.*

The article is not commonly used with proper names
unless the name has been previously mentioned and is
now referred to, or is, for some reason, prominent, as the
name of a well-known and distinguished man.

Κῦρον μεταπέμπεται, *he sends for Cyrus;*
ἀναβαίνει οὖν ὁ Κῦρος, *Cyrus, therefore, goes up.*
Σωκράτης, *Socrates* (any one of the name);
ὁ Σωκράτης, *Socrates,* the celebrated philosopher.
Ἀθῆναι, *Athens;* αἱ Ἀθῆναι, *Athens* (as mentioned before, or as a
   celebrated city).

Obs.—If the proper name is followed by a description which has
   the article, the proper name is without the article, e. g. Σωκράτης
   ὁ φιλόσοφος, *Socrates, the philosopher.* The names of rivers and
   cities are sometimes used thus: ὁ Εὐφράτης ποταμός, *the river
   Euphrates;* ἡ Μένδη πόλις, *the city Mende* (Syntax, 57, Obs.).

---

[a] πᾶσα ἡ πόλις and ἡ πᾶσα πόλις are used for *the whole city,* but
πᾶς is *more emphatic* in the second form.

EXERCISE 5.

VOCABULARY.—*Alcibiades*, Ἀλκιβιάδης. *Assinarus*, Ἀσσί-ναρος. *Athenian*, Ἀθηναῖος. *Babylon*, Βαβυλών, *ἡ. battle*, μάχη. *to besiege*, πολιορκεῖν. *Cyrus*. Κῦρος. *to defend*, ἀμύνειν, with dat. *Demosthenes*, Δημοσθένης. *to fight*, μάχεσ-θαι. *to be general*, στρατηγεῖν. *Gylippus*, Γύλιππος. *island*, νῆσος, *ἡ. to march against*, στρατεύεσθαι ἐπί, with acc. *Nicias*, Νικίας. *now* (conj.), δέ; this word is used in Greek to connect sentences where in English no connecting word is required (Syntax, 125). *to refuse*, οὐκ ἐθέλειν (*to be not willing*). *to retreat*, ἀναχωρεῖν. *river*, ποταμός. *Sicily*, Σικελία. *Syracuse*, Συράκουσαι (nom. plur.).

1. The Athenians sent for Alcibiades. 2. Alcibiades refused to go. 3. The Athenians marched against Sicily. 4. Now Sicily is a large island, with (= *having*) many cities. 5. They besieged the city of Syracuse⁶. 6. Gylippus, the Lacedaemonian, defended the city. 7. The Athenians *fought* many battles, *and* (Ex. 1, 13) retreated. 8. The generals were Nicias and Demosthenes. 9. They were overthrown at the river Assinarus⁶. 10. Cyrus took the city of Babylon⁶.

§ 5. *The Article as a Possessive, and with Abstract Words.*

(1) *My, your, his,* &c., must be translated by the article when it is quite obvious to whom the thing in question belongs.

ἀλγῶ τὴν κεφαλήν, *I have a pain in my head* (Syntax, 54, *Obs.* i.).

But whenever there is any opposition (as when *mine* is opposed to *yours* or any other person's) the possessive pronouns must be used, and the article with them.

λέγω τὴν ἐμὴν πόλιν, οὐ τὴν σήν, *I mean my city, not yours.*

(2) Names of materials and abstract nouns take the article, as ὁ χρυσός, *gold;* ἡ ἀρετή, *virtue.* This is the

case when the material is spoken of as representing the class, and the abstract noun used as a single idea; otherwise, the article is generally omitted (§ 10 (5)).

ὁ χρυσὸς τοῦ ἀργύρου βαρύτερός ἐστιν, *gold is heavier than silver.*
λυσιτελέστερον ἡ ἀδικία τῆς δικαιοσύνης, *injustice (is) more advantageous than justice.*

Exercise 6.

Vocabulary.—*advantageous,* λυσιτελής. *to cling to,* ἀντέχειν, *with gen. country* (as opposed to the *town*), ἀγρός. *first,* πρῶτος. *freedom,* ἐλευθερία. *gold,* χρυσός. *as good as,* ἀντί, *with gen. to have one's head broken,* συντρίβεσθαι τῆς κεφαλῆς. *heavy,* βαρύς. *iron,* σίδηρος. *justice,* δικαιοσύνη. *lead,* μόλυβδος. *or,* ἤ. *riches,* πλοῦτος. *to send,* πέμπειν. *silver,* ἄργυρος. *slave,* οἰκέτης. *stone,* λίθος. *street,* ὁδός, ἡ. *to take place,* γίγνεσθαι. *truth,* ἀλήθεια. *valuable,* τιμήεις. *vice,* κακία. *virtue,* ἀρετή. *wisdom,* σοφία. *wood,* ξύλον.

1. He sent his horse into the city [13] (§ 10 (1)). 2. I have sent my slave into (the) country [13]. 3. He will bring my horse. 4. A fight took place in the street. 5. We all had our heads (*sing.*) broken. 6. Gold is more valuable than silver [8]. 7. Iron is heavier than wood or stone, but lead is heavier than iron. 8. Virtue is better policy (*is more advantageous*) than vice. 9. Wisdom is great riches (*is as good as*). 10. Justice is the first of virtues. 11. Let us cling to freedom and truth.

§ 6. *The Article with Pronouns.*

(1) The article is used with the possessive pronouns, which is not the case in English.

ὁ σὸς δοῦλος, *your slave;* οὑμὸς (= ὁ ἐμὸς) πατήρ, *my father.*

Obs. i.—If the possessive pronoun is a predicate, the article is not used : ἡμέτερος ὁ πυραμοῦς, *the prize* (liter. *the cake*) *is ours.*

Obs. ii.—With *substantives* possession is expressed by the genitive case, e. g. οὐχ ἡμετέρα ἐστὶν ἡ πόλις ἀλλὰ Θηβαίων, *the city is not ours, but the Thebans';* οὐχ ἐν τῇ ἡμετέρᾳ ἐγένετο ἡ μάχη ἀλλ' ἐν τῇ Θηβαίων, *the battle did not take place in our (land), but in the Thebans'.*

(2) When ὅδε, ἐκεῖνος, οὗτος (§ **13**) are used with substantives, the substantive takes the article: ἥδε ἡ πόλις, *this city;* οὗτος ὁ ἀνήρ, *this man;* ἐκείνη ἡ γυνή, *that woman* (or the order may be: ἡ πόλις ἥδε; ἀνήρ (= ὁ ἀνήρ) οὗτος; ἡ γυνή ἐκείνη).

If an adjective is added, it is placed between the article and the substantive, as ἥδε ἡ μεγάλη πόλις, *this great city.*

> *Obs.*—Distinguish between
>
> τούτῳ τῷ διδασκάλῳ χρῶνται, *they employ this teacher;*
> and
> τούτῳ διδασκάλῳ χρῶνται, *they employ this man as a teacher.*

Exercise 7.

VOCABULARY.—*Æschines,* Αἰσχίνης. *black,* μέλας (Prim. 65). *but,* ἀλλά. *has come* (= *is present*), πάρεστι. *deed,* πρᾶγμα. *to fear,* φοβεῖσθαι. *false,* ψευδής. *gain, benefit,* ὠφέλεια. *to intend, to be about to do,* μέλλειν, with infin.[*] *to invade,* εἰσβάλλειν. *Lacedæmonian,* Λακεδαιμόνιος. *land,* γῆ. *loss,* ζημία. *to march into,* στρατεύεσθαι εἰς, with acc. *neither — nor,* οὔτε — οὔτε. *Philip,* Φίλιππος. *rain,* ὄμβρος. *to make a report,* ἀπαγγέλλειν (N.B. *to make a false report* = ψευδῆ ἀπαγγέλλειν. This combination of the neuter adjective plural with the verb is common in Greek). *to say,* φάναι (Prim. 161). *to see,* ὁρᾶν (Prim. 163). *slave,* παῖς, ὁ, ἡ, δοῦλος. *snow,* χιών, ἡ. *swan,* κύκνος. *Theban,* Θηβαῖος. *tree,* δένδρον.

1. In our city law is king. 2. The enemies fear our soldiers. 3. In that land there is (γίγνεται) neither rain nor snow. 4. In this land there are[30] no trees (*there are not trees*). 5. Æschines there (οὗτος) made a false report[26]. 6. 'Philip,' he says, 'is not intending to invade our land, but the Thebans'.' 7. My slave has come, but yours has not come. 8. He said that the deed was mine, not yours. 9. The general marched into the country of the Lacedæmonians. 10. Who in this city ever saw a black swan? 11. The loss is ours, but the gain is our friends'[15].

> *Obs.*—When two clauses are slightly in opposition, they should be united by μέν — δέ. thus, οἱ μὲν ἀπῆλθον οἱ δὲ ἔμενον, *the one party went away, the other remained* (§ 11).

---

[*] μέλλω is generally followed by the future infinitive, sometimes by the present, more rarely by the aorist.

§ 7. *The Article with Participles and Infinitives.*

(1) When joined with participles, the article signifies—

(*a*) The definite person who does (is, &c.) what the participle implies, as οὗτός ἐστιν ὁ ποιήσας, *this is the person who did (it)*.

(*b*) A class of persons (cp. § 3). This is especially the case in the plural, as οἱ τὰ τῆς πόλεως πράττοντες, *those who manage the affairs of the state* (= *public men, politicians*).

Obs.—The article with the participle is thus equivalent to a personal or demonstrative pronoun followed by a relative sentence : ὁ πράττων (= *the (person) doing* =) *he who does* (ὃς or ὅστις πράττει). Cp. § 34.

(2) The infinitive with the article becomes, in effect, a substantive declinable throughout, and answering to the English 'participial substantive' in -*ing*. (Cp. § 31 (3), (4).)

τὸ ταχὺ λαλεῖν, *talking fast* ; τοῦ ταχὺ λαλεῖν, *of talking fast*, &c. ; τὸ πάντας κακῶς λέγειν, *the speaking ill of everybody* ; ἐν τῷ ὁρᾶν, *in seeing*.

Exercise 8.

Vocabulary.—*best*, ἄριστος. *to desire*, ἐπιθυμεῖν, with gen. *to die*, ἀποθνήσκειν. *to escape*, ἐκφυγεῖν. *every one*, πᾶς. *harm*, βλάβη. *to manage the affairs of the city*, τὰ τῆς πόλεως (πράγματα) πράττειν. *possession*, κτῆμα. *to prevent*, κωλύειν. *prosperity* (= *to prosper*), τὸ εὖ πράττειν. *then*, τότε. *to think*, φρονεῖν. *to transgress*, παραβαίνειν. *to make a good use of*, εὖ χρῆσθαι, with dat. *victory* (= *to conquer*), τὸ νικᾶν. *well*, εὖ. *who? what?* τίς; τί;

1. These are they who[11] manage the affairs of the state. 2. This is the person who then escaped. 3. A sound mind (*to think well*) is the best of possessions. 4. What harm is there in seeing this ? 5. Who is to[13] prevent us (*use article and future participle*)? 6. Those who transgress the laws are bad citizens. 7. How sweet is victory! 8. He died at the very moment of conquest (*in the conquering itself*, αὐτός). 9. Every one desires prosperity. 10. Few are there who make a good use of victory.

§ 8. *The Article with Neuter Adjectives, Prepositional Clauses, Adverbs, &c.*

(1) With the *singular* neuter of the adjective the article turns the adjective into an abstract noun; with the *plural* neuter it expresses a class.

> τὸ καλόν. *the beautiful, the honourable* (in the abstract = *beauty, honour*); τὰ καλά, *beautiful* (or *honourable*) *things; whatever things are beautiful; what is beautiful;* or simply, *beautiful things.*

(2) The article can be prefixed to a preposition and its case.

> οἱ ἐν ἄστει, *the people in the city;* οἱ σὺν τῷ βασιλεῖ, *those with the king.*

These clauses are really equivalent to the clauses in § 7 (1), inasmuch as a participle must be understood with the article, οἱ ἐν ἄστει ὄντες, &c.

(3) The article is often used with an adverb.

> οἱ πάλαι, the *long ago* men = *the men of old,* i. e. *the men (being or who were) long ago;* ὁ μεταξὺ χρόνος. *the between time* = *the intermediate time, the interval;* ἡ αὔριον, *adv.* (ἡμέρα, *day* understood), *the morrow, the next day.*

Exercise 9.

Vocabulary.—*advantageous,* συμφέρων.[a] *to ascend,* ἀναβαίνειν. *to avoid,* φεύγειν. *to be badly off,* κακῶς πράττειν. *beloved,* φίλος. *to think oneself better than* (= *to despise*), καταφρονεῖν, with gen. *Brasidas,* Βρασίδας. *brave,* ἀγαθός. *delight,* ἡδονή. *to depart,* ἀποίχεσθαι. *disgraceful,* αἰσχρός. *ever,* ἀεί. *force,* στρατιά. *here,* ἐνθάδε. *large,* μέγας, πολύς. *neighbours,* οἱ πέλας. *of old,* πάλαι. *on,* ἐπί, with gen. *to run down,* κατατρέχειν. *rustic,* ἀγροῖκος. *to seek,* ζητεῖν. *the parts about Thrace,* τὰ ἐπὶ Θράκης (lit. *in the direction of T.*). *trench,* τάφρος, ἡ. *victory,* νίκη. *wall,* τεῖχος, τό. *to win,* νικᾶν.

---

[a] συμφέρων is a participle governing the dative case, e. g. (*a thing*) *advantageous to me* (*to my advantage*), συμφέρον ἐμοί.

1. Let us pursue what is honourable, and avoid what is disgraceful. 2. The beautiful[13] is ever beloved. 3. Beauty has ever been (πέφυκε) a delight to men. 4. Those on the wall ran down to the trench, *and meanwhile* (ἐν δὲ τούτῳ) those in the trench ascended the wall. 5. Those in the country are more rustic than those (gen. Syntax, 23) in the city. 6. Brasidas departed to the parts about Thrace *with* (Ex. 1, *Obs.* i.) a large force. 7. The men of old[14] were brave, and won many victories. 8. The people here are badly off[32]. 9. Every one thinks himself better than his neighbours. 10. Let us seek what is advantageous to the city (*what is for the city's advantage*).

§ 9. *Elliptical Phrases. Position of the Article.*

(1) The substantive to which the article refers is often *understood*, so that the article then stands alone with a genitive. Instances of this have already occurred in the Exercises.

τὰ τῆς πόλεως πράττειν (Ex. 8), where πράγματα may be omitted or retained ; τὰ ἐπὶ Θρᾴκης (Ex. 9), *the parts about Thrace*, where χωρία is understood.

But in some cases the substantive is regularly omitted.

Ἀλέξανδρος ὁ Φιλίππου (sc. υἱός), *Alexander, the son of Philip ;* ὁ Σωφρονίσκου, *the son of Sophroniscus :* εἰς τὴν Φιλίππου (sc. χώραν), *into Philip's country;* ὁ τῆς Ἀθηνᾶς (sc. ναός), *the temple of Athena.*

(2) Though in Greek, as in English, the article precedes the word with which it is used, the position of the article often differs in Greek and English ; thus—

(*a*) ἀνὴρ ὁ ἀγαθός = ὁ ἀγαθὸς ἀνήρ. *the good man ;* or, with repetition of the article, ὁ ἀνὴρ ὁ ἀγαθός.

(*b*) A governed genitive may come between the article and its substantive, as τὸ τῆς γυναικὸς κάλλος. *the beauty of the woman ;* τὸ κάλλος τὸ τῆς γυναικός is also permissible (§ 1 (1), *Obs.* ii.).

(*c*) When an article is used with an infinitive (or a participle), any words governed by or qualifying the verb are placed between the article and the infinitive. as τὸ ταῦτα ποιεῖν ; τὸ πάντας κακῶς λέγειν ; ὁ τούτῳ ξυνών. In the same position is placed all that defines the infinitive or participle, as τὸ ταχέως ἀπελθεῖν, &c.

EXERCISE 10.

VOCABULARY.—*about* (= Lat. *de*), περί, with gen. *admirable*,
θαυμαστός. *after*, μετά, with acc. *against*, ἐπί, with acc.
Aphrodite, Ἀφροδίτη. *army*, στράτευμα. *by*, ὑπό, with gen.
(of agent). *to be put to death* (= *to die*), ἀποθνήσκειν. *Epidamnus*, Ἐπίδαμνος. *from*, ἀπό, with gen. *gulf*, κόλπος.
immediately, εὐθύς. *to inquire*, ἐρωτᾶν. *invasion*, εἰσβολή.
Ionian, Ἰόνιος. *to lead past* (*of a road*), φέρειν παρά, with
acc. *to march* (*of the general of an army*), ἐλαύνειν. *to march*
(*of an army*), πορεύεσθαι. *mountainous*, ὀρεινός. *Peloponnesian*, Πελοποννήσιος. *Persian*, Πέρσης. *poet*, ποιητής. *to
revolt from*, ἀποστῆναι ἀπό. *on the right hand*, ἐκ δεξιᾶς.
road, ὁδός, ἡ. *to sail-into*, εἰσπλεῖν. *Scythian*, Σκύθης. *small*,
ὀλίγος. *teacher*, διδάσκαλος. *truly*, πάνυ. *virtue*, ἀρετή. *with*,
μετά, with gen.

1. Those with the king will march against the son of Philip.
2. The son of Sophroniscus was put to death by the people [5].
3. The army of the Persians marches into the country of the
Scythians. 4. How truly admirable [28] is the wisdom of the poet !
5. The road leads past the temple of Aphrodite. 6. Epidamnus
is a city on the right hand as you enter (*to one* [11] *sailing-
into*) the Ionian Gulf. 7. Immediately after the invasion of
the Peloponnesians, Lesbos revolted from the Athenians. 8.
Wise poets [5] are the teachers of men. 9. The country of the
Athenians is small and mountainous. 10. He used to go
(*imperf.*) to the son of Sophroniscus to inquire (*fut. particip.*) [48]
(of him) about virtue.

§ 10. *The Omission of the Article.*

(1) The article is commonly omitted with the words,
πόλις, *city, state*; ἄστυ, *city, town*; ἀγορά, *market-place*;
τεῖχος, *wall*, when they are used with prepositions. It is
hardly ever used with βασιλεύς, *king*, when the Persian
king is meant.

These words, being in common use, do not require the distinguishing
article ; so we say, 'to town,' 'to market,' &c.

(2) The words, γῆ, *earth*; θάλαττα, *sea*; οὐρανός, *sky, heaven*, frequently omit the article, especially when two or more are used in combination, as κατὰ γῆν καὶ θάλατταν, *by land and sea.* So also, ψυχὴ καὶ σῶμα, *soul and body.* In these cases the English use is a fair guide.

(3) A superlative adjective, when used as a predicate, does not take the article, as πάντων φιλομαθέστατος Κῦρος ἦν, *Cyrus was, of all men, the most fond of learning.*

(4) When two adjectives, relating to one substantive, express ideas which are merely complements one of the other, the article is omitted with the second, as ὁ πάντων δικαιότατος καὶ βέλτιστος, *the most righteous and best of all.*

> *Obs.*—We also find the same omission when two extremes are mentioned, as δηλῶν τὰς μεγίστας καὶ ἐλαχίστας (τῶν νεῶν), '*marking the largest and the smallest of the ships.*' Thuc. i. 10.

(5) Names of arts, virtues, vices, &c., are often used in Greek, as in English, without the article. Cp. § 5 (2).

Pronouns

§ 11. *The Article as a Demonstrative Pronoun.* καὶ ὅς.

(a) When used with μὲν — δέ (Ex. 7, *Obs.*), as ὁ μὲν — ὁ δέ, *the one, the other; this, that,* the article retains its original demonstrative force.

> τοὺς μὲν λυπεῖ ταῦτα τοὺς δὲ τέρπει, *these things give-pain-to some persons, but pleasure-to others.* More than one ὁ δέ may follow on the ὁ μέν.

> *Obs.*—μέν, *indeed*; δέ, *but* (Syntax, 125. 2). Often, however, there is no important opposition between words so connected, the use of μέν being principally to prepare us for a coming δέ. It need not be translated, except when the context plainly requires it, when we may use *indeed.* But in translating from English into Greek, whenever the *second* of two connected clauses has a *but,* the first should have a μέν.

(*h*) In a narrative, ὁ δέ stands (once) in reference to an object already named.

> λύκος ἀμνὸν ἐδίωκεν, ὁ δὲ εἰς ναὸν κατέφυγε, *a wolf was pursuing a lamb, and* (*or but*) *it fled-for-refuge into a temple.*

> *Obs.*—δέ is not only *but,* but also *and,* and sometimes *for.* It is used where no other particle is required, to avoid having a proposition in the middle of a discourse *unconnected* with what goes before. It is often, therefore, omitted when translating into English, and often inserted when translating from English into Greek. Observe the use in the following sentence : 'Αλέξανδρος, ἔτι παῖς ὤν, πολλὰ τοῦ Φιλίππου κατορθοῦντος, οὐκ ἔχαιρεν, ἀλλὰ πρὸς τοὺς συντρεφομένους ἔλεγε παῖδας· Ἐμοὶ δὲ ὁ πατὴρ οὐδὲν ἀπολείψει. τῶν δὲ παίδων λεγόντων ὅτι Σοὶ ταῦτα κτᾶται· Τί δέ ὄφελος ; εἶπεν, ἐὰν μὲν πολλὰ ἔξω, πράξω δὲ μηδέν. *Alexander, while yet a child, when Philip was successful in many* (*enter-prises*) *was not pleased, but said to the boys who were brought up with him, 'My father will leave nothing for me* (*to do*).' *When the boys replied that,* '*He is acquiring these things for you ;*' *he said,* '*What benefit* (*will it be*) *if I am to possess much and do nothing ?*'

(*c*) ὅς, the relative pronoun, can also be used, of a person, as a demonstrative in the phrase καὶ ὅς, &c.

> καὶ ὃς ἐξαπατηθεὶς διώκει ἀνὰ κράτος, *and he, being deceived, pursues at full speed.* ἦ δ' ὅς, *said he.*

Exercise 11.

Vocabulary.—*to admire,* θαυμάζειν. *to consider,* οἴεσθαι. *Corinthian,* Κορίνθιος. *daughter,* θυγάτηρ. *to deceive,* ἐξαπατᾶν. *dog,* κύων. *Dorian* (*woman*), Δωρίς. *enemy, hostile,* ἐχθρός. *to fly for refuge,* καταφεύγειν. *to give,* διδόναι. *to hear,* ἀκούειν. *to loose,* λύειν. *meadow,* λειμών, ὁ. *money,* χρήματα, τά. *mother,* μήτηρ. *nothing,* οὐδέν. *to reproach,* ὀνειδίζειν, with dat. *to ride,* ἐλαύνειν. *sheep,* ὄις, ἡ. *ship,* ναῦς. *to speak, say,* εἰπεῖν. *at full speed,* κατὰ κράτος. *to be taken,* ἁλῶναι (ἁλίσκεσθαι). *temple,* ναός.

1. A dog was pursuing a sheep, and it fled for-refuge into a house. 2. Some [19] admire the mother; others the daughter. 3. And they, being deceived, fly for refuge into a temple. 4. And he, riding at full speed, escapes *his pursuers* [11]. 5. The city he considered to be his enemy, but your enemies (to be) his friends. 6. *My father was* Polybus of Corinth, and my mother Merope, a Dorian. 7. *Thus he spoke* to his friends, and they,

on hearing it (*part.*), went away. 8. Some he reproached, to others he gave money, to others he said nothing. 9. He loosed the horse, and it went away to the meadow. 10. Three of the ships were taken, the rest⁵ escaped.

4. Say: Those pursuing (him). 6. To me there was a father. 7. He said these (things).

§ 12. *αὐτός.*

(*a*) **αὐτός** is *self*, when it stands in the *nominative without* a substantive, or in *any case with* one.

αὐτὸς ἔφη, *he himself said it* (*ipse dixit*); αὐτὸς ὁ δοῦλος, *the slave himself* (or ὁ δοῦλος αὐτός); τοῦτο μᾶλλον φοβοῦμαι ἢ τὸν θάνατον αὐτόν, *I fear this more than death itself* (or αὐτὸν τὸν θάνατον); αὐτὸς ἦλθε, *he came of his own accord.*

The substantive may have the article, or it may not—

ὑπὸ λόφον αὐτόν, *under the very crest, just under the crest* (or ὑπ᾽ αὐτὸν τὸν λόφον);

but with persons the article is generally kept.

(*b*) In an *oblique* case, without a substantive, **αὐτόν** (αὐτήν, &c.) is *him* (*her*, &c.), and unless it is the first word of a sentence, it never means *self.*

ἔδωκεν αὐτοῖς τὸ πῦρ, *he gave them fire*; εἶδον γὰρ αὐτόν, *for I saw him*; αὐτὸν γὰρ εἶδον, *for I saw the man himself.*

(*c*) **ὁ αὐτός** is *the same*, literally, *the self.*

τὰ αὐτὰ καὶ λυπεῖ καὶ τέρπει, *the same things give pain and pleasure.*

(*d*) In the dative case, singular or plural, **αὐτός**, with a substantive, expresses accompaniment.

αἱ νῆες αὐτοῖς τοῖς ἀνδράσιν ἀπώλοντο, *the ships perished along with their crews,* 'crews and all.'

(*e*) **αὐτός** is often used with the ordinal numerals (Prim. 87) to express the number of persons united in any enterprise or undertaking, thus: Περικλῆς πέμπτος αὐτός, *Pericles with four others*; lit. *himself the fifth.*

EXERCISE 12.

VOCABULARY.—*ambassador*, πρεσβευτής —πρέσβυς (for the plur. πρέσβεις is used). *to choose*, αἱρεῖσθαι. *clothing, clothes*, ἐσθής, ἡ, ἱμάτια, τά. *crew*, ἄνδρες. *earth*, γῆ. *Euthycles*, Εὐθυκλῆς. *to fall*, πίπτειν (Prim. 164). *fifth*, πέμπτος. *five*, πέντε. *food*, σῖτος. *god*, θεός. *letter*, ἐπιστολή. *not*, οὐ, with indic.; μή, with imperat. *now*, νῦν. *one*, εἷς. *pool*, λίμνη. *recess*, μυχός. *return*, κατιέναι. *Sparta*, Σπάρτη. *standing*, ἑστώς. *to step into*, εἰσβαίνειν εἰς. *to take*, αἱρεῖν. *take down*, καθαιρεῖν. *Tantalus*, Τάνταλος. *tell, announce*, ἀγγέλλειν. *tenth*, δέκατος. *Theramenes*, Θηραμένης. *to* (= *after*), μετά, with acc. *trireme*, τριήρης. *twice*, δίς. *Xenoclides*, Ξενοκλείδης.

1. The Athenians took five ships, and one (of them) with the crew. 2. The triremes were taken with their crews. 3. The gods took him down to the recesses of the earth, horses and all. 4. He fell into the river, clothes and all. 5. Xenoclides, *the son of*[15] Euthycles, was general of the Corinthians, with four others. 6. Theramenes was chosen ambassador to Sparta, with nine others. 7. He did not send a letter, but told me himself. 8. There I saw Tantalus himself, standing in a pool. 9. I shall go to him, but he will not return to me. 10. Who will now give them money, fool, or clothing? 11. They came *of their own accord*. 12. We are *alone*. 13. I did not see *the master*, but the servant. 14. Do not say the same thing twice. 15. No one can step into the same river twice.

11, 12, 13. Use αὐτός.

§ 13. *Demonstrative Pronouns. Relative Pronouns.*

(1) It is important to distinguish accurately between the demonstrative pronouns, ὅδε, οὗτος, ἐκεῖνος.

(*a*) ὅδε is the person here—who is present, whom we see—the person in immediate proximity.

(*b*) οὗτος is the person there, some one seen, but not regarded as in immediate proximity. If ὅδε is a person standing by me, οὗτος may be a person in another part of the room. It is also used of some one referred to in thought, or in a previous speech. ὅδε is sometimes called the *deictic* pronoun (pronoun of *pointing at*) ; οὗτος, the *anaphoric* pronoun (pronoun of *reference to*).

Hence οὗτος is the pronoun used for the opponent in a law-suit = Lat. *iste;* it is also joined with the second personal pronoun, as οὗτος, σὺ πῶς δεῦρ᾽ ἦλθες; *you there, why did you come hither?* or with imperative, as οὗτος, βλέφ᾽ ὧδε, *you there, look this way.*

The adverbs derived from ὅδε, οὗτος are ὧδε, οὕτως, but ὧδε alone has a local meaning, ' *hither.*'

(c) ἐκεῖνος is *that man*, referring to a person more remote, whether in time, distance, or thought.

> *Obs.* i.—τόδ᾽ ἐκεῖνο, *this is that* (which I heard long ago, or have had long in my thoughts; the phrase is often nearly = it has come at last); ἐκεῖν᾽, ἐκεῖνο γεννιότατον τῶν ἐμῶν, *that, that was my chef-d'œuvre*, referring to an act in past life (lit. *that was the most noble of my actions*). ὅδ᾽ ἐκεῖνος ἐγώ, *here am I, the far-away man* (*whom you supposed to be at a distance*).

> *Obs.* ii.—τεκμήριον δὲ τούτου καὶ τόδε, ' *of this* (*which has been stated*) *this* (*which follows*) *is also a proof.*' Clyde, Syntax, § 30. οὗτος refers to what has gone before, ὅδε to what is to come.ᵃ

(2) Of the relative pronouns,

(a) ὅς is simply, ' *who.*'

(b) ὅσπερ is, ' *the very person who.*'

(c) ὅστις is, ' *whosoever*,' but ὅστις is also used in clauses which describe or give the character of a single person, or denote him as one of a class, ' *any one who.*'

> ἐκεῖνος οὐκ ἔστ᾽ ἀνὴρ ἄβουλος, ὅστις εἰς κακὸν πεσὼν ἀκεῖται, *he is not a foolish man, who, when he has fa'len into misfortune, accepts remedies.*

> *Obs.* i.—The Greeks say πᾶς ὅστις, *every one who;* but in the plural πάντες ὅσοι, *all who* (lit. *all as many as*), not πάντες οἵτινες.

> *Obs.* ii.—The noun with οὗτος, ὅδε, ἐκεῖνος, takes the article, as shown in § 6, (2).

---

* ' *Est ὅδε venturi; quod dictum est, respicit οὗτος.*'

C

Exercise 13.

Vocabulary.—*to be*, εἶναι, γίγνεσθαι. *to beat*, παίειν, τύπτειν. *country*, χώρα. *to delay*, μέλλειν. *to do*, ποιεῖν, πράττειν. *no one*, οὐδείς. *to pelt*, βάλλειν. *very* (*person*), αὐτός (§ **12**). *to lay waste*, τέμνειν (lit. *to cut*, Prim. 167). *to shuffle*, εἰς τριβὰς ἐλαύνειν. *why?* τί; *wolf*, λύκος. *to do wrong* (*to make a mistake, to err*), ἐξαμαρτάνειν (Prim. 167).

1. This man is shuffling. 2. You there, why do we delay? 3. In that country [10] the men become wolves. 4. How beautiful is this city [10]! 5. This is the man, the very man, pelt him, beat him. 6. You there, what are you doing? 7. These are they *who did the deed* [47] (*partic.*, § **7**). 8. No one who [71] is a good citizen acts thus. 9. This is the person who [47] conquered the enemy. 10. The general laid waste the rest (of the) country. 11. In this he did wrong; but in the rest (*of his actions*) he has been a good citizen.

8. Say: *does these things*. 11. τἆλλα, cp. § **3**.

§ **14.** *Reflexive Pronouns.*

(*a*) '*Myself*,' '*yourself*,' '*himself*,' are translated by ἐμαυτόν, σεαυτόν, ἑαυτόν, when the *self* is not emphatic. To express '*self*' emphatically, αὐτός must be detached and precede the pronoun, as αὐτὸν ἐμέ, αὐτὸν σέ, &c.

(*b*) αὐτός (nom.) is used for *himself* with the infinitive in indirect speech, when the subject of the main verb and the infinitive is the same (Syntax, 157 (*a*), below, § **30** (3)).

> ἔφη αὐτὸς ποιῆσαι, *he said that he did it himself*; ἔφη οὐκ ἐκείνους ἀλλ' αὐτὸς στρατηγεῖν, *he said that not they, but himself, was general*. Contrast this idiom with the Latin, *dixit se fecisse*.

(*c*) In a dependent sentence (or in a clause with accusative and infinitive), ἑαυτόν is often used (like *se*) of the subject of the main sentence.

> νομίζει τοὺς πολίτας ὑπηρετεῖν ἑαυτῷ, *he thinks that the citizens are his servants*.

(*d*) '*Own*' (possessive) is expressed by the genitive of the reflexive pronouns, as ἔφη πάντας τοὺς ἀνθρώπους τὰ ἑαυτῶν ἀγαπᾶν, *he said that all men love their own things*.

'*His own*' is expressed by the genitive singular, '*their own*' by the genitive plural.

Exercise 14.

Vocabulary.—*to accustom*, ἐθίζειν (aug. εἴθιζον, εἴθισμαι. For the passive = *to be accustomed*, εἴωθα is often used). *to come into*, εἰσιέναι. *to confer benefits on*, εὖ ποιεῖν, with acc. *to be contented with, love*, ἀγαπᾶν, with acc. *gold* (*of money*), χρυσίον. *to order*, κελεύειν. *no other person*, οὐδεὶς ἄλλος. *he said*, ἔφη, *he said that*, ἔφη, with infinitive (§ 17). *to serve*, ὑπηρετεῖν, with dat. *to show* (*or prove*) *false*, ψευδῆ καθιστάναι. *state* (*city*), πόλις. *to think*, νομίζειν. *to wish*, ἐθέλειν.

1. Accustom yourself to be contented with your own (*lot*). 2. He thinks that the citizens have conferred benefits upon him. 3. I accustom myself to serve the state. 4. I will give the gold into your own hands (*to you yourself*). 5. He said that he wished to do it himself[24]. 6. He said that Alcibiades did not come into his[9] house as a friend. 7. He thinks that the citizens are his enemies. 8. I will do it myself. 9. I will not show myself false to the city. 10. He ordered the servant to give the money to himself, and to no other (*person*).

§ 15. 1. ἄλλος, ἕτερος, &c.

ἄλλος and ἕτερος differ as the Latin *alius* and *alter*. ἄλλος is *another*, where there are many; ἕτερος, where there are only two, e. g. ἄλλοι πάντες, *all others;* but ἡ ἑτέρα χείρ, *the other hand*. But ἕτερος is often used of another class of things, while ἄλλος is used of other members of the same class.

> τὸ ἕτερον στράτευμα, *the other army, of two;*
> οἱ ἕτεροι, *the opposite party;*
> ἕτερον ποτήριον, *a different cup;*
> but
> τὸ ἄλλο στράτευμα, *the rest of the army;*
> οἱ ἄλλοι, *the rest of the same party;*
> ἄλλο ποτήριον, *one cup more.*

Obs. i.—ἄλλος is sometimes to be translated, *in addition;* e. g. οὐ γὰρ ἦν χόρτος, οὐδὲ ἄλλο δένδρον οὐδέν, *for there was no grass, nor yet any tree.* (Clyde, Greek Syntax, § 28 (2). a.)

Obs. ii.—ἄλλος, like *alius*, is often repeated: ἔπαιον ἄλλος ἄλλον, *one beat the other*; ἔφυγον ἄλλος ἄλλῃ, *they fled in different directions.*

2. *The Pronominal Correlatives* (Prim. 99).

INTERROGATIVES.		INDEFINITE.	DEMONSTRATIVE.	RELATIVE.
DIRECT.	INDIRECT.			
τίς; *who?*	ὅστις, *who.*	τις, *any, some.*	ὅδε, &c., § 13, *this.*	ὅς, ὅστις, *who.*
πότερος; *which of two?*	ὁπότερος, *which of two.*	ποτερός, *one of two.*	ἅτερος (ὁ ἕτερος), *the one of two.*	
ποῖος; *of what sort?*	ὁποῖος, *of what sort.*	ποιός, *of some sort.*	τοιόσδε, τοιοῦτος, *of that sort.*	οἷος, *of what sort, as.*
πόσος; *how great?*	ὁπόσος, *how large.*	ποσός, *of any size.*	τοσόσδε, τοσοῦτος, *of that size.*	ὅσος, *of which size (number), as.*

EXAMPLES.

Interrogative.—σὺ εἶ τίς ἀνδρῶν; ὅστις εἰμ' ἐγώ; *what man are you? who am I (do you ask)?* ἔστιν δὲ ποῖον τοῦπος; *of what nature is his speech?* ἤρετο ὁποῖον ἦν τὸ ἔπος, *he asked of what nature was his speech.*

Demonstrative.—ὁ Κῦρος ἀκούσας τοῦ Γωβρύου τοιαῦτα τοιάδε πρὸς αὐτὸν ἔλεξεν, *Cyrus having heard this from Gobryas, replied to him as follows:* τοιαῦτα μὲν οἱ Κερκυραῖοι εἶπον· οἱ δὲ Κορίνθιοι μετ' αὐτοὺς τοιάδε. τοιοῦτος is used of what has gone before, τοιόσδε of what is to come. (Cp. οὗτος and ὅδε, § 13, *c*; and for the further use of interrogatives, §§ 55, 56.)

Demonstratives and Relatives combined.—οὔπω τοιοῦτον εἶδον θηρίον οἷον σὺ λέγεις, *I never yet saw such an animal as you describe;* οὐκ ἔξεστί μοι κλαῦσαι τοσόνδε ὅσον θέλω, *I am not allowed to weep as much I wish.*

Obs.—The distinction between τοσόσδε and τοσοῦτος is not great; both words are used of extent and number: *so great, so many.*

Indefinite.—ἤρετό τις, *some one asked;* ἀνήρ τις, *some man* (§ 1). τις is often added to other pronouns: ποῖός τις, τοιοῦτός τις, &c. τί οὖν λέγει ποτερὸς ὑμῶν, *what, then, does either of you say?* δεῖ ποιὸν εἶναι τὸν λόγον, *the argument must be of a certain nature.*

Exercise 15.

Vocabulary.—*to ask*, ἔρεσθαι, ἐρωτᾶν. *bowman*, τοξότης. *brother*, ἀδελφός. *to imitate*, ἀπομιμεῖσθαι. *to know*, εἰδέναι. *matter*, πρᾶγμα. *to mean*, λέγειν. *multitude*, πλῆθος, τό. *neither (of two)*, οὐδέτερος. *never*, οὔποτε. *ought*, δεῖ, impers. (e. g. τί δεῖ ποιεῖν (sc. ἐμέ); *what must I, ought I to do?*). *peltast*, πελταστής. *to receive*, δέχεσθαι. *to rule*, ἄρχειν, with gen. *to say*, λέγειν. *to suffer*, πάσχειν. *talent*, τάλαντον. *ten*, δέκα. *thousand*, χίλιοι.

1. Who is this man? Do you ask who it is? It is my brother. 2. The rest of the soldiers went to the other camp. 3. What is this [74] you are asking? I do not know what you mean. 4. I never saw so great a multitude of men as were then in the city. 5. The matter was on this wise (*of such a nature*). 6. They sent a thousand bowmen, and as many peltasts *in addition*. 7. He received a second (sum of) ten talents. 8. I ask which of you two did this. Neither of us. 9. You too are a man, and rule over others like yourself (*of such a nature*). 10. I do not know in what numbers (*how many*) the men were. 11. No one has suffered such (calamities) as I have. 12. He says one thing and thinks another. 13. Which of you two imitated the other? 14. What ought (I) to say to such a man?

§ 16. *Number and Gender.*

(1) In Greek the plural neuter is often used where in English the singular would be found; as for instance with pronouns and adjectives: εἶπε ταῦτα, *he said this* (lit. *these words*); δίκαια λέγεις, *you say what is just.*

(2) The neuter article *plural* (rarely *singular*) with a genitive case (or a possessive pronoun) is used in an indefinite way for anything which relates to or proceeds from a person; τὰ ἐκ τῶν θεῶν φέρειν χρή, *we ought to bear what comes from the gods;* τὰ τῆς τύχης, *fortune, accidents;* εὖ φρονῶ τὰ σά, *I am careful of your interests.*

(3) The neuter plural of the superlative adjective, and the neuter singular of the comparative, is used for the adverb, as αἴσχιστα διετέλεσεν, *he lived in a most disgraceful way;* σοφώτερον ποιεῖς, *you act more wisely.*

(4) With adjectives used as predicates the neuter is often found, though the subject be masculine or feminine.

ἡ ἀρετή ἐστιν ἐπαίνετον, *virtue is a praiseworthy thing.*

Obs.—The verb ἐστίν is often omitted: ἐπαίνετον ἡ ἀρετή.

(5) The adjectives, πολύς, *many, much,* and ἥμισυς, *half* —and *superlatives* when used with a *genitive*—generally take the gender of the substantive which is in the genitive case.

ἡ πολλὴ (ἡ πλείστη) τῆς γῆς, *the greater part of the land;* ὁ ἥμισυς τοῦ χρόνου, *the half of the time.*

(6) With a neuter plural nominative, the verb stands in the singular, as δῶρα θεοὺς πείθει, *gifts persuade the gods;* unless persons or living creatures are meant, in which case the verb *may* be in the plural.

Exercise 16.

Vocabulary.—*Attica,* ἡ Ἀττική. *to bear,* φέρειν. *disgraceful,* αἰσχρός. *to go on an expedition,* στρατεύειν, στρατεύεσθαι. *forefathers,* πρόγονοι. *good,* ἀγαθός. *to live, to spend life,* διατελεῖν. *nation,* ἔθνος, τό. *to plant,* φιτεύειν. *to plough,* ἀροῦν. *in my power,* ἐπ' ἐμοί. *praiseworthy,* ἐπαίνετος. *to ravage,* δῃοῦν. *to render services = to serve,* ὑπηρετεῖν, with dat. *in my time,* ἐπ' ἐμοῦ.

1. The enemy laid waste half the country.   2. He spent half his life *in a most disgraceful way.*   3. The Peloponnesians ravaged the greater part of Attica.   4. Let us bear what comes from the gods[15].   5. Accustom yourselves to bear what comes from the gods.   6. This is good.   7. Many nations will go[30] on the expedition.   8. These things took place[30] in the time of our forefathers.   9. These things are not in my power.   10. Alci-

biades *rendered many* [57] *great services* [27] to his state. 11. Wisdom is praiseworthy [28]. 12. He planted half the land, the other half he ploughed.

2. Use neut. plur. of superlative. 10. Use πολλά with the verb. 12. Use μέν — δέ (§ 11).

§ 17. *Verbs of Saying, Thinking, &c.*

i. (1) φημί, *I say*, is generally used in the present and imperfect indicative; λέγω, *I say*, in the present and imperfect indicative, in the present infinitive and imperative.

λέγω is generally used of *statements*, φημί of *conversation*. But φημί is also used in an emphatic sense, *to assert* (implying that the assertion is false); in this sense φάσκειν, φάσκων, ἔφασκον, are used for the infinitive, participle, and imperfect (though ἔφην may also be used). οὐ φημί is *I say no, I deny*.

λέγω is also used in an emphatic sense with τι, as λέγει τι, *he makes a (right) statement; he is right*.

(2) εἶπον, *I said*, has no present. It is the past tense (in use) of λέγω, and refers to statements rather than conversation. ἔφη, for instance, and not εἶπον, is used parenthetically in quoting a conversation, e. g. *This, he said, is true*, is τοῦτ᾽, ἔφη, ἀληθές ἐστι; but εἶπεν is used of proposals made in the public assembly, e. g. Δημοσθένης εἶπεν, *Demosthenes proposed*.

ὡς εἰπεῖν or ὡς ἔπος εἰπεῖν is *so to say*.

(3) *I will say* is ἐρῶ. *I have said* is εἴρηκα, pass. εἴρημαι.

(4) In introducing a quoted or indirect statement (*I say, he said, that*), φημί is usually followed by the infinitive with the accusative; εἰπεῖν is followed by a subordinate clause beginning with ὡς or ὅτι, *that*, and λέγειν by either the infinitive or ὡς, ὅτι (Syntax, 157, 159).

(5) ἀποκρίνομαι, *I answer;* ἀποδείκνυμι, *I show;* πυνθάνομαι, *I learn;* ἐνθυμοῦμαι, *I reflect,* are followed by ὅτι
or ὡς. νομίζω, *I think;* δοκῶ, *I think,* take the accusative
and infinitive.

ii. The verb in the quoted or indirect clause beginning
with ὡς or ὅτι is in the indicative; or, when the verb
signifying *to say* is in the past tense, in the optative.

> λέγει ὅτι οὐδὲν αὐτῷ μέλει, *he says that he does not care.*
> ἔλεγεν (εἶπεν) ὅτι οὐδὲν αὐτῷ μέλοι (ἔμελεν), *he said that he did not care.*

> *Obs.*—In the construction with the accusative and infinitive, past
> time is often expressed by the aorist = English pluperfect, e. g.
> ἔφη ταῦτ᾽ ἁμαρτεῖν, *he said that he had done this wrong.* But
> the aorist is also used where we use the present, simply to give
> the meaning of the verb, e. g. οὐδεὶς οἷός τέ ἐστιν ἀποδεῖξαι, *no
> one is able to show.*

iii. But sometimes after a main verb in the past tense,
the verb of the dependent clause is in the present indicative, as εἶπεν ὅτι οὐδὲν αὐτῷ μέλει. Here the actual words
spoken are given with a change of pronoun, οὐδέν μοι
μέλει becoming οὐδὲν αὐτῷ μέλει, and the ὅτι introduces
this clause, without any alteration in the verb.

Thus in Greek we have a variety in the use of moods
in indirect speech which is not allowed in Latin.

> i. *He says (said) that the general is present.*
> φησὶ (ἔφη) τὸν στρατηγὸν παρεῖναι.
> λέγει (ἔλεγεν) τὸν στρατηγὸν παρεῖναι—
>   or ὅτι (ὡς) ὁ στρατηγὸς πάρεστι.
>   (εἶπεν) ὅτι (ὡς) ὁ στρατηγὸς πάρεστι

> ii. *He said that the general was present.*
> ἔφη τὸν στρατηγὸν παρεῖναι.
> ἔλεγεν τὸν στρατηγὸν παρεῖναι—
>   or ὅτι (ὡς) ὁ στρατηγὸς παρῆν—
>   or ὅτι (ὡς) ὁ στρατηγὸς παρείη.
> εἶπεν ὅτι (ὡς) ὁ στρατηγὸς παρῆν—
>   or ὅτι (ὡς) ὁ στρατηγὸς παρείη.

> iii. *He said that the general was present.*
> εἶπεν ⎱
> ἔλεγεν ⎰ ὅτι (ὡς) πάρεστιν ὁ στρατηγός.

EXERCISE 17.

VOCABULARY.—*to be able*, οἷός τε εἶναι. *bear in mind*, μεμνῆσθαι. *to buy up*, συνωνεῖσθαι. *corn*, σῖτος. *corn-seller*, σιτοπώλης. *death*, θάνατος. *every one denies*, οὐδείς φησι. *to be dishonourable in one's office*, οὐ καλῶς ἄρχειν.[a] *to furnish* (*find*), *provide*, παρέχειν. *from goodwill*, ἐπ' εὐνοίᾳ. *to be guilty of a breach of the law*, παρανομεῖν τι. *according to law*, κατὰ νόμον. *to make money*, κερδαίνειν. *to acknowledge a mistake*, μεταγιγνώσκειν.[b] *necessaries*, τὰ ἐπιτήδεια. *in my opinion — ought*, δοκεῖ μοι, followed by acc. and infin. (lit. *it seems good to me that*). *orator*, ῥήτωρ. *perhaps*, ἴσως. *the poor*, οἱ ἀπόρως διακείμενοι.[c] *to punish*, ζημιοῦν. *the rich*, οἱ ἔχοντες. *to sail away*, ἐκπλεῖν. *to show*, ἀποδεικνύναι. *to be ill-, well-treated*, κακῶς, εὖ πάσχειν. *to be willing*, ἐθέλειν.

1. I said that the rich ought to find necessaries for the poor. 2. They say that the best and wisest (men) are most willing to acknowledge a mistake. 3. No one is able to show that he was dishonourable in his office. 4. They said that he sailed away from a desire to make money. 5. It is said that those who have been badly treated bear it in mind longer *than those who*[11] have been well (treated). 6. Some (ἔνιοι) of the orators said that (they) ought to be punished with death. 7. I said that in my opinion the corn-sellers ought to be punished according to law. 8. Perhaps they will say that they bought up the corn from goodwill to the city. 9. They said that they had been guilty of this breach of the law from goodwill to you. 10. Every one denied[11] that he knew him.

4. Say: desiring. 5. Those who have; use article and participle according to § 7. 1 (*b*). 9. To you; use the possessive pronoun with the substantive.

---

[a] Literally: *to govern, manage an office, not well*. This combination of verb and adverb is common in Greek; cp. εὖ πάσχειν, and note [c].

[b] Literally: *to change one's mind*, implying that the change is acknowledged.

[c] διακεῖσθαι with adverbs is a common paraphrase in Greek = English, *to be — off*, e. g. εὖ διακεῖσθαι, *to be well off*; κακῶς διακεῖσθαι, *to be badly off*, *to be in a bad state*.

Exercise 18.

Vocabulary.—*accuser*, κατήγορος. *all of you*, ὑμεῖς πάντες. *to answer*, ἀποκρίνεσθαι. *anything = everything*, πᾶν. *to consider*, νομίζειν. *to defeat, conquer*, νικᾶν. *to be conquered*, ἡττᾶσθαι. *to declare = to say*, φάναι, λέγειν. *money*, χρήματα. *none of the citizens*, οὐδεὶς τῶν πολιτῶν. *offensive*, δυσχερής. *to give orders*, προστάττειν, with dat. *it is permitted to me*, ἔξεστί μοι. *Platæan*, Πλαταιεύς. *to receive*, λαμβάνειν. *three hundred*, τριακόσιοι. *unjustly*, ἀδίκως. *violent*, βίαιος.

1. He answered that he knew the man. 2. *The rest* (§ **15**, 1) declared that they did not know him, but one (man) said that he knew that none of the citizens had (*optative*) this [10] name. 3. Not even Pancleon considers himself to be a Platæan. 4. The accuser says that I am receiving money unjustly from the city. 5. I think that all of you are acquainted with (*know*) my life. 6. He says that I am offensive and violent. 7. It is permitted to me to do this. 8. He thinks that he may (*it is permitted to him to*) do anything. 9. When they heard this [47] they went away, thinking that they were defeated. 10. They went away without saying anything. 11. He declared that it was not possible for him (*that he was unable*) to do this. 12. No one is able to show how these things happened [30]. 13. He said that three hundred soldiers had come into the city. 14. He said that he was general, and that the others had no power (*it was not permitted to the others*) to give any orders [27].

10. Without saying anything = saying nothing.

§ **18.** *The Tenses.*

Tenses are used to express the time of an action (or state). The use of the tenses in Greek, especially in the moods beside the indicative, is a marked peculiarity of the language, and must be carefully noted in reading. Much that we express by the use of auxiliary forms is in Greek expressed by the use of different tenses (Syntax, 66—68); for instance, *I was accustomed to do* may be expressed simply by the imperfect tense.

(1) An action may be spoken of as (*a*) past, present,

or future, and (*b*) as continuous, momentary, or completed. Hence we get nine tenses, thus—

	CONTINUOUS.	MOMENTARY.	COMPLETE.
Past {	*I was doing,* ἔπραττον.	*I did,* ἔπραξα.	*I had done,* ἐπεπράχειν.
Present {	*I am doing,* πράττω.	*I do,* πράττω.	*I have done,* πέπραχα.
Future {	*I shall be doing,* πράξω.	*I shall do,* πράξω.	*I shall have done,* [πεπράξω.]

Obs. i.—All the past tenses begin with the augment, and as the augment is confined to the indicative mood, it follows that *past time* in Greek is expressed in the indicative mood only.

Obs. ii.—The Greeks do not, as a rule, distinguish in the indicative mood the present-continuous and the present-momentary. πράττω is *I am doing,* or *I do.* So also in the future, πράξω is *I shall be doing,* or *I shall do.* But in the other moods than the indicative, the distinction between these two kinds of time is marked by the use of the present and the aorist tenses.

Obs. iii.—Hence the aorist is constantly used in Greek where we use the present, e. g. οὐχ οἷός τέ εἰμι τοῦτο πρᾶξαι, *I am not able to do this;* μὴ τοῦτο κλέψῃς, *do not steal this,* whereas μὴ κλέπτε is rather *do not be a thief.*

Obs. iv.—The Greeks often express actions in momentary time which we express in completed time, i. e. they use the aorist where we use the pluperfect, e. g. *when he had done this, he went away,* is in Greek, *when he did this, he went away,* ἐπειδὴ τοῦτ' ἔπραξε, ἀπῄει. So also with the participle, τοῦτο πράξας ἀπῄει, *having done this, he went away.* In English we have no aorist participle, i. e. no participle of momentary time; we must translate ἐλθὼν εἶδε, *on his arrival he saw;* εὖ ἐποίησας ἀφικόμενος, *you did a kindness in coming; it was kind of you to come.*

(2) As a general rule, all past actions, spoken of without regard to their continuance or consequences, are put in the aorist indicative, which is thus the common tense for narration.

ἀπέθανε, *he died;* ἡ πόλις ἑάλω, *the city was taken.*

When, on the other hand, it is intended to mark the

consequences of the action as still in existence, the perfect is used, ἡ πόλις ἑάλωκε, *the city has been taken, is now captive.* Hence states of body or mind are put in the perfect.

> τέθνηκε, *he is dead;* σεσωσμένος, *saved, safe.*

(3) The imperfect, besides denoting a continuous action—*I was doing*—is also used in Greek to denote an action begun and not completed, or a habitual repeated action.

> ἐμισθοῦτο τὴν αὐλήν, *he wished (or attempted) to hire the court;*
> ἔτυπτεν αὐτόν, *he kept beating him.*

EXERCISE 19.

VOCABULARY.—*Andocides,* Ἀνδοκίδης. *better,* κρείττον. *to confess,* ὁμολογεῖν. *towards day,* πρὸς ἡμέραν. *to demand,* πράττεσθαι (lit. *to get for oneself*). *democracy,* δημοκρατία (*during the democracy* = *when the democracy was,* δημοκρατίας οὔσης, gen. absol. § 37). *door,* θύρα. *either — or,* ἤ — ἤ; in questions, *was it either — or?* πότερον — ἤ; (Syntax, 150.) *to entreat, beseech,* ἱκετεύειν. *estate,* χωρίον. *to show excessive pity, favour,* κατελεεῖν, with acc., καταχαρίζεσθαι, with dat. *to fasten — to,* δεῖν — ἐκ (lit. *to bind — from*). *handle,* ῥόπτρον. *impossible,* ἀδύνατον. *to kill,* ἀποκτείνειν. *to let go,* ἀφίεσθαι, with gen. *to make mention of,* μιμνήσκεσθαι, with gen. (Prim. 166). *misfortune,* δυστυχία. *it is necessary,* ἀνάγκη ἐστί. *the next night,* ἡ ἐπιοῦσα νύξ. *not,* with the infinitive mood, μή (Syntax, 115). *of = about,* περί, with gen. *olive-tree enclosed in a fence),* σηκός. *on,* ἐν. *to open,* ἀνοιγνύναι (Prim. 155). *you ought to hear,* προσήκει ὑμῖν ἀκοῦσαι. *to pass over,* ἐᾶν. *to produce,* παρέχεσθαι. *to show,* ἐπιδεικνύναι. *shrine,* τὸ ἱερόν. *a sum of money,* ἀργύριον. *to take away,* ἀφαιρεῖσθαι. *to think (regard as),* ἡγεῖσθαι. *thirty,* τριάκοντα (*in the rule of the thirty (tyrants),* ἐπὶ τῶν τριάκοντα). *to transgress the law,* παρανομεῖν. *valour,* ἀρετή. *when,* ἐπειδή. *witness,* μάρτυς. *youth, young man,* νεανίσκος.

1. It is necessary to tell you all *that has happened*[14] (= the facts). 2. When it was towards day, he came (ἧκεν) and opened the door. 3. He entreated (*repeatedly*) me not to kill him, but to demand a sum-of-money. 4. They showed their[9]

valour even in misfortune. 5. They let-go the youth, and began-to-beat me. 6. The rest I will pass over, but what I think you ought to hear, of this I will make mention. 7. He fastened his horse to the handle of the shrine, and in the next night (*gen.*) he took it away. 8. It is impossible for you to show either excessive pity or favour to Andocides. 9. He confessed that he did it. 10. Was it better for me to transgress the laws during the democracy, or during (the rule of) the thirty tyrants? 11. I showed that there was no olive-tree on the estate, and produced witnesses.

> 11. That there was not an olive-tree.

§ 19. *The Moods.*

The moods (διαθέσεις) express the mode or form in which an expression is made. These modes or forms are numerous. An action, for instance, may be stated *as a fact* in past, present, or future time, &c.; or the expression may take the form of a *command*, a *question*, a *contingency*, a *wish*, a *purpose*. But there are not different moods to correspond to all these forms; there is no such thing, for instance, as an interrogative mood, distinct from the other moods. The same grammatical forms are also used to express a wish and a purpose, &c.

The Greek language is commonly said to have five moods: the indicative, the imperative, the subjunctive, the optative, the infinitive.

The use of the indicative and imperative is easily understood—it is much the same in Greek and English, except in regard to the tenses. The difficulty is rather to understand rightly the use of the infinitive, the subjunctive, and the optative.

The infinitive for the present may be left out of sight. It is not a mood in the same sense as the other moods, because it cannot express *person* or *number*; in fact, it is not, strictly speaking, a verb at all, but only a verbal substantive, expressing the action of the verb in a general manner (Syntax, 85 ff.). But in indirect speech, as we have seen, it can represent a verb.

The subjunctive and optative remain. These moods are generally represented in English by some form of auxiliary verb, *may, might, should, could,* &c.

The term subjunctive implies that the mood, so called, can only be used in dependent clauses—that is, subjoined to some other clause. In Attic Greek this is true, though there are one or two exceptions: e. g. the aorist subjunctive is used in prohibitions, as μὴ κλέψῃς, *do not steal;* the subjunctive 1st person plural represents the imperative, as μένωμεν, *let us remain;* and the subjunctive can be used in interrogatives implying deliberation (mostly in 1st person singular and plural), as τί φῶ ; *what am I to say?*

In the older language the subjunctive is sometimes used as an emphatic sort of future.

τί γένηται ; *what will happen?* οὐκ ἔστιν οὐδὲ γένηται, *there is not, and cannot be.*

The optative is so called because it is used to express a wish ; but this is but a small part of the use of the optative, as will be seen from the following sections.

The chief use of the subjunctive and optative moods is in dependent clauses. When the tense of the verb in the dependent clause is in any way connected with the tense in the main clause, the general rule is that a subjunctive mood follows a primary tense, an optative a historic tense, in the same way that a present subjunctive in Latin follows a primary tense, and an imperfect subjunctive in Latin follows a historic tense.[a]

---

[a] For this reason the two moods are sometimes spoken of as the primary and historic conjunctives. The terms are convenient for use, but they are nevertheless inaccurate and misleading. We can say in Greek, εἶπεν ὡς ἔλθοι, but we cannot say λέγει ὡς ἔλθῃ (except in the sense, *in order that he may come*). Nor is there any necessary connexion between the optative and past time. For παρῆν ἵνα ἴδοιμι

πάρειμι ἵνα ἴδω,
adsum ut videam, } *I am here that I may see.*

παρῆν ἵνα ἴδοιμι,
aderam ut viderem, } *I was present in order that I might see.*

§ 20. *Optative and Subjunctive in Independent Sentences.*

(1) A wish, which may still be fulfilled, is expressed in the optative, as ἔλθοι, *may he come.* If the wish is negative, μή must be used: μὴ ἔλθοι, *may he not come.*

εἴθε, εἰ, εἰ γάρ, are often added to the optative (cp. § 62 (5)).

(2) Commands and prohibitions are expressed by the imperative and subjunctive: φέρε ἴδω, *come! let me see;* ἴωμεν, *let us go.* In *prohibitions,* if the *subjunctive* is used, the *aorist* tense is required, as μὴ ποιήσῃς τοῦτο, *don't do this,* except in the 1st person singular or plural.

μὴ δοκῶμεν, *let us not think.*

The present tense expresses a habit, the aorist a definite act: μὴ ποίει, *do not do,* of a habit; μὴ ποιήσῃς, *do not do,* of a definite act (§ 18, *Obs.* iii.).

(3) Questions implying deliberation are expressed in the subjunctive.

τί φῶ; *what am I to say?* τί δρῶμεν; *what are we to do?*

Sometimes βούλει; *do you wish?* is prefixed, as βούλει μένωμεν; *do you wish us to remain?*

Obs.—μή with the *imperative* of the *aorist* in the second person is not usual in Attic (Madvig).

---

we might substitute παρῆν ὀψόμενος (or βουλόμενος ἰδεῖν); and for πάρειμι ἵνα ἴδω, πάρειμι ὀψόμενος. If a general definition is to be given, the subjunctive may be defined as the mood of *purpose,* the optative as the mood of *wishing;* and in independent clauses the subjunctive denotes what is regarded as **near** and **definite,** while the optative denotes what is regarded as remote and indefinite.

EXERCISE 20.

VOCABULARY.—*to be absent*, ἀπεῖναι. *to acquit*, ἀφιέναι. *captive* (*prisoner*), αἰχμάλωτος. *to deliberate*, βουλεύεσθαι. *depositions* (*evidence*), μαρτυρία. *to escape* (*run away*), ἀποδρᾶν. *to fear*, φοβεῖσθαι. *god*, θεός. *how?* πῶς; (in indirect questions), ὅπως.ᵃ *how many?* πόσοι; ὁπόσοι, ὅσοι. *law*, νόμος. *to set at liberty*, i. e. *to ransom*, λύεσθαι. *to be at a loss*, ἀπορεῖν. *misfortune*, συμφορά. *to obey*, πείθεσθαι, with dat. *parent*, γονεύς. *to plot against*, ἐπιβουλεύειν, with dat. *to portion* (*give a dowry to*), ἐκδιδόναι. *to be present*, παρεῖναι. *to reproach*, ὀνειδίζειν, with acc. of thing, dat. of person. *to be silent*, σιγᾶν. *sister*, ἀδελφή. *truth* (*true things*), τἀληθῆ.

1. Let me read you the depositions. 2. Come then, let me tell you how many of the captives[29] I set at liberty myself. 3. How are we to speak about these things? 4. Will ye receive us, or are we to go away? 5. Shall we speak or be silent? 6. I am at a loss how to portion my sister. 7. I am deliberating how I am to escape you. 8. Do you wish me to tell you the truth[26]? 9. Do not reproach any one with misfortune. 10. Take the depositions *and* read them. 11. Fear the gods, honour your parents, obey the laws. 12. Do not[33] plot against the thirty when absent (*particip.*), and acquit them when present (*particip.*).

§ 21. *Sentences of Purpose. Indirect Questions.*

(1) A dependent sentence signifying the intention *to, in order to, in order that, with a view to*, can be expressed in Greek by a dependent clause beginning with ὅπως, ὡς, ἵνα, *that.*

---

* In § 15, 2, we saw that in dependent or indirect questions, after verbs of asking, deliberating, &c., the rule is to use—

not τίς ; *who?* but ὅστις.

not πόσος ;	ποῖος ;	πηλίκος ;
(*quantus?*)	(*qualis?*)	*how old or big?*
but ὁπόσος.	ὁποῖος.	ὁπηλίκος.

So also

not πότε ;	ποῖ ;	ποῦ ;	πῶς ;	πόθεν ;	πῇ ;
when?	*whither?*	*where?*	*how?*	*whence?*	*how? whither?*
but ὁπότε.	ὅποι.	ὅπου.	ὅπως.	ὁπόθεν.	ὅπη.

But the *direct* interrogatives are nevertheless very frequently used in indirect questions, as ἠρώτα με τίς εἴην, *he asked me who I was.*

(*a*) If the verb in the main clause is in a primary tense (present, perfect, future), the verb in the dependent clause is in the subjunctive mood.

πάρειμι ἵνα ἴδω, *I am here to see; in order that I may see.*

(*b*) If the verb in the main clause is in a historic tense (an augmented tense), the verb in the dependent clause is in the optative mood.

παρῆν ἵνα ἴδοιμι, *I was there to see; in order that I might see.*

(2) In indirect questions:

(*a*) The indicative is used when the verb in the main clause is in a primary tense : πόθεν ἥκεις ; *whence do you come?* πόθεν ἥκω ἔρει ; *do you ask whence I come?*

(*b*) If the verb in the main clause is in a historic tense, the optative may be used, as ἤρετο πόθεν ἥκοι. *he asked whence he came.* (πόθεν ἥκει *is also possible, but not* πόθεν ἥκῃ).

(*c*) If the question is deliberative, the subjunctive is used when the tense in the main clause is primary, as ἀπορῶ τί φῶ, *I do not know what I am to say.* After a historic tense this subjunctive may pass into an optative, as ἠπόρει τί δρῴη, *he did not know what to do.*[a]

(3) Verbs of asking and deliberating are often followed by εἰ (§ 22). Here, also, primary tenses are followed by the indicative, and historic tenses by the optative.

(1) ἐρωτῶ, εἰ τοῦτ' ἀληθές ἐστι, *I ask if this is true.*
(2) ἠρώτα, εἰ τοῦτ' ἀληθὲς εἴη, *he asked if this was true.*

When the clause beginning with εἰ represents a deliberative subjunctive, the subjunctive *can* be retained : εἰς τὰ χρηστήρια ἔπεμψε, εἰ στρατεύηται ἐπὶ τοὺς Πέρσας, *he*

---

[a] This, however, represents τί δράσω : (fut. indic.) as well as τί δρῶ (subj.), there being no distinction. in this form of construction, between questions for information and deliberative questions.

*sent to the oracles (and inquired) if he should march against
the Persians,* where εἰ στρατεύηται is the indirect form of
στρατεύωμαι ;

EXERCISE 21.

VOCABULARY.—*to accept,* παραλαμβάνειν. *to announce,
bring news,* ἀπαγγέλλειν. *Aphobus,* Ἄφοβος. *to ask,* ἔρεσθαι,
ἐρωτᾶν. *building,* οἴκημα. *to burn,* κατακαίειν. *to capture
(seize),* καταλαμβάνειν. *to converse with,* διαλέγεσθαι, with
dat. *to do something with,* χρῆσθαι τι, with dat. *Elatea,*
Ἐλάτεια. *to set fire to,* ἐμπιπράναι. *to give up,* παραδιδόναι.
helper, σύνεργος. *if,* εἰ. *to have need of,* δεῖσθαι, with
gen. *to pay (give),* ἀποδιδόναι, with dat. of person. *prytany
(public officer at Athens, see* Dict. Ant.), πρυτανεῖς. *Theban,*
Θηβαῖος. *to be troubled with,* πράγματα ἔχειν ὑπό, with
gen. *when,* ὅτε. *whether — or,* εἴτε — εἴτε (Syntax, 124).
to do wrong to, ἀδικεῖν, with acc.

1. Cyrus thought that he had need of friends, in order that
he might have helpers. 2. I asked Aphobus if any persons
were present when he accepted the money. 3. They asked if
they should give up the city. 4. He gave him money, that he
might not be troubled by him. 5. One came with-a-message
(announcing) to the prytaneis that Elatea was captured. 6. They
deliberated whether they should burn the Thebans by setting-
fire-to (*particip.*) the building, or should do something else (with
them). 7. Are we to do wrong to all our citizens in order that
thirty may serve us? 8. Having no one with whom to converse, he went away. 9. He sent him to [13] carry the news (*announce the matter*) to Cyrus. 10. I shall ask Cyrus if he is
willing to pay the money.

8. With whom he could converse (*optative*).

§ 22. *On εἰ and ἄν. Conditional Propositions.*

(Syntax, 176 ff.)

(1) The conjunction εἰ (like our *if*) has the two mean-
ings of *if* and *whether;* hence it is not only used in
indirect questions, as in the last section, but in clauses
introducing a hypothesis or supposition. It takes the
indicative or optative.

Obs.—εἰ + ἄν = ἐάν, ἤν, &c., always takes the subjunctive.

(2) ἄν (Syntax, 132) is a particle which we cannot translate in English. It indicates an implied condition :

λέγοιμ' ἄν, *I would say* (i. e. *if I were asked*) ;

or refers to a condition already stated:

εἴ τι ἔχοιμι, διδοίην ἄν, *if I should have anything, I would give it.*

Obs. i.—In conditional sentences, ἄν with the subjunctive is always in the protasis, never in the apodosis ; ἄν with the indicative or optative is always in the apodosis, never in the protasis.

Obs. ii.—The *if*-clause is the protasis ; the clause which answers to *if* is the apodosis.

(3) The commonest forms of conditional propositions in Greek are the following :—

(*a*) εἰ βροντᾷ καὶ ἀστράπτει,
     if it thunders, it also lightens.
     εἰ ἐβρόντησε καὶ ἤστραψεν,
     if it thundered, it also lightened.
     εἴ τι ἔξω, δώσω,
     if I shall have anything, I will give it.

This form of hypothesis, which merely connects two statements in the simplest manner, may be used with any tense of the indicative mood.

(*b*) ἐάν = (εἰ ἄν) τι ἔχωμεν. δώσομεν,
     if we have anything, we will give it.

Here the use of the subjunctive with ἄν represents the clause in which it occurs as somewhat uncertain.[a]

(*c*) εἴ τις ταῦτα πράττοι, μέγα μ' ἂν ὠφελήσειε,
     if any one should do (or *were to do*) *this, he would do me a great service.*

In this form of the hypothesis the prospect of decision is not kept in view. The statement is vague. There is no

---

[a] In English we have no exactly corresponding expression ; *if I have* is too near the indicative, *if I should have* is too near the optative. It would be possible to say in Greek, εἴ τι ἔξω, *if I shall have*, but this would give a definite reference to a future time, which is not implied in the subjunctive with ἄν. This form of conditional proposition is used when we speak with uncertainty, but with a prospect of decision, and in making general statements.

certainty that the person will act in the manner indicated ; *if* he does, the result indicated will follow.[a]

(*d*) εἴ τι εἶχεν, ἐδίδου ἄν,
    if he had anything, he would give it.
    εἰ ἔπραξε τοῦτο, καλῶς ἂν ἔσχεν,
    if he had done this, it would have been well.
    τῶν ἀδικημάτων ἂν ἐμέμνητο τῶν αὑτοῦ, εἴ τι περὶ ἐμοῦ γεγράφει,
    *he would have made mention of his own misdeeds, if he had
    proposed anything concerning me.*

Observe—

(i.) By placing a hypothesis in past time, the Greeks represent it as impossible.

> Hence all forms of conditional sentences, which represent the condition as no longer possible, are expressed in the augmented tenses of the indicative mood.

(ii.) Conditions and consequences which are represented as having duration, and as continuing up to the present time, are placed in the imperfect ; conditions and consequences referring to some moment in past time, are expressed in the aorist.

> his is one of the instances (cp. **18.** (1), *Obs.* iv.) in which the *have*, *had* of the English perfect and pluperfect are employed in translating a Greek aorist ; but the aorist is used in Greek because the statement, if not hypothetical, would be in that tense (*I had something, and I gave it*).[b]

(iii.) When the *perfect* would be used in a sentence not hypothetical, the *pluperfect* is used in the hypothetical form ; e. g. *I have had something, and I have given it*, would require the pluperfect, *if I had had, I would have*

---

[a] In English we often say, *if a person did this, he would do me a great favour*, using the indicative in the protasis, though we do not intend to speak of anything but a mere supposition. We must not be misled by this idiom, which is less exact than the Greek, but remember the difference between *if it was* and *if it were*—where the forms of the verb allow a distinction analogous to the distinction between the indicative and the optative in Greek. In every statement which means, *if* this *were true*, that *would also be true*, the optative is to be used in both clauses.

[b] Conditional propositions with the imperfect are sometimes not easily distinguished in translation from propositions with the aorist ;

given it. Thus the Greek, by means of the aorist and pluperfect, preserves differences which can hardly be expressed in English.

Lastly, a condition may be spoken of with definite reference to past time, while the consequence is regarded as continuing up to the present. In this case the protasis is placed in the aorist, the apodosis in the imperfect.

(e) εἰ ἐπείσθην, οὐκ ἂν ἠρρώστουν, *if I had (then) been persuaded, I should not (now) be out of health.*

Taken out of the hypothetical form, this sentence becomes : *I was not persuaded, and I am out of health.*

Obs.—ἄν is not to be joined with the primary tenses of the indicative or with any tense of the imperative.

EXERCISE 22.

VOCABULARY.—*to be so,* οὕτως ἔχειν. *to benefit, do a service,* ὠφελεῖν, with acc. *to be found guilty of,* ἁλίσκεσθαι, with gen. *to hurt, injure,* βλάπτειν, with acc. *mina,* μνᾶ. *murder,* φόνος. *not only — but also,* οὐχ ὅτι — ἀλλὰ καί. *Philip,* Φίλιππος.

1. If I have anything, I will give it [40]. 2. If you were to do this, you would confer the greatest [27] benefit upon me. 3. If any one should do this, he would greatly [27] injure me. 4. If I had a mina, I would give it to the slave. 5. If any one were to do this, he would do the greatest injury to the state. 6. If the wise were to manage the affairs of the state [15], they would confer a great benefit upon all the citizens. 7. If this be so, I will go away at once. 8. If you were really wise, you would admire the beauty of virtue [1]. 9. If the citizens were wise, they would have killed not only Xenoclides, but also Philip. 10. If you should be found guilty of murder, the citizens will put you to death.

---

the meaning is nevertheless different : εἰ ἦσαν ἄνδρες ἀγαθοί, οὐκ ἄν ποτε ταῦτα ἔπασχον, *if they had been brave men, they would never have suffered this treatment;* this refers to a series of acts in the past : οὐκ ἂν νήσων ἐκράτει, εἰ μή τι καὶ ναυτικὸν εἶχεν, *he would never have become master of the islands, if he had not been in possession of a fleet;* here the reference is to a past state. The person spoken of was master of the islands for some time, and was possessor of a fleet (Goodwin, Moods and Tenses, § 19 (2)).

§ 23. *Conditional Propositions in Indirect Narration.*

(1) After ὡς or ὅτι, with verbs of saying (§ 17), conditional propositions are unchanged where the main verb is in a primary (present, perfect, future) tense.

> λέγει ὅτι εἴ τι ἔχει, δώσει,
> *he says that if he has anything, he will give it.*
> λέγει ὅτι ἐάν τι ἔχῃ, δώσει, &c.

But when the main verb is in a historic tense:

(*a*) Those forms of conditional propositions which have the indicative (present and future) or subjunctive in the protasis (§ 22 (3), *a* and *b*), change these moods into the optative, and the indicative future of the apodosis *may* become the future optative.

> ἐάν τι ἔχῃ (or εἴ τι ἔχει, or ἕξει), δώσει,
>   becomes
> ἔλεγεν ὅτι εἴ τι ἔχοι, δώσει, or δώσοι.

(*b*) The forms with the optative and the past tenses of the indicative in the protasis, and ἄν in the apodosis (§ 22 (3), *c* and *d*), remain unchanged.

> εἴ τι ἔχοι, δοίη ἄν,
> εἴ τι εἶχεν (ἔσχεν), ἐδίδου ἄν, ἔδωκεν ἄν,
>   remain unchanged.

(2) When the verb of saying takes the infinitive, the following changes occur :—

(*a*) Instead of the indicative future in the apodosis, we have the infinitive future ; and in the protasis, εἰ with the optative takes the place of ἐάν with the subjunctive, if the main verb is in a historic tense.

> εἴ τι ἔχοι (ἔχει may also be used) ἔφη δώσειν.

If the main verb is in a primary tense, the protasis remains unchanged.

> εἴ τι ἔχει (or ἐάν τι ἔχῃ), φησὶ δώσειν.

(*b*) Instead of the optative with ἄν in apodosis, we have the infinitive with ἄν.

> εἴ τι ἔχοι, ἔφη δοῦναι ἄν.

(c) Instead of the imperfect or aorist with ἄν in apodosis, we have the present or aorist infinitive with ἄν.

εἴ τι εἶχεν, ἔφη δοῦναι ἄν.

Thus, where we should have had in the apodosis:

| ποιήσω, | ⎰ ποιοῖμ' ἄν,
⎱ ἐποίουν ἄν, | ποιήσαιμ' ἄν,
ἐποίησα ἄν, | πεποιήκοιμ' ἄν.
ἐπεποιήκειν ἄν. |

we shall have:

| | ποιήσειν, | ποιεῖν ἄν, | ποιῆσαι ἄν, | πεποιηκέναι ἄν. |

EXERCISE 23.

VOCABULARY.— *to arrange, equip, furnish,* κατασκευάζειν. *blessings (goods),* ἀγαθά. *to come in (of money),* προσιέναι. *to deprive,* στερεῖν, fut. in passive sense, στερήσεσθαι. *to happen to know,* τυγχάνειν εἰδώς (§ 35 (2)). *to inflict, suffer injury,* ποιεῖν, πάσχειν κακῶς. *to inhabit,* οἰκεῖν, with acc. *to be master of,* ἄρχειν, with gen. *mines,* μέταλλα. *a large sum of money,* χρήματα πάμπολλα. *to pity,* ἐλεεῖν. *to have it in my power,* ὑπάρχειν ἐμοί (ὑπάρχειν is used impersonally). *to praise,* ἐπαινεῖν. *properly,* ὡς δεῖ. *to be proved to be,* ἐπιδειχθῆναι ὤν (§ 35, (3) b). *sea,* θάλαττα. *so long as,* ἕως, with indic. *would simply say that =* would say so much (τοσοῦτον) *that.*

1. He said that if you were to do this, you would do him the greatest[27] service. 2. I said that if any one were to do this, he would greatly injure me. 3. He said that, if he had a mina, he would give it to the slave. 4. He said that if any one were to do this, he would do the greatest injury to the state. 5. I think that each of you, if any one were to ask him what he did not happen (*opt.*) to know, would simply say that he did not know. 6. If he is proved to be a good citizen, I think that you ought to praise him. 7. If the mines were properly arranged, I think that a large sum of money would come in from them. 8. They ought to know that if they pity him, they will be deprived of other greater blessings. 9. If the Athenians inhabited an island, they would have had it in their power to inflict injuries without suffering any (*but to suffer nothing*), so long as they were masters of the sea. 10. He declared that he would not go away unless he received a present.

§ 24. ἀν in Apodosis ; ἀν with Infinitive and Participle.

(Cp. § 34 on the Participle.)

(1) In conditional propositions the protasis is often dropped, and the apodosis alone remains, i. e. we say, *I would, I should,* do this or that—meaning, *if I had the opportunity, if I might.* Hence, in Greek:

(*a*) The optative with ἀν is equivalent to our *would, should,* and sometimes to our *may, might.*

> ἡδέως ἂν θεασαίμην ταῦτα,
> *I would gladly see this ;* or, *I should like to see this.*
> ἄνθρωπον ἀναιδέστερον οὐκ ἄν τις εὕροι,
> *one could not find a more shameless fellow.*

Sometimes the optative with ἀν is even equivalent to a future, the Greeks preferring the more indirect and doubtful mode of expression to the direct future.

> λέγοιμ' ἄν, *I will tell you (with your permission) ;* οὐκ ἂν φύγοις, *you cannot escape ;* εἴποι τις ἄν, φήσειέ τις ἄν, *some one will (or may) say.*

(*b*) The indicative aorist with ἀν is equivalent to our *should have been ;* οὐκ ἂν εὗρον αὐτόν, *I should not have found him.*

> *Obs.*—Often, both in these clauses, and in those with the optative with ἀν, the condition (protasis) is expressed by a participle.
> ζητῶν οὐκ ἂν εὗρον,
> *if I had sought, by seeking, I should not have found.*

(2) (*a*) ἀν gives to the infinitive and participle the same force that it gives to the optative and indicative.

> πόσον ἂν οἴει εὑρεῖν τὰ σὰ κτήματα πωλούμενα : *how much do you think that your possessions would fetch* (lit. *find*) *if they were sold !* = πόσον ἂν εὕροι — εἰ πωλοῖτο ;

If for the present, πωλούμενα, we substitute the aorist participle, πωληθέντα (πραθέντα), we may translate, *how much do you think that they would have fetched, if they had been sold ?* = πόσον ἂν εὗρεν, εἰ ἐπράθη ;

So with the active participle : τἆλλα σιωπῶ, πολλὰ ἂν
ἔχων εἰπεῖν, *about the rest I am silent, though I should
have much to say,* where πολλὰ ἂν ἔχων εἰπεῖν = καίπερ
πολλὰ ἂν ἔχοιμι εἰπεῖν.

Sometimes ὡς is added to the participle in this construction to express the alleged object or intention with
which an act is done.

αἰτεῖ μισθόν, ὡς οὕτως περιγενόμενος ἂν τῶν πολεμίων, *he asks for
pay, as being thus likely to conquer the enemies.*

Here ὡς οὕτως περιγενόμενος ἄν is = οὕτω γὰρ ἄν, ὡς
φησι, περιγένοιτο (cp. § 36).

(*b*) Thus ἄν with the infinitive is often equivalent to a
future infinitive. This is the common way of expressing
the future after verbs of *hoping, thinking, trusting, knowing, confessing,* &c., when the future is in any way
dependent on a condition expressed or implied.

κάρτ' ἂν εὐτυχεῖν δοκῶ (ἐμέ),
I think that I should be very fortunate,
= κάρτ' ἂν εὐτυχοῖμι.

ὁμολογῶ ταῦτ' ἂν ἀληθῆ εἶναι,
I confess that this would be true,
= ταῦτ' ἀληθῆ ἂν εἴη.

ἤλπισεν ἂν δείξαι,
he hoped that he would show.

(3) The optative with ἄν, and also the indicative with
ἄν, is very common in questions with τίς; πῶς;

τίς ἂν νομίζοι;
who would think!

τίς ἂν εὖρεν;
who would have found? &c.

πῶς ἄν; with the optative, is also at times used to
express a wish.

πῶς ἂν ὀλοίμην;
would that I might perish.

πῶς ἂν ἔλθοι,
I wish he would come.

EXERCISE 24.

VOCABULARY.—*I should like to* —, ἡδέως ἄν, with opt. of the verb. *that is, no good man ;* say : *at least* (γε) *being good.* *messenger*, ἄγγελος. *to get money*, χρήματα λαβεῖν. *to please*, ἀρέσκειν (i. e. *to satisfy*), with dat. *to venture*, τολμᾶν. *to be well for*, καλῶς ἔχειν (impers.), with dat. of person.

1. I should like to know, what I should have suffered (*what would have become of me*), if this had happened. 2. I should like to ask who this (person) is. 3. It would have been well for you, if this had happened. 4. No one would have done this [17]. 5. No one, that is, no good man, would have done this [17]. 6. I will tell you what I heard from the messenger. 7. I think that you would like to hear why this happened. 8. He went away to Philip, *because he thought he would* get money (*part. with* ἄν). 9. What would not such a man venture to do? 10. How could I please such people?

EXERCISE 25.

VOCABULARY.—*ally*, σύμμαχος. *clearly*, σαφῶς. *to contribute money*, εἰσφέρειν χρήματα. *to find*, εὑρίσκειν (Prim. 166). *happily*, εὐδαιμόνως. *justly*, δικαίως. *to live*, ζῆν. *not to know a thing*, ἀγνοεῖν τι. *to prove*, ἐπιδεικνύναι. *rather* — *than*, ἥδιον — ἤ. *slavish*, ἀνδραποδώδης. *strength*, ἰσχύς, ἡ. *ten times*, δεκάκις. *to be at one's wits' end*, εἰς πολλὴν ἀπορίαν καθεστηκέναι.

1. I do not know how I could prove the matter more clearly. 2. I am at my wits' end (to know) what I could do to please these men (*what doing* (part.) *I could please*). 3. Oh that I might [36] live more happily! 4. Who could have been found wiser? 5. You will not escape from those who [11] are pursuing you. 6. Some one will say that the strength of the Athenians consists in the ability of their allies to contribute money (*that this is the strength of the Athenians if their allies be able*, &c.). 7. What can I do to benefit you (*what doing*)? 8. I think that he would rather die ten times than do this [17]. 9. Socrates thought that persons who did not know [41] this would justly be called slavish. 10. I do not think that a wiser man could have been found.

§ 25. *Compounds with ἄν. Relative Clauses.*

(1) (*a*) The compounds of ἄν (ἐάν, ὅταν, ἐπειδάν, &c.) regularly take the subjunctive after a verb in a primary tense.

> παρέσομαι, ἐάν τι δέῃ,
> *I will come (or be with you), if there be any need.*
>
> τότε δὴ, ὅταν ἃ χρὴ ποιῇς, εὐτυχεῖς,
> *then only, when you do what you ought, are you prosperous.*

(*b*) The same rule applies to relatives with ἄν (ὃς ἄν, ὅστις ἄν): οὓς ἂν ἴδῃ εὐτάκτως καὶ σιωπῇ ἰόντας, ἐπαινεῖ, *whomsoever he sees marching in good order, and in silence, he praises.*

> *Obs.*—To relatives and conjunctions the addition of ἄν often gives the force of our *ever: ὃς ἄν* (= *quicunque, si quis*), *whoever, any one, who;* and in the plural, *all who; ὅταν, whenever,* &c.

(2) After a historic tense, and in indirect narration, these compounds with ἄν, relatives, &c., may (*a*) remain unchanged with the subjunctive; or, (*b*) their place may be taken by the simple words, εἰ, ὅτε, ἐπειδή, and the relatives *without* ἄν, with the *optative.*

> Thus
> παρέσομαι ἐάν τι δέῃ
> becomes
> (*a*) ἔφη παρέσεσθαι ἐάν τι δέῃ, ⎫ *he said that he would be present,*
> (*b*) ἔφη παρέσεσθαι, εἴ τι δέοι, ⎭ *if there were any need.*

> *Obs.*—In this use the optative often denotes what has taken place frequently in past time : *optative of indefinite frequency.*
> ὑπερῷον εἶχεν ὁπότε ἐν ἄστει διατρίβοι, *he had an upper chamber whenever he stayed in town;*
> ἔπραττεν ἃ δόξειεν αὐτῷ, *he did what (in each case) seemed good to him;*
> οὓς ἴδοι εὐτάκτως καὶ σιωπῇ ἰόντας, ἐπῄνει, *he used to praise those whom (at any time) he saw marching in good order and silence.*

(3) When these compounds of ἄν and relatives with ἄν occur with the aorist subjunctive, that tense sometimes

marks the completion of the action, and thus answers to
the Latin future perfect.

ἐπειδὰν ἅπαντα ἀκούσητε, κρίνατε,
when you have heard all, judge.

διαφθερεῖ ὅ τι ἂν λάβῃ,
he will destroy whatever he takes (ceperit).

EXERCISE 26.

VOCABULARY. — *to join (as an ally)*, προστίθεσθαι. *market-
place*, ἀγορά. *you may go away*, say : *it is possible for you,
&c.*, ἔξεστί σοι. *to make necessary*, ἀναγκάζειν. *to punish*,
ζημιοῦν. *to stay*, i. e. *to pass time*, διατρίβειν. *whenever*,
ὁπόταν, ὁπότε. *to be wise*, σωφρονεῖν. *to do wrong*, πλημμελεῖν,
lit. *to strike a false note.*

1. If you are wise, you will do this. 2. Whenever I come
to the city, I see Socrates conversing in the market-place. 3.
When you have done this, you may go away. 4. Whoever does
this must be put to death. 5. When you have seen, you will
know. 6. Whenever he stayed in the city, he *used-to-come*
(*imperf.*) to our house. 7. When you have proved this, I will
step down. 8. Whomsoever he saw doing wrong, he used to
punish. 9. Whomsoever you join, they will conquer. 10. Whatever the circumstances make necessary, about this I will speak.

EXERCISE 27.

VOCABULARY. — *to abandon*, προίεσθαι. *to advance*, ἐπιέναι.
amusement, παιδιά. *to attack*, ἐπίκεισθαι. *to encamp*, αὐλίζεσθαι. *to be engaged in serious business*, σπουδαῖόν τι πράττειν.
guard, φύλαξ. *to set guards*, φύλακας καθιστάναι. *to help*,
ἀρκεῖν, fut. ἀρκέσειν. *to indulge (in an amusement)*, χρῆσθαι, with
dat. *judges*, say : *the judging* (particip. and article, § 7, (1) *b*).
to judge, δικάζειν. *justice*, τὸ δίκαιον (§ 8 (1)). *to obtain*, διαπράττεσθαι. *prison*, δεσμωτήριον. *to publish a proclamation
of death*, κηρύττειν θάνατον. *to retire*, ὑποχωρεῖν, ἀναχωρεῖν
(the first in the sense of *making room for a person*). *to*, παρά,
with acc., ὡς, with acc. (of persons only). *to want*, δεῖσθαι.

1. Whenever the prison was opened, we *used to go* (*imperf.*)
to Socrates. 2. Now I am going to the king ; when I have
obtained what [67] I want, I will take you to Hellas. 3. They in-

dulged in this amusement whenever they were not engaged in
more serious business. 4. He said that [35], whenever he went into
the city, he saw Socrates talking in the market-place. 5. He
said that he saw no one who could help him. 6. He published
a proclamation, that whoever did this would be put to death.
7. Whenever they came where it was necessary to encamp,
they set guards. 8. Whenever the Athenians advanced, they
retired ; and when they retired, they attacked them. 9. When
you have managed the affairs of the state [15] well, you shall manage
mine also. 10. Men praise the judges when they do not (μή)
abandon justice.

6. Say : He published a proclamation of death if any one should
do this.

§ 26. *The Negatives οὐ and μή* (Syntax, 114 ff).

(1) The direct negative in Greek is οὐ (negative of
fact), which is used in all direct and independent clauses,
and in indirect clauses when it is the denial of an actual
fact that is made, i. e. after ὅτι, ὡς (*that*) ; and with ἐπεί,
ἐπειδή (*when, after, as, since*). οὐκ ἐθέλει, *he does not
choose*; λέγει ὡς οὐκ ἐθέλει, *he says that he does not choose*.
οὐκ ἂν γένοιτο, *it cannot be*; οὐκ ἂν ἦλθεν, *he would not
have come*; λέγει ὡς οὐκ ἂν ἦλθεν, *he says that he would
not have come*. τί οὐκ ἐγένετο ; οὐδέν ἐστιν ὅ τι οὐκ
ἐγένετο.

οὐ is also used, even with the infinitive, after verbs of
saying and *thinking*, &c.: οὐκ ἐθέλειν φησί, *he says that
he does not choose*; νομίζει οὐ καλὸν εἶναι, *he thinks that it
is not honourable*. μὴ δοκῶμεν δρῶντες κακὰ οὐκ ἀντ-
τίσειν κακά.

(2) When the negative is in any sense dependent, i. e.
when it will only hold good under certain conditions—
when it refers to a supposed case or purpose, or expresses
a *fear, solicitude*, or *care*, i. e. when it is = to our *lest* or
whether, μή is used (negative of conception).

(*a*) μή is used in all *prohibitions*, whether with the imperative or the subjunctive mood, as μὴ κλέψῃς, μὴ κλέπτε, and in wishes with the optative mood, as μὴ γένοιτο.

(*b*) μή is used with all conditional conjunctions, εἰ, ἐάν (ἤν, ἄν), ὅταν, ἐπειδάν, and with ὅτε, ὁπότε, when a condition is implied.

> εἰ μηδὲν ἔχει, πῶς δώσει;
> *if he has nothing, how can he give it?*
> ὅταν μὴ δύνωμαι, παύσομαι.
> *when I am able, I will stop.*

(*c*) μή is used with all conjunctions expressing intention or purpose, ἵνα, ὅπως, ὡς, &c.

> ἄπειμι, ἵνα μὴ ἴδω,
> *I will go away, in order that I may not see.*
> τοῦτ' ἐποίει, ἵνα μὴ ἔλθοι,
> *he did this, in order that he might not come.*

(3) In negative propositions, indefinite pronouns and adverbs should be translated into Greek by the corresponding negative forms.

(*a*) Hence the particles for *neither — nor* (οὔτε — οὔτε μήτε — μήτε) are to be used after a negative, where in English we use *either — or;* and, similarly, *no, nobody, nowhere,* must be used for *any, anybody, anywhere.*

> ἀπῆλθεν ἵνα μηδεὶς μήτε ἴδοι μήτε ἀκοῦσαι, *he went away, that no one might either see or hear.*

(*b*) The forms compounded with οὐ and μή, as οὐδείς, οὔτε, μηδείς, μήτε, are to be used according as the principal negative of the proposition is οὐ (or a compound of οὐ) or μή (or a compound of μή).

Exercise 28.

VOCABULARY.—*to be in danger,* κινδυνεύειν. *to detect,* ἐξελέγχειν. *to be disobedient,* ἀπιστεῖν. *to know,* ἐπίστασθαι. *to let be, leave alone,* ἐᾶν. *misfortunes,* τὰ κακά. *to order — not, to forbid,* ἀπαγορεύειν. *painful,* ἀλγεινός. *unless,* εἰ μή.

1. If it seems good to you, do so; if not, let it be. 2. He did not think that it was honourable to go away *when the city was in danger* (gen. absol., § 37). 3. Neither he nor his father said anything [41] about the matter. 4. Say [33] nothing that is not true, that you may not be detected *in falsehood* (*speaking false things*). 5. He says that he will not come unless you go away. 6. I could not, and may I never know (how) to be disobedient to my father. 7. There is no one who [71] does not say that this is true. 8. He ordered him not to go into the city. 9. Do not say anything to any one [41] about the matter. 10. There is nothing painful or disgraceful, which (*such as*) I have not seen in my misfortunes.

§ 27. *The Negative continued, μή.*

(1) (*a*) When μή is used with relative sentences, it implies that the negative does not directly and simply deny an assertion in respect to some particular person or thing, but that the negative is conditional or general, and extends to a class, or to all persons or things of such a nature as the thing named (Ex. 27, 3).

τίς δοῦναι δύναται ἑτέρῳ, ἃ μὴ αὐτὸς ἔχει; *who can give to another what he has not got himself?*

Here the negative is conditional (if he has not got it himself), or denotes a class (belonging to the class of things which he does not possess). Hence ὃς μή in Greek is = *qui non* with the subjunctive in Latin.

(*b*) μή is used with adjectives and participles in the same conditional and general sense: τὰ μὴ καλά, *what is not honourable* (of a whole class of things); ὁ μὴ ποιῶν, *one who does not do* (speaking generally) ; μὴ ποιῶν, *without doing* (conditional) ; ὁ μηδὲν εἰδὼς Οἰδίπους, *the (Edipus, who* (as you imply) *knows nothing.*

(2) μή is used with infinitives (but cp. § 26, 1).

τὸ μὴ τιμᾶν γέροντας ἀνόσιον, *it is wrong (unholy) not to honour old men.*

ὥστε, *so that,* with the infinitive, takes μή; with the indicative, οὐ.

ἀσφάλειάν σοι παρέξονται, ὥστε σε μηδένα λυπεῖν, *they will afford you security, so that no man shall annoy you ;*
πράγματα παρεῖχον ὥστε οὐκέτι ἐδύνατο τὸ στράτευμα πορεύεσθαι, *they harassed them, so that the army was unable to advance any farther.*

Exercise 29.

Vocabulary.—*it is agreed,* δοκεῖ.[a] *to belong to, to be becoming to,* or *for,* προσήκειν, with dat. *brave,* ἀνδρεῖος. *dangerous,* σφαλερός. *foolish,* μωρός. *human affairs,* τὰ ἀνθρώπινα. *lasting,* βέβαιος. *not — yet,* οὔπω. *punishment,* ζημία. *to repent,* μεταμέλειν (impersonal, μεταμέλει μοι, *I repent*). *servant,* οἰκέτης. *to set sail,* ἐκπλεῖν. *strong,* ἰσχυρός. *to summon,* παρακαλεῖν. *unprepared,* ἀπαράσκευος. *to make use of,* χρῆσθαι, with dat. *to vote,* ψηφίζεσθαι.

1. I do not think that I know what I do not know. 2. Vote such[27] (measures) that you will never repent of them (*of which you will never repent*). 3. Do you not see how dangerous it is to say or do what one (τις) does not know ? 4. What use could one make of a strong or brave man, if he were not wise ? 5. I came so unprepared that I did not summon either[d] friends or servants or any other person. 6. It has been agreed that the ships shall not set sail yet. 7. Consider that there is nothing lasting in (*gen.*) human affairs. 8. They will be worthy of punishment, if they (shall) take what does not belong to them. 9. What army could conquer without (*not having*) generals? 10. No one that is not foolish would do such a thing.

---

* Use the aorist infinitive after δοκεῖ, § 33 (2).

§ 28. ὅπως, *with Verbs of Striving, &c.* οὐ μή.

I.

(1) After verbs of *striving* (*considering, planning*), ὅπως is often found with the future indicative to express the object of the endeavour.

φρόντιζε ὅπως τοῦτο ποιήσεις, *consider how you will do this.*
φρόντιζε, ὅπως μηδὲν αἰσχρὸν ποιήσεις, *take care to do nothing disgraceful.*

(2) When the intention is to be marked strongly, i. e. when instead of *how* we can say *in order that*, the subjunctive may be used.

οὐκ οἴει σοι ἄξιον ἐπιμεληθῆναι, ὅπως διασωθῇ ἡ πόλις; *do you not think it worth your while to take care that the city be saved?*

II.

When these constructions occur after a historic tense in the main clause, the optative may take the place of the indicative or subjunctive (but the future optative is rarely used).

ἐπεμελεῖτο ὅπως διασωθείη, *he considered how he might escape.*

But more frequently the construction is not changed even after a past tense, as, ἔπραξεν, ὅπως ἐπὶ τοῖς ἐχθροῖς ἡ πόλις ἔσται, *he took measures that the city might be in the power of the enemy.*

III.

The verb on which ὅπως depends is sometimes omitted, and ὅπως with the future or subjunctive becomes equivalent to an imperative.

ὅπως ἀνὴρ ἔσει, *see that you behave like a man.*
ὅπως μὴ ποιήσητε, ὃ πολλάκις ὑμᾶς ἔβλαψεν, *be sure not to do what has often been detrimental to you.*

IV.

(*a*) οὐ μή with the aorist subjunctive and indicative future is a strong negative.

οὐ μὴ γένηται τοῦτο, *this will assuredly not happen.*
οὐ σοι μὴ μεθέψομαι, *I will not follow you.*

E

(*b*) οὐ μή with the *second person* of the indicative future and an interrogative, is a strong prohibition.

οὐ μὴ λαλήσεις; *don't talk.*[a]

EXERCISE 30.

VOCABULARY.—*argument,* λόγος. *army,* στράτευμα. *as — as possible,* use the superlative adjective with ὡς, e. g. *as good as possible,* ὡς βέλτιστος. *bring in (apply),* προσφέρειν. *to consider,* φράζεσθαι, φροντίζειν. *cowardly,* δειλός. *to cross,* διαβαίνειν. *food,* σιτία, τά. *freedom,* ἐλευθερία. *to go out from,* ἐξέρχεσθαι ἐκ. *to keep (a peace),* ἄγειν. *peace,* εἰρήνη. *to pity,* οἰκτίζειν. *to save, keep safe, preserve,* διασώζειν. *shepherd,* ποιμήν, ὁ. *to take measures,* προθυμεῖσθαι (lit. *to be anxious or zealous*), ἐπιμελεῖσθαι (lit. *to take care, be careful*), παρασκευάζειν (lit. *to make preparations*), πράττειν.

1. Take care that one day (ποτέ) you will not pity yourself. 2. Do not bring in a cowardly argument. 3. He shall never go out from this [10] land. 4. Consider how you will escape from these misfortunes. 5. Seuthes orders Xenophon to take measures for the crossing of the army (lit. *to take care that the army may cross*). 6. The shepherd ought to take measures that his [9] sheep may have food. 7. It is a noble thing to take measures that the citizens may be as good as possible[64]. 8. See that ye show yourselves worthy of the freedom which[67] ye possess. 9. We ought not only to vote the peace, but also to take measures for keeping it (lit. *how we shall keep it*). 10. He took every means that the city might be preserved (*for preserving the city*).

§ 29. μή, μὴ οὐ, *with Verbs of Fearing. Repetition of the Negative.*

I.

(1) After expressions of fear, solicitude, uncertainty, &c., μή is used with the *subjunctive* or *indicative.* The subjunctive expresses the apprehension vaguely (*may be*);

---

[a] The construction in *a* has been explained by the ellipse of some word signifying to fear, thus: οὐ (δέος ἐστὶ) μή —, *there is no fear that,* &c. This explanation does not suit the use of the indicative future, either in negations, as οὐ μὴ μεθέψομαι, *I will not follow you,* where the insertion of δέος fails to explain the mood or tense; or in

⌣ the *indicative* is used when the speaker wishes to intimate his conviction that the thing feared, &c., has or will really come to pass.

> *Obs.*—After a historical tense the subjunctive becomes the optative; the indicative is changed into the optative present or aorist (the future optative is rare), or retained, with an alteration of tense.
>
> φοβοῦμαι μὴ θάνω, *I fear that I may die;* ἐφοβούμην μὴ θάνοιμι, *I feared that I might die.*
>
> φοβοῦμαι μὴ εὑρήσομεν, *I fear that we shall find;* ἐφοβούμην μὴ εὕροιμι, *I feared that I should find* (μὴ εὑρήσοιμι, Goodwin, Moods and Tenses, § 26 (*b*)).
>
> φοβοῦμαι μὴ ἡμαρτήκαμεν, *I fear that we have made a mistake;* (ἐφοβούμην μὴ ἡμαρτηκότες ἦμεν, *I feared that we had made a mistake.*)

⌣ (2) When it is feared that the thing has *not* taken place, or will *not* take place, μὴ οὐ is used. Hence—

> φοβοῦμαι μή,
> *I fear that it will* = *vereor ne.*
> φοβοῦμαι μὴ οὐ,
> *I fear that it will not* = *vereor ut,* or *ne non.*

The moods and tenses are the same after μὴ οὐ as after μή.

(3) The notion of fear is often not expressed before μὴ οὐ, and the verb in this construction is generally in the subjunctive.

> ἀλλὰ μὴ οὐκ ᾖ διδακτόν, *but perhaps it is a thing which cannot be taught.*

II.

⌣ (1) The Greeks often repeat the negative particle, where in English it is not repeated.

> *I cannot either speak or be silent,* becomes
> *I cannot neither speak nor be silent,*
> οὐ δύναμαι οὔτε λέγειν οὔτε σιγᾶν.
>
> *No one said anything,*
> οὐδεὶς οὐδὲν εἶπεν.

---

prohibitions, as οὐ μὴ λαλήσεις; it seems best to refer both idioms (the subjunctive and the indicative, with or without the interrogative) to one source, and to say that μή is here added to οὐ because the idioms express not only a fact (or question), but also a determination on the part of the speaker.

(2) Sometimes, when a verb expressing a negative idea is followed by an infinitive, the negative is expressed with the infinitive, where it is omitted in English. This is especially the case after verbs signifying *to forbid, to deny, to hinder*, &c.

> ἀπαγορεύω μὴ ἐξελθεῖν, *I forbid you to go out.*
> ἀρνοῦμαι μὴ δεδρακέναι, *I deny that I did it.*

(3) When a negative is added to any of the above verbs, it is repeated with the infinitive following. Thus:

> ἀρνοῦμαι μὴ δεδρακέναι becomes
> οὐκ ἀρνοῦμαι μὴ οὐ δεδρακέναι.

Obs. i.—This double negative. μὴ οὐ, is also used after such expressions as δεινὸν εἶναι, αἰσχρὸν εἶναι, αἰσχύνεσθαι, and after such negative expressions as *to be unable, impossible, not right*, &c.

Obs. ii.—μὴ οὐ is also sometimes used with the participle, and with ὥστε and infinitive after negative expressions.
The repetition of οὐ in these constructions brings the general negation expressed by μή into more direct reference to the particular case mentioned.

III.

Cases in which two negatives cancel each other must be carefully distinguished from the cases in which the negative is repeated.

> οὐδὲν τούτων οὐκ ἐποίησεν,[a] lit.: *nothing of this he did not do*, i. e. *he did all this*, is to be carefully distinguished from οὐκ ἐποίησεν οὐδὲν τούτων, *he did not do any of these things.*

EXERCISE 31.

VOCABULARY.—*to attack*, προσβάλλειν. *one's country*, ἡ πατρίς. *to deny*, ἀπαρνεῖσθαι. *for*, ὑπέρ. *irremediable*, ἀνήκεστον. *to labour with*, συμπονεῖν, with dat. *to prevent*, ἀπείργειν, κωλύειν (κωλύειν, as a rule, is *not* followed by μή).

---

[a] In οὐδὲν τούτων οὐκ ἐποίησεν we have a compressed form of expression (§ 58). The sentence is = to οὐδὲν τούτων ἦν ὃ οὐκ ἐποίησεν, and each verb has its own negative.

1. There was no one to whom he did not tell this. 2. He did not tell this to any one. 3. Do not tell this to any one. 4. He denied that he went into the city. 5. He did not deny that he went into the city. 6. I prevented him from going into the city. 7. No one was prevented from going into the city. 8. I am afraid that some evil will happen to me. 9. He was afraid that the enemy would come into the city. 10. I am afraid that I have done an irremediable mischief [56]. 11. I am afraid that the servant will not come from the country *with* (*particip.*) the horse. 12. It is shameful not to labour with the good.

Exercise 32.

1. I fear his coming to some harm (*lest he should suffer something*). 2. I feared the boy would come to some harm. 3. I fear we shall find that these things are [75] not so. 4. I knew that they would prevent the king from coming into the country. 5. I fear that we have treated them ill. 6. Nothing prevents this from being true. 7. It is not right not to choose to fight for one's country. 8. I fear this will happen. 9. The general forbade his [9] soldiers to attack the enemy. 10. There is no one who would not be willing to do this.

§ 30. *The Infinitive* (Syntax, 85 ff.).

The use of the infinitive in Greek is more extensive than in Latin, and therefore nearer to the use in English. It includes, not only the Latin infinitive, but often also the supine in -*u*, and the participle in -*dus*.

(1) The infinitive is added to verbs and adjectives as a complement or extension of the notion contained in the verb or adjective.

δεινὸς εὑρεῖν, *clever at finding;* ἄνθρωπος πέφυκε φιλεῖν, *it is the nature of man to love.*[a]

---

[a] The infinitive is really the case of a verbal noun of agency, which has gradually attained a wider and more adverbial use. φιλεῖν is, literally, *in loving;* εὑρεῖν, *in finding,* or *for finding.* This original use is most difficult to trace in the *accusative and infinitive,* e. g. λέγει αὐτὸν ἀπελθεῖν, *he says that he went away;* but even here the strict grammatical translation appears to be, *he speaks of him in having gone away,* i. e. the accusative is really 'governed' by λέγει, and the infinitive forms the complement of the assertion.

Hence the infinitive often expresses the *purpose* or *object* of an action.

παρέχω ἐμαυτὸν ἐρωτᾶν, *I offer myself to be questioned;* μανθάνειν ἥκομεν, *we are come to learn.*

Obs.—The infinitive *active* is used where we should use the *passive,* e. g. ἐρωτᾶν, not ἐρωτᾶσθαι. So ἡδὺς ἀκούειν, *sweet to be heard, to hear.*

(2) The particle ὥστε, *so that,* is used with the infinitive to express a *consequence* or *result;* or if the consequence is regarded as having actually taken place, 'as an independent fact,' the indicative may be used.

Obs.—The usual negative with the infinitive is μή — (cp. **27,** (2)).
οὕτως ἀνόητός ἐστιν, ὥστε πόλεμον ἀντ' εἰρήνης αἱρεῖσθαι,
he is so senseless as to choose war in preference to peace.
οὕτως ἀνόητός ἐστιν, ὥστε πόλεμον ἀντ' εἰρήνης αἱρεῖται,
he is so senseless that he actually chooses war in preference to peace.

(3) The accusative and infinitive is used in Greek as in Latin, with this exception, that when the subject of the infinitive is the same as the subject of the principal verb, the nominative case is retained, even before the infinitive.

Κλέων ἔφη οὐκ αὐτὸς ἀλλὰ Νικίαν στρατηγεῖν, *Cleon said that not himself, but Nicias, was general.*[a]

Here, in Latin, we should have *se* before the infinitive.

Cleo se imperatorem esse negavit.

Exercise 33.

Vocabulary.—*to give advice,* συμβουλεύειν, with dat. *to be ashamed,* αἰσχύνεσθαι. *to be a beggar,* πτωχεύειν. *to be born,*

---

[a] This idiom is one of the most distinctive characteristics of Greek, and when we find something similar in Latin, as in Virgil's *sensit medios delapsus in hostes,* we must suppose an imitation of the Greek construction, unless, indeed, the translation of this passage is, 'Having fallen into the midst of the enemy, he found it out.'

πεφυκέναι. *to burn,* καίειν. *to have compassion,* συγγνώμην
ἔχειν, *with dat. competent,* ἱκανός. *to consider,* λογίζεσθαι.
to cut, τέμνειν. *death,* θάνατος. *to desire (long for),* ἐρᾶν, *with*
gen. (*lit. to love*). *to desire (wish),* βούλεσθαι. *to determine,*
γνῶναι. *to entreat,* δεῖσθαι. *to give up,* παραδιδόναι. *to guard,*
φυλάττειν. *housekeeper,* οἰκονόμος. *to judge,* γνῶναι. *to leave,*
καταλείπειν. *to manage (a house),* οἰκεῖν, *with acc. to offer,*
παρέχειν. *Phliasians,* Φλιάσιοι. *prepared (ready),* ἕτοιμος.
it is right, it is a duty, προσήκει. *to be situated (in a certain*
condition), καθεστάναι. *to be a slave,* δουλεύειν. *to undergo*
(*endure, suffer*), ὑπομένειν. *to be willing,* ἐθέλειν. *worth*
while, ἄξιον.

1. I offer myself to be cut and burnt [44]. 2. The Phliasians
gave up their city to the Lacedaemonians to guard. 3. Xenophon
left the half [29] of his army to guard the camp. 4. Themistocles
was most competent to speak and judge and act (use *aorist*).
5. They were prepared to undergo any dangers. 6. There is
no one so foolish as to desire death. 7. They said that they
were prepared to undergo any dangers, but that their friends
were not. 8. It is right to be willing to listen to those who
desire to give advice. 9. It is not pleasant to have many
enemies. 10. It is worth-while to consider the position of the
affairs of Philip (*the affairs of Philip in what (position) they*
now are situated). 11. You were not born to be a slave.
12. I am ashamed to be a beggar. 13. I entreat you to have
compassion upon me. 14. I determined to cross the river. 15.
It is the part of (*gen.*) a good housekeeper to manage his house
well.

§ 31. *Infinitive continued. Subject and Predicate.*
Infinitive with Article.

(1) We saw (§ 30 (3)) that when the subject of the
infinitive was the same as the subject of the principal
verb, the nominative case was retained. But this subject
is generally omitted before the infinitive when it has
been expressed or assumed with the principal verb.

> ἔφη σπουδάζειν, *he said that he was in haste.*
> συνειπεῖν ὁμολογῶ, *I confess that I assented.*

When the subject of the infinitive is thus omitted, because expressed with the principal verb, an adjective agreeing with it, or a substantive (in apposition, as predicate, &c.), is put in the case in which the omitted substantive would have been, i. e. in the nominative.

> ὁ ᾽Αλέξανδρος ἔφασκεν εἶναι Διὸς υἱός, *Alexander used to say that he was the son of Zeus.*

Here the subject before εἶναι is omitted, but υἱός, the predicate, is in the nominative.

In *oratio obliqua* this would, of course, become λέγουσι τὸν ᾽Αλέξανδρον φάσκειν εἶναι Διὸς υἱόν, with accusative for nominative.

> ἔφη τριταῖος ἐλθεῖν, *he said that he came on the third day.*
> ὁμολογοῦσιν ἐχθροὶ εἶναι, *they confess that they are enemies.*

(2) After εἶναι, γίγνεσθαι, καλεῖσθαι, &c., an adjective or substantive, which forms the predicate with the infinitive, is mostly put in the same case as the noun of which it is predicated.

> ἐδέοντο αὐτοῦ εἶναι προθύμου, *they entreated him to be zealous;*
> ἔξεστί μοι γενέσθαι εὐδαίμονι, *it is possible for me to become happy.*

(3) The neuter article is often added to the infinitive, which then becomes a neuter noun, capable of declension in the singular.   Cp. § 7 (2).

> τὸ ὑγιαίνειν, *health.*
> τοῦ ὑγιαίνειν, *of health,* &c.

(a) In the genitive, the infinitive with the article sometimes denotes a *motive* or *purpose.*

> ἐτειχίσθη δὲ καὶ ᾽Αταλάντη, τοῦ μὴ λῃστὰς κακουργεῖν τὴν Εὔβοιαν, *and Atalanta also was fortified, that robbers (or pirates) might not damage Euboea.*

---

* It is also possible to say ἐδέοντο αὐτοῦ εἶναι πρόθυμον. The difference between this and ἐδέοντο αὐτοῦ εἶναι προθύμου is the same as the difference between *they entreated him that he would be zealous,* and *they entreated him to be zealous;* i. e. in the former the adjective agrees with a subject understood, αὐτόν supplied from αὐτοῦ.

(*b*) A *preposition* with the article and infinitive may be equivalent to a sentence introduced by a conjunction.

οὐδὲν ἐπράχθη διὰ τὸ ἐκεῖνον μὴ παρεῖναι, *nothing was done, because he was not present* (= ὅτι ἐκεῖνος οὐ παρῆν), *owing to his absence.*

(*c*) When the infinitive with the article has a separate subject, it, following the general rule, is in the *accusative.*

οὐκ ὀρθῶς ἔχει τὸ κακῶς πάσχοντα ἀμύνεσθαι ἀντιδρῶντα κακῶς, *it is not right when one suffers wrong to avenge himself by doing wrong in return.*   (Cp. λῃστάς in *a*, ἐκεῖνον in *b*.)

(4) The infinitive with the article is often to be translated by a substantive.

τὸ πολλὰ ἀπολωλεκέναι, *our numerous losses;* τὸ ἐπιτιμᾶν, *finding fault, criticism;* τὸ εὖ πράττειν, *prosperity,* &c.

Hence, conversely, abstract substantives in English are often to be expressed in Greek by the infinitive of the cognate verb with the article.

prosperity = τὸ εὖ πράττειν, &c.[a]
owing to his absence = διὰ τὸ ἐκεῖνον μὴ παρεῖναι.

Obs.—Though abstract words and modes of expression are common both in Greek and English, it does not follow that abstract forms or words in English are always to be rendered by abstract forms or words in Greek ; for instance, 'a life of virtue' would certainly not be translated by the words βίος ἀρετῆς, but by some such phrase as 'to pass life in doing just things.' And even when abstract words are used in Greek, it should be remembered that in Greek they have *gender,* which gives them a sort of personification which is not present in the English.

---

[a] The infinitive thus used, 'still retains its regimen as a verb,' i. e. it governs cases, &c., as in the example, τὸ πολλὰ ἀπολωλεκέναι, where πολλὰ is the accusative after the verb, or τὸ ἄγγελον πέμπειν, *the sending a messenger;* 'and any quality or circumstance attributed to it must be expressed, not adjectivally, but adverbially,' as in τὸ εὖ πράττειν (Clyde, Greek Syntax, § 6, Obs. 1). Of course, τὸ καλὰ πράττειν is correct, but it means, *the doing honourable things.*

EXERCISE 34.

VOCABULARY.—*to be a great advantage for,* πολλῷ προσέχειν πρός, with acc. *to criticise, find fault with,* ἐπιτιμᾶν, with dat. *the fact that,* use τό with the infinitive, e. g. τὸ ἐλθεῖν αὐτόν, *the fact that he came, the fact of his coming. foolish,* ἀνόητος. *to be foolish,* κακῶς φρονεῖν. *to fortify,* τειχίζειν. *with full power, autocratic,* αὐτοκράτωρ. *to hate,* μισεῖν. *incentive,* ἀφορμή. *to long for,* ἐπιθυμεῖν, with gen. *to lose,* ἀπολλύναι (perdere). *lord,* κύριος. *neglect,* ἀμέλεια. *to persuade,* πείθειν, or better, aorist, πεῖσαι. *to put down to,* τιθέναι, with gen., e. g. τιθέναι μωρίας, *to put down to folly. to put in rapid execution, to execute rapidly,* τὸ ταχὺ πράττειν. *ruler,* ἄρχων. *to succeed, success,* τὸ εὖ πράττειν. *undeservedly,* παρὰ τὴν ἀξίαν. *warlike schemes, plans,* τὰ τοῦ πολέμου. *worse,* χείρων.

1. I long to become ruler with full powers. 2. I do not think that I am worse than the others (*gen.*). 3. It is possible for you to become better than others [5]. 4. They entreated him to become their ally. 5. Our numerous *losses* in the war one might justly put down to our neglect. 6. *Criticism,* one may say, (is) easy. 7. To foolish men [5] undeserved *success* is an incentive to *folly.* 8. The fact that Philip, in his single self (εἷς ὤν), is lord of all is a great advantage for (πρός) the rapid execution of warlike schemes. 9. He persuaded them that he was a god. 10. Nothing was done, because all the soldiers hated the general. 11. The city was fortified, that no one might [33] do an injury to the citizens. 12. He went away that no one might [33] see him.

5. Say: That we have lost many things.

§ 32. *Infinitive continued.*

(1) The usual construction, described in § 30 (3), is retained even when the infinitive mood is introduced by the article or ὥστε.

   (*a*) πρὸς τὸ συμφέρον ζῶσι, διὰ τὸ φίλαυτοι εἶναι,
     *they make self-interest the object of their lives (live with a view
     to self-interest) because they are lovers of themselves.*

   (*b*) ἐκπέμπονται ἐπὶ τῷ ὅμοιοι τοῖς λειπομένοις εἶναι,
     *they are sent out on the understanding that they are to be equal
     (to be on an equal footing) with those that are left behind.*

(*c*) μηδεὶς τηλικοῦτος ἔστω παρ᾿ ὑμῖν ὥστε, τοὺς νόμους παραβὰς,
μὴ δοῦναι δίκην,
*let no one be so powerful amongst you as not to be punished if
he transgresses the law.*

Obs.—Of course, when the subject is different, the accusative is
used : οὐδὲν ἐπράχθη διὰ τὸ ἐκεῖνον μὴ παρεῖναι, *nothing was done,
because he was not present.*

(2) A simple infinitive, and sometimes an accusative
and infinitive, is added to assertions in order to limit
them, with ὡς or ὅσον in the sense of *so, so far as* : ὡς
εἰπεῖν, *so to say;* ὅσον ἐμὲ εἰδέναι, *so far as I know.*
Sometimes the infinitive is used alone, without ὡς : δοκεῖν
ἐμοί, *in my opinion.*

EXERCISE 35.

VOCABULARY.—*ambitious,* φιλότιμος. *to attack,* ἐπιέναι,
ἐπελθεῖν. *to beat off,* ἀμύνεσθαι. *to be the beginning of,*
ἄρχειν. *to conjecture,* ἐπεικάζειν. *equal,* ὅμοιος. *to excel,*
προέχειν. *lovers of self,* φίλαυτοι. *to manage well (of a form
of political constitution),* καλῶς πολιτεύειν. *to prefer,* βούλεσθαι
μᾶλλον. *in preference to,* ἀντί, with gen. *to be highly prized
by,* τίμιος εἶναι, with dat. *to suffer punishment,* δίκην διδόναι.
to have never tasted, ἄγευστος εἶναι, with gen. *on an understanding that,* ἐπὶ τῷ, with inf.

1. They choose war in preference to peace, because they have
not tasted the evils of war. 2. They undergo every labour
because they are ambitious. 3. All men, so to say, are lovers
of self. 4. I am come *on an understanding that* I am to be on
an equal footing with (*equal to*) the other citizens. 5. He will
not do this, so far as I conjecture. 6. In my opinion that day
was the beginning of great evils to the Athenians. 7. Demo-
cracies, when well managed (*part.*), excel in being more just. 8.
They do everything to avoid (ὥστε μή) suffering punishment.
9. You prefer to beat off their attack, instead of attacking them
yourselves. 10. To become citizens *of your city* (παρ᾿ ὑμῖν) is
highly prized by all men.

§ 33. *The Aorist Infinitive. The Infinitive after* δοκεῖν, ἐλπίζειν, μέλλειν, *&c.*

(1) The aorist infinitive is used in two different modes, which must be carefully distinguished.

(*a*) It is sometimes a *preterite*, as in the indicative. This is the case when it is used, without ἄν, after verbs of *saying* and *feeling* (*declarandi et sentiendi*), and sometimes when an accusative and infinitive is used with the article.

Ἐπύαξα ἐλέγετο Κύρῳ δοῦναι πολλὰ χρήματα,
it was said that Epyaxa gave (ἔδωκεν) *much money to Cyrus.*

τὸ μηδεμίαν τῶν πολέων ἁλῶναι πολιορκίᾳ, μέγιστόν ἐστι σημεῖον τοῦ
διὰ τούτους πεισθέντας τοὺς Φωκέας ταῦτα παθεῖν,[a]
the fact that none of the cities was taken by siege is a very great proof that the Phocians were persuaded into their misery owing to these men.

(*b*) In other uses the aorist infinitive has not a *past* signification, but differs only from the present as a momentary from a continuous tense (cf. § 18).

λέγειν δυνατώτατος, *very able to speak* (present); γνῶναι ἱκανώτατος, *very capable of forming an opinion* (aorist); τὸ γῆμαι, *marriage.*

(2) (*a*) After δοκεῖ, impersonal, *it seems good,* use infinitive present or aorist: δοκεῖ λέγειν, δοκεῖ ἀπελθεῖν.

(*b*) After δοκῶ, personal, *I am likely to, I think that,* use infinitive aorist with ἄν: δοκεῖτέ μοι τοῦτο ἂν παθεῖν.

(*c*) After μέλλω, *I am likely to, I intend to,* use infinitive future; more rarely infinitive present or aorist: μέλλω ἄρξειν, μέλλει γίγνεσθαι, γενέσθαι.

(*d*) After ἐλπίζω, *I hope,* &c., use the future infinitive, or aorist with ἄν, more rarely the aorist without ἄν: ἐλπίζω τοῦτο ἔσεσθαι, *I hope that this will take place,* τοῦτ᾽ ἂν γενέσθαι.[b]

---

[a] In other words, the aorist has a past sense in the infinitive when it represents an aorist indicative.

[b] τοῦτ᾽ ἂν γενέσθαι may be = to τοῦτο ἂν γένοιτο, or to τοῦτο ἂν ἐγίνετο, *he hoped that this would happen,* or *that it would have happened.*

(*e*) After ὑπισχνοῦμαι, *I promise,* &c., the future infinitive will be found, where in English the present is in use.

ὑπέσχετο τοῦτο ποιήσειν, *he promised to do this.*

Obs.—ὑπέσχετο ποιῆσαι is also possible. Cp. Goodwin, Moods and Tenses, § 23, 2, n. 3.

EXERCISE 36.

VOCABULARY.—*basely,* κακῶς. *to hope,* ἐλπίζειν. *hope,* ἐλπίς. *to inhabit,* οἰκεῖν. *to intend,* μέλλειν. *necessity,* ἀνάγκη. *what is right,* τὰ δίκαια. *to save,* σώζειν. *when,* ὅτε.

1. *It is said that* the Cyclopes inhabited the island. 2. He declared that he went away himself [24] when Cyrus came. 3. It is better to die ten times than to live basely. 4. This they will not do, if they intend to do what is right. 5. I hope that Cyrus will come. 6. There is a hope that the enemy will not come into the country. 7. *It seems to me that they* would never have done [40] this if they had not been compelled (*if there had not been a necessity*). 8. He was unwilling either [41] to go away or to remain. 9. *It seems to me that Philip* would not have done [40] this if he had intended to keep the peace. 10. There was no hope that their affairs would ever become better. 11. There is no hope of saving the city.

Obs.—The Greeks often use a *personal* construction where we use an *impersonal,* e. g. instead of *it is (was) said that he,* they say, *he is (was) said;* instead of *it seems, seemed that he,* they say, *he seems, seemed,* &c.

§ 34. *The Participle.*

Greek is distinguished from English and from Latin by the wide use of participles. Speaking generally, we may distinguish two uses.

(1) *The Participle with the Article* (§ 7 (1)).—The participle with the article is equivalent to a verbal substantive.

ὁ ποιῶν = *the doer.*

It may often be paraphrased by a relative clause: ὁ ποιῶν = ὃς ποιεῖ, ὁ ταῦτα ποιῶν = ὃς ταῦτα ποιεῖ. Regarded as a substantive, the participle with the article may be the subject or the predicate of a sentence, or may stand in apposition to another noun: ὁ ἀδικήσας ἔφυγε, οὗτός ἐστιν ὁ ἀδικήσας, Αἰσχίνης ὁ ποιήσας ἔφυγε.

(2) *The Participle without the Article.*—The participle without the article is part of the predication, i. e. it is closely connected with the verb of the sentence, and defines the action in some way or other.

ἐκεῖνος λαβὼν ἀπῴχετο, *he, having taken, went away.*

The participle without the article may thus represent a descriptive relative sentence, or a temporal or causal sentence (*when he had taken; because he had taken*) in close connexion with the verb. Hence—

(*a*) Relative sentences, and sentences introduced by *when, after, if, since, because, although,* &c., may often be translated into Greek by omitting the relative or conjunctive, and turning the verb into a *participle.*

ποιήσας ἀπῴχετο, *when he had done this, he went away;* ἀδικήσας ἔφυγε, *because he had done wrong, he ran away;* ὄρνιν εἶχε τίκτουσαν ᾠα, *he had a hen, which laid eggs* (*he had a hen, and it laid eggs*).

When the relative clause describes a permanent attribute, or is otherwise not in close relation with the verb as part of the predicate, the article is to be added to the participle: οἴκτειρε τὴν τεκοῦσαν, *have pity on her who bore you, your mother;* ἀπέκτεινε τὸν ἀδικοῦντα, *he slew the person who was doing wrong* (τὸν ἀδικοῦντα = a substantive); ἀπέκτεινεν ἀδικοῦντα, *he slew him when he was doing wrong* (ἀδικοῦντα = predicate).

(*b*) Two verbs connected by *and* in English, may in Greek be rendered by a verb and participle, especially in the past tense (Ex. 1, 13).

he took and went away, λαβὼν ἀπῴχετο.[a]

---

[a] This gives the relation of the tenses more accurately than the participial translation, *having taken, he went away,* which confuses the aorist and perfect participle. The two actions expressed by λαβών and ἀπῴχετο are intended to be simultaneous, but such a relation can only be expressed in English by using two verbs.

(c) The English verbal substantive in -*ing*, under the government of a preposition, may often be translated into Greek by a participle agreeing with the nominative case of the sentence.

ληιζόμενοι ζῶσιν, *they live by plundering.*

EXERCISE 37.

VOCABULARY.—*to be deposed*, ἐκπίπτειν τῆς ἀρχῆς (lit. *to fall out of the government*). *the facts*, τὰ γενόμενα. *to fear*, δεῖσαι, *of rational apprehension*. *from*, παρά, with gen. *to meet*, ἀπαντᾶν, with dat. *to meet with*, τυγχάνειν, with gen. *mercy*, ἔλεος. *to give an opinion*, γνώμην εἰπεῖν. *pity*, αἰδώς, οἷς. *to pity*, οἰκτείρειν. *punishment*, τιμωρία. *to set out*, πορεύεσθαι (*to a person*, ὡς, with acc.). *to step down*, παραβαίνειν. *three*, τρεῖς, τρία. *truth*, ἀλήθεια. *to be a tyrant*, τυραννεύειν.

1. When I had said this, I went away. 2. When he said this, the general ordered him to step down. 3. I met Philip as he was going away. 4. After being tyrant three years Hippias was deposed. 5. I learnt this while yet a child. 6. The person who gave this opinion was Pisander. 7. Is it more just to pity the dead man, or her who killed him (*part.*)? 8. She killed him *without fear* of gods or men. 9. If she were to meet with neither pity nor mercy from you, she would meet with the most righteous (*just*) punishment. 10. Tissaphernes sets out to the king *with* [71] about 500 horsemen. 11. I shall be saved by telling the facts truly (*with* (μετά) *the truth*).

§ 35. *Participle continued.*

(1) The future participle is used to express a purpose; it may, of course, be added either to the subject or object of the sentence, and be used with or without the article.

ἔρχομαι ὑμῖν ἐπικουρήσων,
I am coming to aid you.

τὸν ἀδικοῦντα παρὰ τοὺς δικαστὰς ἄγειν δεῖ δίκην δώσοντα,
he who wrongs another should be taken before the judges to be punished (lit. *to pay the penalty*).

ἄνδρας τοῦτο ποιήσοντας ἐκπέμπει,
he sends out men to do this.

οὔπω ὁ λωφήσων παρῆν,
the person who would set him at liberty was not yet present.

(2) Many verbs have the complement of the predicate in the participle, where in English the infinitive, participial substantive in *-ing*, or a dependent sentence would be used. Such are verbs expressing *continuance* or *cessation*, *pleasure* or *shame*, &c.

> διατελεῖ τοῦτο ποιῶν, *he continues doing this.*
> παύεται τοῦτο ποιῶν, *he is stopped from, or ceases, doing this.*

Such verbs are διατελῶ, διάγω, κάμνω, ἀπείρηκα, παύομαι, ἐκλείπω, χαίρω, ἥδομαι, ἀγανακτῶ, αἰσχύνομαι, ἄχθομαι, ἄρχω, ὑπάρχω, ἀδικῶ, εὖ or καλῶς ποιῶ, &c. (Madvig, Greek Syntax, § 177).

Especially worthy of notice are τυγχάνω, λανθάνω, and φθάνω.

> ἔτυχον παρόντες, *they happened to be present ;*—λανθάνω τι ποιῶν, *I escape notice while doing something,* i. e. (*a*) *I do it unknown to myself; I do it unconsciously;* (*b*) *I do it unknown to others,* i. e. *I do it secretly ;*—ἔφθην αὐτοὺς ἀφικόμενος, *I was before them in arriving,* i. e. *I arrived before them ;*—οὐκ ἂν φθάνοις ποιῶν τοῦτο, *you cannot do this too soon ;* or, with an interrogative : οὐκ ἂν φθάνοις ποιῶν τοῦτο ; *won't you do this at once !*

(3) Many verbs that signify *emotions*, *perceptions by the senses*, *knowledge*, and *recollection*, take the *participle*.

(*a*) When used actively, the participle agrees with the object.

> οἱ Ἕλληνες οὐκ ᾔδεσαν Κῦρον τεθνηκότα,
> *the Greeks did not know that Cyrus was dead.*

(*b*) When used intransitively or passively, so that the subject of the participle and verb is the same, the participle is in the nominative.

> ἐξελέγχθη ἀδικήσας.
> *he was convicted of crime.*
>
> ἴσθι λυπηρὸς ὤν,
> *know that you are troublesome.*

So ὁρῶ, αἰσθάνομαι, ἀκούω, πυνθάνομαι, μανθάνω, οἶδα, μέμνημαι, δηλῶ, ἀποφαίνω, ἐξελέγχω, &c. (Madvig, § 178).

Obs.—With some verbs a slightly different meaning is conveyed by the use of the participle and the infinitive.

αἰσχύνομαι λέγων,
I am ashamed while I speak;
αἰσχύνομαι λέγειν,
I am ashamed to speak, (and therefore do not speak).

φαίνομαι ποιῶν,
I am seen doing; I obviously do;
φαίνομαι ποιεῖν,
I seem to do (whether I do or not).

So οἶδα ποιῶν, *I know that I do;* οἶδα ποιεῖν, *I know how to do.*

EXERCISE 38.

VOCABULARY.— *it will be to our advantage to,* ἄμεινον ἔσται ἡμῖν, with particip. *for his own benefit,* ἑαυτοῦ ἕνεκα. *to compel,* ἀναγκάζειν. *I am conscious of,* σύνοιδ᾽ ἐμαυτῷ, with particip.[a] *to convict,* ἐξελέγχειν. *to delight in doing,* χαίρειν ποιῶν. *to despise,* καταφρονεῖν, with gen. *to do — to,* ἐργάζεσθαι, with double acc. (§ 39 (2)). *guilty,* αἴτιος. *harm,* συμφορά. *to help,* ἐπικουρεῖν, with dat. *I am here,* πάρειμι. *obvious, clear,* φανερός. *to take refuge with,* καταφεύγειν ἐπί, with acc. *I repent,* μεταμέλει μοι (*it repents me*), with particip. *to break a truce,* σπονδὰς λύειν.

1. I am here to help you. 2. The allies sent ambassadors to Lacedaemon to announce the victory. 3. If you do this, know that you will suffer for it. 4. He delights in being praised, because [16] he is ambitious. 5. You are doing wrong in beginning the war and breaking the truce. 6.[b] It is clear that you despise me. 7.[b] It was obvious to all that the Thebans would be compelled to take refuge with us. 8. I am conscious that I have been wronged. 9. Philip has been convicted of doing everything for his own benefit. 10. I shall be shown to have been guilty of no harm, but [19] to have done much good to the city. 11. I repent having done this. 12. It will be to our advantage to keep the peace.

---

[a] The participle may be in the nominative or dative: σύνοιδ᾽ ἐμαυτῷ, οὐδ᾽ ὁτιοῦν σοφὸς ὤν, or σύνοιδ᾽ ἐμαυτῷ οὐδὲν ἐπισταμένῳ.

[b] Use the personal construction (cp. Ex. 36, *Obs.*).

F

§ 36. *Participle continued.* ἅτε, ὡς, *with Participles.*

(1) The particle ἅτε (frequently strengthened by δή, ἅτε δή) is used with a participle when we denote a *ground* or *reason* which we allege (in *our* opinion) as *naturally accounting for the action, conduct,* &c., that we are relating of *another person.*

> ὁ Κῦρος, ἅτε παῖς ὤν, ἥδετο τοῖς τοιούτοις,
> *Cyrus, as being a boy (as was natural in a boy), took delight in such things.*

(2) The particle ὡς is often added to participles which express the *intention* or *supposition* with, or under which, an action is done.

> ἀγανακτοῖσιν ὡς μεγάλων τινῶν ἀπεοτερημένοι,
> *they are vexed, thinking themselves deprived* (lit. *as having been deprived*) *of some great advantages.*
> Ἀρταξέρξης συλλαμβάνει Κῦρον, ὡς ἀποκτενῶν,
> *Artaxerxes arrests Cyrus with the intention of putting him to death.*

EXERCISE 39.

VOCABULARY.—*about,* περί, with gen. *to allow, stand by and see,* περιορᾶν. *to anticipate,* φθάνειν (Prim. 167). *to be ashamed,* αἰσχύνεσθαι. *calamity,* συμφορά. *to cease,* παύεσθαι. *to continue,* διατελεῖν. *to escape notice,* λανθάνειν (Prim. 167). *messenger,* ἄγγελος. *to do great mischief to,* μέγα κακὸν ποιεῖν, with acc. *mortal,* θνητός. *to perceive,* αἰσθάνεσθαι (Prim. 167), with gen. *to speak well of,* εὖ λέγειν, with acc.

1. You cannot go away too soon [50]. 2. The enemy arrived at the city before (us) [50]. 3. Philip, *as was natural for* an ambitious man, did everything for *his own interests* (for the sake of himself). 4. They took them away with *the intention of putting* them to death. 5. They entered the city *without being observed* [50]. 6. *Unknown to myself* I have fallen [50] into a great calamity. 7. He happened to be in the city when the messenger came. 8. They went away *under the impression that they were conquered.* 9. *It is evident that he can* [54] not speak well of his friends, nor treat them well. 10. *Unknown to them-*

selves they have done great mischief to the city.   11. I am not ashamed of speaking the truth about myself.   12. I remember that I heard [51] these things from Pericles.   13. All his life long (*acc.*) he continued to talk (converse) in the market-place.   14. He perceived that the enemy had arrived before him in the country.   15. Cease speaking.   16. I know that I am mortal.   17. I will not stand by and see you injured (*I will not allow you being injured*).   18. I cannot tell you the facts *for shame* (part.).

§ 37. *Genitive Absolute, &c.*

(1) It often happens that the cause, time, manner, &c., attending an action cannot be expressed by the participle in agreement with the subject or object, inasmuch as they are connected with some person or thing distinct from the subject or object, e. g. *I came because he asked me,* where the cause is connected with *he,* a person who is not the subject of the verb *came.* In this case the participle of the verb expressing the time, cause, &c., and the substantive to which it belongs (*asked, he*), are added to the sentence in the genitive case. This is the so-called *genitive absolute.*[*]

> οὐκ ἂν ἦλθον δεῦρο, ὑμῶν μὴ κελευσάντων,
> *I should not have come hither if you had not bidden me.*
>
> ἐμοῦ καθεύδοντος, ἀπῆλθον.
> *they went away while I was asleep.*
>
> τούτων οὕτως ἐχόντων, ἄπειμι,
> *this being the case, I will go away.*

In the first instance given, the same thing might be expressed thus, οὐκ ἂν ἦλθον δεῦρο, μὴ ὑφ' ὑμῶν κελευσθείς, *I should not have come hither if I had not been bidden by you,* where the participle can be made to agree with the subject of the sentence.

Obs. i.—The *genitive* absolute in Greek corresponds to the *ablative* absolute in Latin, but in comparing the two constructions it

---

[*] The term absolute merely implies that the genitive is not in direct connexion with any particular word (verb, substantive, &c.) in the sentence, but with the sentence generally.

must be borne in mind that the Greeks have a large number of
active participles which do not exist in Latin. Hence the Greeks
often use the active where in Latin the passive is used, employing
at the same time the simple participle instead of the 'absolute'
construction, e. g. *his dictis abibant* becomes ταῦτ' εἰπόντες
ἀπῇεσαν. On the other hand, the Greeks prefer the absolute
construction in the *active* to the *simple* participle in the *passive*,
i. e. ὑμῶν μὴ κελευσάντων is more common than μὴ ὑφ' ὑμῶν
κελευσθείς.

Obs. ii.—The particles ὡς and ἅτε are added to the *absolute* construction with the same meaning as to the simple participle, e. g.
ἐσιώπα ὡς πάντων εἰδότων, *he was silent under the impression
that all knew.*

(2) The participles of *impersonal* verbs are put absolutely in the *accusative*, without a *substantive in agreement*,
and in the neuter gender.

> διὰ τί μενεῖς ἐξὸν ἀπιέναι;
> *why do you remain, when you are at liberty to go away?*

So δέον ἀπιέναι, *when, whereas*, &c., *you ought to go
away* (participle of δεῖ). δόξαν (δεδογμένον) ἡμῖν ἀπιέναι,
when we have determined to go away (participle of δοκεῖ,
placet).

(3) The adverbs ἅμα and μεταξύ are often added to
participles (especially in the personal use) to imply that
the action of the main verb occurs at the same time as
the action of the participle.

> μεταξὺ δειπνῶν ἀνέστη, *he rose up during dinner*; ἅμα ἰόντες
> ἐτόξευον, *as they went, they shot.*

EXERCISE 40.

VOCABULARY.—*at once*, αὐτίκα. *to call*, καλεῖν. *court*, αὐλή.
to be finished, πεπράχθαι. *sources of gain*, κέρδη, τά. *Hellas*,
Ἑλλάς, ἡ. *to come to help*, βοηθεῖν, with dat. *Pelasgians*,
Πελασγοί. *to play*, παίζειν. *to refrain from*, ἀπέχεσθαι, with
gen. *to reign*, βασιλεύειν. *in the reign of Cyrus*, ἐπὶ Κύρου
βασιλεύοντος. *to be silent*, σιγᾶν, σιωπᾶν. *to spend*, ἀναλίσκειν. *statue*, εἰκών, ἡ. *to unveil*, ἐκκαλύπτειν.

1. Why do you remain, *when we have determined to* come to

---

* *Accusatives Absolute:*—δεδογμένον, *when it is determined*; δέον,
when (you) ought; also, *when it is a duty*; *when it becomes (you)*;

the help of our[9] friends? 2. Why are you silent, *when you ought
to* speak? 3. Why do you remain, now that *you have an opportunity to* depart? 4. *This being determined (since this is determined),* we cannot set out *too soon*[50]. 5. This being the case, I will
go away at once. 6. These things took place *in the reign of* Cyrus.
7. When the Pelasgians possessed the (land) now called Hellas,
the Athenians were Pelasgians. 8. Though their friends bade
them, they refused to come in person[20]. 9. Though many were
present, no one came to my help. 10. He went away under
the impression that the business was finished. 11. The general
retired, *under the impression that* the enemy would not attack.
12. While playing, Menexenus enters from the court. 13. As
he said this, he unveiled the statue. 14. Will you choose
something else, when it is possible to rule over all Asia? 15.
Many *when they have spent* their money, do not refrain from
sources of gain, from which they refrained previously *because
they thought* them disgraceful.

Exercise 41.

Vocabulary.—*to confirm,* βεβαιοῦν. *false arguments,* οἱ
λόγοι οἱ ἐψευσμένοι (*for* their, my *false arguments,* add ὑπ'
ἐκείνων, ὑπ' ἐμοῦ, &c., with the part.). *to foresee,* προορᾶν.
the future, τὸ μέλλον. *to give orders,* προαγορεύειν. *Greek,*
Ἕλλην. *What has induced you?* τί μαθών, μαθόντες; *or* τί
παθών, παθόντες; *for the moment,* εἰς τὸ παραυτίκα. *to obtain,*
φέρεσθαι (lit. *to carry off for oneself*). *to be in a person's
power,* ἐπί τινι εἶναι. *to put on the rack, to rack,* στρεβλοῦν.
to be rid of, ἀπηλλάχθαι, with gen. (the perfect denotes a
state, cp. § 18 (2)). *torture,* βάσανος, ἡ. *to tell the truth,* τῇ
ἀληθείᾳ χρῆσθαι, τὰ ἀληθῆ λέγειν. *to undertake,* ἐπιχειρεῖν.

1. It was in their power to put an end *to his sufferings*. 2.
This he did, *in the expectation that* he would gain (fut., § 33,
2 (*d*)) his freedom, and *from a desire* to be rid, for the moment,
of the torture. 3. They gave orders to put him on the rack,

παρόν, παρέχον, *when there is an opportunity;* ἐξόν, *when it is
possible (from external circumstances);* ἐνόν, *when it is possible
(from the nature of the thing).* In the same way any adjective in
the neuter can be used with the participle ὄν (from ἐστί): ἄδηλον ὄν,
it being doubtful; δῆλον ὄν, αἰσχρὸν ὄν, &c.

because he *did not* tell the truth. 4. When he knew that he would be put to death, he at once *began to* tell (*imperf.*) the truth. 5. By saying this he confirmed the truth of his former assertion (*he confirmed his former assertions as having been spoken true*). 6. I am destroyed by their false arguments, *under the impression that they are true.* 7. He knew that he would cease *to be racked,* when he said what they approved (*what seemed good to them*). 8. How little can we men *foresee* about the future, *and* how much do we undertake! 9. What has induced you to do this? 10. What has induced them to go away so quickly (*adj.*)? 11. Cyrus is said to have asked the *Greeks present* (*those present of Greeks*) *who the* Lacedæmonians were *that* they gave (*pres.*) such orders to him.

§ 38. *The Accusative.*

(1) (*a*) The rules given in the Latin grammar with regard to the construction of verbs with nouns are often inapplicable to Greek, e. g. the Greek uses the accusative in cases where in Latin the dative or genitive is required.

ἀδικῶ, βλάπτω (acc.),	*noceo* (dat.).
πείθω (acc.),	*persuadeo* (dat.).
κολακεύω (acc.),	*adulor* (dat.).
οἰκτείρω, ἐλεῶ (acc.),	*misereor* (gen.).
ὠφελῶ, εὐεργετῶ (acc.),	*opitulor* (dat.).

(*b*) Intransitive verbs of motion, when compounded with a preposition, often become transitive.

βαίνω, *I walk* (intrans.); παρα-, ὑπερ-βαίνω (active), *I transgress.*

So διέρχομαι, διαπλέω, μετέρχομαι, &c.

(*c*) κατά often gives a transitive sense to intransitive verbs, and at the same time implies *with destruction.*

πολεμέω, *I am at war* (intrans.); but κατα-πολεμέω, *I war-down, destroy by war* (active)

So καθιπποτροφῶ τὴν οὐσίαν, *I waste my property by keeping horses.*

(2) Two accusatives.

(*a*) With verbs of *making, showing, exhibiting, naming,*

calling, &c., a second accusative is often added to the accusative of the object. This accusative forms part of the predicate—is the complement of the predicate—and if a substantive is in apposition to, or if an adjective is in agreement with, the accusative of the object (Syntax, § 8, 9).

οἱ στρατιῶται Ἀλκιβιάδην στρατηγὸν εἵλοντο, *the soldiers chose Alcibiades general.*
φίλον σε ἡγοῦμαι, *I consider you a friend.*[a]

(*b*) With verbs of *demanding*, *depriving*, *teaching*, &c., two accusatives, one of the person, the other of the thing, can be used.

> διδάσκω σε μουσικήν,
> *I teach you music.*
> Θηβαίους χρήματα ᾔτησαν,
> *they asked the Thebans for money.*

In the passive of these verbs, the accusative of the person becomes the *nominative*; the accusative of the thing remains unaltered.

> Θηβαῖοι χρήματα ᾐτήθησαν,
> *the Thebans were asked for money.*
> διδάσκομαι μουσικήν,
> *I am taught music.*

Obs.—The Accusative Absolute.—The participles of impersonal verbs, when used alone (cf. (§ 37 (2)) p. 68, note) or with a pronoun, e. g. δεδογμένον δ' οὐδέν, *when nothing had been settled*, are used in the accusative case, for the same purposes as the genitive in the genitive absolute. And sometimes the *accusative absolute* is used of persons, the clause being introduced by ὡς (§ 37 (1), *Obs.* ii.): οὐκ ἀξιοῦντες τοῦ Ἀλκιβιάδου υἱέος τοσαύτην δειλίαν καταγνῶναι, ὡς ἐκεῖνον πολλῶν ἀγαθῶν, ἀλλ' οὐχὶ πολλῶν κακῶν αἴτιον γεγενημένον, *not thinking it right to charge such cowardice upon the son of Alcibiades as if he (A.) had been the source of great blessings to the state, and not the source of great evils.* (Cf. Clyde, Greek Syntax, § 64 (*d*).) This construction is mostly found in the orators and Plato.

---

[a] This construction is not, of course, confined to the accusative. When a verb takes a genitive or dative, the complement is added in the genitive or dative, as φίλῳ σοι χρῶμαι, *I treat you as a friend.*

EXERCISE 42.

VOCABULARY.—*barbarian*, βάρβαρος. *bee*, μέλισσα. *child*,
τέκνον. *to clothe*, ἀμφιεννύναι. *to conceal*, κρύπτειν. *crown*,
στέφανος. *to dance away*, ἀπορχεῖσθαι. *deserter*, αὐτόμολος.
the affairs of the enemy, τὰ ἐκ τῶν πολεμίων. *to flatter*,
θωπεύειν. *forefathers*, πρόγονοι. *husband*, ἀνήρ. *to indict*,
γράφεσθαι. *life*, ψυχή. *to make (king)*, καθιστάναι. *meadow*,
λειμών, ὁ. *miserable*, ἄθλιος. *mortal*, βροτός. *parents*,
οἱ τεκόντες. *poor*, πτωχός. *to put on (of clothes)*, ἐνδύειν.
to remind, ἀναμιμνήσκειν. *more than is right*, καιροῦ πέρα.
to run away, ἀποδιδράσκειν. *for the sake of*, χάριν, ἕνεκα,
with gen. *to spend in horse-breeding*, καθιπποτροφεῖν. *to
strip*, ἐκδύειν. *tall*, μέγας. *tunic*, χιτών, ὁ. *to wander across*,
διέρχεσθαι. *to wonder at*, θαυμάζειν, with acc.

N.B.—*to put on oneself*, ἐνδύεσθαι, *on another*, ἐνδύειν. *to strip oneself*, ἐκδύεσθαι, *another*, ἐκδύειν; but the 2 aor. Act. is used intransitively.

1. I have often wondered (*aor.*) by what arguments *those who
indicted* [11] Socrates persuaded the Athenians that he was worthy
of death.　2. Do not benefit [33] mortals more than is right.　3.
It is right that children should benefit parents.　4. It is disgraceful to flatter any one for the sake of gain.　5. You are
doing wrong to the Greeks by breaking the peace.　6. I pity
him, though he is my enemy.　7. The bee wanders across the
meadow. 8. Hippoclides! you have danced (*aor.*) your wife away!
9. Having spent all his money in keeping horses, he ran away
out of the country.　10. We wished to make Ariaeus king.　11.
Lysander received a gift of crowns (*crowns as a gift*) from
(ἀπό) the cities.　12. The Greeks called all the rest (of mankind)
barbarians.　13. I consider this the most miserable of cities.
14. The Thebans were attempting to take Messene from us.
15. I will remind you of the virtues of your forefathers.　16.
Diogiton concealed from his daughter the death of her husband.
17. Do you, a poor man (*being poor*), say this of the general ?
18. He took the life of my only child.　19. He asked the
deserters about the affairs of (ἐκ) the enemy.　20. The tall boy,
having stripped the small boy of his [9] large tunic, put it on, and
clothed the small boy in his own small tunic.

§ 39. *Accusative continued.*

(1) "The rule of the Latin language that every noun
which can be the subject of the passive verb in the

The Accusative.

nominative, must be in the accusative with the active
verb, is not the rule of the Greek language." An object
which is in the genitive or dative may become the
nominative of the verb. Thus—

ἡγεμονεύειν τινός, but οὐκ ἠξίουν οὗτοι ἡγεμονεύεσθαι ὑφ' ἡμῶν.

Hence also verbs which govern an accusative and dative in
the active, as ἐπιτρέπω τὴν δίαιταν τῷ Σωκράτει, *I entrust
Socrates with the arbitration*, often retain the accusative
in the passive, while the dative becomes the nominative:
ὁ Σωκράτης ἐπιτρέπεται τὴν δίαιταν.

(2) Any intransitive verb can take an accusative of a
noun of *kindred* meaning—the so-called *cognate* accusative. This accusative admits a wide use; anything
which limits or defines the cognate notion, in the way of
apposition, being put in the accusative. Thus, πόλεμον
πολεμεῖν, ζῆν βίον, ὕπνον κοιμᾶσθαι, are instances of the
cognate accusative in the stricter sense; but in ῥεῖν γάλα
the use is more extended, γάλα being in apposition to a
cognate substantive such as ῥόον.

By uniting this accusative with the ordinary accusative
of the object, a verb may govern two accusatives.

ἐνίκησε τοὺς βαρβάρους (acc. object) τὴν ἐν Μαραθῶνι μάχην (acc.
cognate), *he conquered the barbarians in the battle of Marathon.*

(3) Verbs which cannot take an accusative of the
object are often found with the accusative neuter of a
pronoun, or of a numeral adjective, or an adjective which
can express the extent of the action.[a]

σμικρόν τι ἀπορῶ, *I have a little difficulty.*
δέομαι μέτρια ὑμῶν, *I make a moderate request to you.*
τί σοι χρῶμαι; *what am I to do with you?*

[a] This use of the pronoun and adjective is really a development of
the cognate use: σμικρόν τι ἀπορῶ is = σμικράν τινα ἀπορίαν ἀπορῶ,
δέομαι μέτρια is = δέομαι μετρίαν δέησιν, and so with other cases.
There is no reason to suppose an ellipse of κατά.

EXERCISE 43.

VOCABULARY.—*to agree with,* ὁμολογεῖσθαι, with dat. *already,* ἤδη. *arbitration,* δίαιτα. *battle,* μάχη. *bird,* ὄρνεον. *to command, give a command,* ἐπιστέλλειν τινί τι (the pass. = *to receive commands*). *to be cold,* ῥιγοῦν. *contrary,* ἐναντίος. *to be afflicted with disease,* νόσον νοσεῖν. *to entrust to,* ἐπιτρέπειν, πιστεύειν τινί (pers.) τι. *to share exile,* συμφεύγειν. *government,* ἀρχή. *to be hungry,* πεινῆν, with irregular contraction into -ῆν for -ᾶν (Prim. 119, *Obs.*). *to do many grievous injuries to,* πολλὰ καὶ μεγάλα ἀδικεῖν τινα.[a] *to make a just request,* δίκαια δεῖσθαι.[b] *last,* τελευταῖος. *to live a life,* βιοῦν βίον. *not worth living,* ἀβίωτος. *to be lucky, to have good luck,* εὐτυχεῖν. *a piece of good luck,* εὐτύχημα, τό. *Marathon,* Μαραθών, ῶνος. *to exact an oath,* ὅρκον ὁρκοῦν (lit. *to cause a person to swear an oath*). *to sing,* ἐπᾴδειν. *to suffer pain, to be in pain,* λύπην λυπεῖσθαι. *at that time = then,* τότε.

1. I have had the arbitration entrusted to me.   2. The general was entrusted with the government of the city.   3. The Corinthians, having received the commands, went away.   4. My friend shared this exile with me.   5. When they had experienced [47] this piece of good luck, the enemy went away.   6. We are afflicted with the contrary disease.   7. At that time he was already suffering from his last illness.   8. The life that you have lived is not worth living.   9. No bird sings when it is hungry or cold, or suffers any other pain.   10. I say nothing of (ἐῶ) the rest [5] (of the) battles in which the enemy were defeated.   11. Miltiades defeated the Persians in the battle at Marathon.   12. He exacted the most stringent (μέγιστος) oaths from all the soldiers.   13. In this one thing I cannot agree with you.   14. Do not send me away when I make a just request of you.   15. The enemy have done the city many grievous (μέγας) injuries [27].

---

[a] Observe that in Greek two adjectives which agree with the same substantive are usually united by καί; hence in Greek say, *many and great,* not *many great.*

Carefully distinguish this use from δικαίων δεῖσθαι, *to be in need of justice;* ῥώμης δεῖσθαι, *to need strength.*

§ 40. *Accusative of Limitation, Time, &c.*

(1) The accusative is used with nouns and adjectives, intransitive verbs, and participles, to limit the idea expressed by the noun, adjective, &c., to a particular part or circumstance (Syntax, 12 ff.) :

καλὸς τὸ σῶμα, *beautiful in body,*

where the beauty is limited and specified ;

τύπτομαι τὴν κεφαλήν, *I am struck on the head,*

where the part injured is specified.[a]

The accusative so used is called an *accusative of respect,* or of the *part affected,* or of *limitation,* or of *extent.*

(2) The accusative is used to express duration of time, and the distance of one place from another, as—

πολὺν χρόνον ἀπῆν, *he was absent a long time.*
τρεῖς ὅλους μῆνας ἐν Μακεδονίᾳ ἐμένομεν, *we remained three whole months in Macedonia.*
ἀπέχει δέκα σταδίους, *it is distant ten stades.*

(3) *Adverbial uses of the Accusative.*—Among these are τοὐναντίον (= τὸ ἐναντίον), *on the contrary ;* τὸ λεγόμενον, *as the saying is ;* τὴν ταχίστην, *as soon as possible* (supply ὁδόν = *by the shortest route*) ; τὸ σὸν μέρος, *so far as you are concerned ;* τὸ λοιπόν, *for the future* (the neuter article, both in the singular and the plural, is often used to introduce adverbial phrases of this kind); δίκην, *like ;* χάριν, *for the sake of,* &c.

On the use of the accusative in general, observe—

i.—The Latin rule about the accusative with verbs of motion is not applicable to Greek. The simple accusative, without a preposition,

---

[a] The relation implied by this accusative could be expressed more definitely by using the preposition κατά, *as to ;* but there is no reason to suppose an ellipse of κατά in order to explain the construction.

is found with verbs of motion in Greek, but equally with countries and towns.

οὐ γὰρ ἂν δέσποιν' ἐμὴ Μήδεια πύργους γῆς ἔπλευσ' Ἰωλκίας (Eur. Med. 6).

οὐ γάρ τι φαύλως ἦλθε Πολυνείκης χθόνα (ib. Ph. 110).

θάλαμον ἀνύτουσαν (Soph. Ant. 805), &c.

But the facility for compounding verbs with prepositions is so great in Greek, and the use of prepositions so much more frequent in Greek than in Latin, that the preposition, in one form or other, generally accompanies verbs of motion, especially in prose, e. g. εἰσιέναι τὴν πόλιν, ἰέναι εἰς τὴν πόλιν, &c. With *persons*, ὡς and πρός are the prepositions mostly in use.

ii.—In regard to the accusative, Greek differs from Latin chiefly in regard to the use of what is sometimes called the 'internal' accusative, i. e. the accusative of cognate signification in the wider sense, and the accusative of limitation.

Exercise 44.

Vocabulary.—*to* ache, κάμνειν. alike (adv.), ὁμοίως. *to have come*, ἥκειν. *to be in good, bad condition*, εὖ, κακῶς ἔχειν. *to be distant from*, ἀπέχειν, διέχειν. haste, σπονδή. head, κεφαλή. impious, ἀνόσιος. innumerable, ἄπειρος. journey, ὁδός, ἡ. judgment, γνώμη. leg, σκέλος, τό. middle, μέσος. mile, reckon eight stades for a mile, e.g. 10 miles = 80 stades. mind, διάνοια. not — yet, οὐ — πω. number, multitude, πλῆθος. *to be — old*, εἶναι — γεγονώς (lit. *to be — born*). *to have a pain*, ἀλγεῖν. river, ποταμός. six hundred, ἑξακόσιοι. stade, στάδιον, plur. -ιοι, -α. *to support*, τρέφειν. theatre, θέατρον. third, τρίτος. through, διά, with gen. *to be wont to, to love to*, φιλεῖν.

1. The soldiers were in good bodily condition (*in good condition as to their bodies*). 2. In all, the soldiers were six hundred in number. 3. Through the middle of the city flows a river, by name Cydnus. 4. I have a pain in my head[9]. 5. Put yourselves in mind (*become in mind*) for a short time in the theatre. 6. He was not yet twenty years old. 7. The journey shall be hastened night and day alike (*there shall be haste on the journey* (gen.)). 8. The army was distant from the city about ten miles. 9. This is the third year that[a] I have not had to support (*have ceased supporting*) my mother. 10. On the third day after the general had arrived, the ships sailed away (*when the general had come*[55] *the third day*).

[a] For *this is the third year that*, say, *for this third year* (acc. of time).

11. Do you see *to what* (ἵνα) you have come, though a man of sound judgment (*good as to judgment*)? 12. For the future we will keep the peace. 13. He went away as quickly as possible [64] to the city. 14. By acting in this way [17], I shall be rid of the whole business. 15. The barbarians invaded Greece in innumerable multitudes (*innumerable in number*). 16. So far as you were concerned, the city was captured. 17. My father has now [a] been absent three years. 18. The king and the Greeks were about thirty stades distant from each other. 19. My legs ache with the long journey (*I ache as to my legs, having gone a long way*). 20. On hearing [47] this, he advances an argument (*speaks a speech*) of all most impious. 21. Evil men are wont to speak evil of the good.

§ 41. *The Genitive.* [b]

The genitive in Greek is not only equivalent to the genitive in Latin, but also covers many uses of the Latin ablative. As an ablative it can be used with prepositions.

(1) The genitive is used in exclamations, as τῆς ἀναιδείας, *what impudence!* τῶν ἀλαζονευμάτων, *what humbug!*

---

[a] *Now* can often be translated by οὗτος in agreement with the acc. of time, e. g. *now three years = this third year.*

[b] The fundamental idea of the genitive as a *genitive* would seem to be *connexion with* in a wide sense, as for instance, a part is connected with the whole, &c.; as an *ablative* the genitive signifies *motion, removal from.* Hence one and the same case seems to represent two opposite ideas, *motion from, connexion with.* This difficulty is sometimes explained by the statement that all separation implies previous connexion (Madvig, § 46). It is better to regard the combination of genitive and ablative in Greek as accidental; the ablative originally ended in -*t*, the genitive in -*s*, but as Greek changed a final -*t* into -*s*, it is obvious that the two forms would tend to become identical.

Where the genitive was different in form from the ablative, the ablative remains in form; thus κακῶς in form is the ablative of κακός, of which the genitive is κακοῦ (κακοῖο), &c.; but in use the genitive took the place of the ablative, which became an adverb.

(2) The genitive is used with adverbs of time and place, as τρὶς τῆς ἡμέρας, *thrice in the day;* ποῦ γῆς; *where in the world?* &c.

Obs. i.—Wherever in English *a* is = *each,* as, e. g. in *thrice a day, twice a year, a* must be translated by *the* in Greek.

Obs. ii.—τρὶς τῆς ἡμέρας = *ter die;* ποῦ γῆς = *ubi terrarum?*

(3) Numerals, superlatives, and all partitive expressions, as adjectives, participles with the article, &c., take a genitive.

οἱ δεῖς Ἑλλήνων, *none of the Greeks, no Greek;* ἡ μεγίστη τῶν νόσων, *the greatest of diseases;* οἱ φρόνιμοι τῶν ἀνθρώπων, *wise men;* ὁ ἥμισυς τοῦ χρόνου, *half the time.*

So, where we use the word *some,* the Greeks use the genitive.

ἔδωκά σοι τῶν χρημάτων, *I gave you (some) of my money;* πίνειν ὕδατος, *to drink (some) water;* ἐσθίειν κρεῶν, *to eat (some) meat* (ἐσθίειν κρέα would be, *to eat meat* as a habit).

(4) The genitive also expresses the material of which a thing is made (*genitive of material*), and also it is used in *descriptions* of the most general character (expressing *qualities, properties, circumstances,* &c.).

στέφανος ὑακίνθων, *a crown of hyacinths;* πλίνθων ἐξῳκοδομήθη, *it was built of bricks;* ἦν γὰρ ἀξιώματος μεγάλου, *he was of great consideration.*

Obs.—When a further description is added to a possessive pronoun, this description is added in the genitive, e. g. διαρπάζουσι τἀμὰ τοῦ κακοδαίμονος, *they are plundering my property, unhappy me!* In the plural this would be, τὰ ἡμέτερα τῶν κακοδαιμόνων.

Exercise 45.

Vocabulary.—*to be advanced in years* (*age*), πόῤῥω τῆς
ἡλικίας εἶναι. *ancient,* παλαιός. *consideration,* ἀξίωμα. *figure,*
σχῆμα. *foolishness,* ἀβουλία. *from,* παρά, with gen. *golden,*
χρύσεος. *to imitate,* μιμεῖσθαι, with acc. *injustice,* ἀδικία.
till late in the day, μέχρι πόῤῥω τῆς ἡμέρας. *lily,* κρίνον. *to
plunder,* διαρπάζειν. *to rob,* ἀποστερεῖν, with double acc.
sensible, φρόνιμος. *to sleep,* καθεύδειν. *thrice,* τρίς. *violet,*
ἴον. *wine,* οἶνος. *year,* ἔτος.

1. I will place a crown of violets upon the boy's head [1]. 2.
The mother placed a crown of lilies on *her* [9] daughter's head.
3. Let us imitate sensible persons [5]. 4. I will come to you three
times *a* [3] year. 5. If he were not [40] a person of great consideration,
the citizens would have put him to death. 6. If he had not been
advanced in years, he would not have died. 7. He is stricken
with the worst of diseases [1], foolishness. 8. They *used to sleep*
till late in the day. 9. I will give to each of those present a
golden crown. 10. He refused to give pay to any of the
soldiers. 11. Unhappy me! my possessions are being plundered.
12. See! the ambassadors are come from the king [18]; what
figures! 13. He gave him some wine to drink. 14. For half
the time [29] he was away in Macedonia. 15. What injustice! I
am robbed of half my possessions. 16. Some [19] of the citizens
perished, some escaped. 17. The Phrygians were thought to
be the most ancient of mankind.

§ 42. *Genitive with* εἰμι, γιγνομαι, *&c.*

(1) The partitive genitive may be used as a predicate
with the verbs εἰμί, γίγνεσθαι, &c., where in English we
should say *one of.*

Κριτίας τῶν τριάκοντα ἦν.
Critias was one of the thirty, was among the thirty.

But εἰς may also be inserted.

τῶν εἰς τὴν πολιν ἀνηλωκότων τὴν οὐσίαν εἰς ἐγω φανησομαι γεγενη-
μένος, *I shall be found to have been one of those who spent
their substance on the city.*

Obs.—εἶναι αἰσχρόν, τῶν αἰσχρῶν, τῶν αἰσχρων τι, ἐν τῶν αἰσχρῶν,
are all = *to be disgraceful ; to be a disgraceful thing.*

(2) The genitive with εἰμί (generally ἐστί, used impersonally) denotes what is *proper to, what suits* or *accords with* the person or thing placed in the genitive.

οὗτοι δικαίου ἐστὶν ἀνδρὸς τὰ τοιαῦτα πράττειν,
it is not the part of, it does not become, it is not like, a just man to do such things.

(3) The genitive of *quality* (cp. § 41 (4)) may appear as a predicate with εἰμί, γίγνομαι.

ταῦτα μεγάλης δαπάνης ἐστί, *this is a matter involving (requiring) great expense.*

So also the genitive of *material*, &c. (cp. § 41 (4)).

φοίνικος αἱ θύραι ἦσαν, *the doors were of palm-wood.*

Obs.—The genitive of quality requires to be accompanied by an adjective, defining the general quality more precisely.

(4) The genitive may also be used with the neuter pronoun (or the word ἕν), to denote something *in*, or *on the part of* some person.

τοῦτό μοι ἔδοξε τῶν κατηγόρων ἀναισχυντότατον,
this seemed to me the most shameless thing in the accusers.

So also of things :

ἃ διώκει Αἰσχίνης τοῦ ψηφίσματος, ταῦτ' ἐστιν,
what Æschines attacks in the decree, is this (Madvig, § 53).

Exercise 46.

Vocabulary.—*to accuse*, κατηγορεῖν. *base*, αἰσχρός. *to blame*, μέμφεσθαι. *breadth*, εὖρος, τό. *to choose*, καταλέγειν. *to come, arrive*, ἀφικεῖσθαι. *what time of day?* πηνίκα τῆς ἡμέρας; *to desert, abandon*, προδιδόναι. *dilatoriness*, τὸ μέλλον. *especially*, μάλιστα. *folly*, μωρία. *foundation*, κρηπίς, ἡ. *honeycomb*, κηρίον. *to hunt after*, θηρᾶν, with acc. *impossible things*, ἀμήχανα. *income*, πρόσοδος, ἡ. *late*, ὀψέ. *to march against*, ἐπιστρατεύειν. *plethron* (100 feet), πλέθρον. *polished*, ξεστός. *to sail*, πλεῖν. *to lose one's senses*, ἄφρων γενέσθαι. *shameless*, ἀναίσχυντος. *Thrasylus*, Θρασύλος. *trierarch*, τριήραρχος. *to go far in wisdom*, πόρρω ἐλαύνειν τῆς σοφίας. *years old*, use gen. of ἔτος, *e.g.* τριῶν ἐτῶν εἶναι, *to be three years old*; but cp. also Voc. 11.

1. Thrasylus was chosen one of the trierarchs in Sicily. 2. The general said he[24] was not one of those who sailed to[11] the city. 3. To desert allies is one of the basest of things. 4. It is the mark of a good man to love his[9] city. 5. Do not be ashamed of the dilatoriness which they especially blame in you (*gen.*). 6. This I consider the most shameless (thing) in him, that he betrayed the city. 7. It is not for every man to sail to Corinth. 8. Does it then (ἄρα) become a just man to injure his[9] enemies ? 9. The river is four plethra in breadth. 10. The foundation was of polished stone. 11. It shows great folly to hunt after things impossible. 12. The boy was more than twelve years old. 13. He had an income of twenty minae a[3] year. 14. Thebes is (situated) in Bœotia[a] (§ 41 (2)). 15. The enemy marched against Pharsalus in Thessaly.[a] 16. All who (ὅσοι) ate any of the honeycombs lost their senses. 17. At what time of day did the messenger come ? 18. This person[10], who accuses his father, is going far in wisdom. 19. It was late in the day when the messenger came.

§ 43. *Genitive with Verbs.*

(1) Verbs relating to the *senses*, except *sight*, take the genitive. ἀκούειν, *to hear*, generally takes an *accusative* of the *sound*, and a *genitive* of the *person* producing it; but in both constructions exceptions will be found.

> ἀκούω παιδίου κλαίοντος, *I hear a child crying.*
> ᾔσθετο τῆς φωνῆς, *he heard (perceived) the voice.*

(2) Verbs signifying *to touch, lay hold of, cling to,* &c., take a genitive.

> ἔχεσθαί τινος, *to cling to something (to be next to it)*; ἅπτεσθαι
> νεκροῦ, *to touch a corpse.*[b]

---

[a] Use the article with the name of the country, *not* with the name of the town.

[b] The difference between λαβεῖν τινα, *to catch a person*, and λαβέσθαι τινός, *to lay hold of a person*, seems to be, that in the one case the action of the verb extends to the *whole* of the object, in the other to a *part* only. The genitive is, therefore, partitive.

(3) Most verbs that express such notions as *freeing from, keeping off from, ceasing from, deviating* or *departing from*, &c., take the genitive. Such verbs are, e. g. ἀπαλλάττειν, *to rid of*; εἴργειν, *to exclude*; παύειν, *to make to cease, to stop*; ἁμαρτάνειν, *to miss, to err*; διαφέρειν, *to differ*, and others.

> *Obs.*—When these verbs are transitive, they can, of course, take an accusative, as well as the genitive, e. g. εἴργειν τινὰ τῆς ἀγορᾶς, *to exclude a person from the market-place.*

(4) Most verbs that express *remembering* or *forgetting, caring for* or *despising, sparing, aiming at* or *desiring, ruling over* or *excelling, accusing of* or *condemning*, take the genitive; but not without many exceptions. Such verbs are: μέμνημαι, *I remember*; ἐπιλανθάνομαι, *I forget*; φείδομαι, *I spare*; ἐπιθυμῶ, *I desire*; ἐρῶ, *I love*; καταγιγνώσκω, *I condemn*, &c.

> *Obs.* i.—Though we can say in Greek, διώκειν, φεύγειν, εἰσάγειν, δικάζεσθαι, γράφεσθαί τινα δειλίας—putting the person in the *accusative*, and the crime in the *genitive*—the compounds of κατα- which 'denote accusation and condemnation' take a *genitive* of the person, and an *accusative* of the crime, e. g. κατηγορεῖν μωρίαν τῶν στρατηγῶν, *to charge the generals with folly.* In the passive, the accusative becomes the nominative, the genitive is unchanged: μωρία κατηγορεῖται τῶν στρατηγῶν.

> *Obs.* ii.—Verbs compounded with ἐκ, ἀπό, &c., frequently repeat the preposition, e. g. ἐκβαίνει ἐκ τοῦ πλοίου, and τοῦ πλοίου, *to go out of the boat.* Of the two constructions, the repetition of the preposition is the most common when 'the *local* notion is prominent.' Cf. Madvig, § 57 (*b*).

Of the two constructions, that in which the preposition is used with the verb and not with the noun is probably the older. The first use of the so-called prepositions was as adverbs, to define more accurately the direction of the action signified by the verb. In this way the addition of a preposition to a verb made the verb capable of taking more than one case, e. g. αὐτοὺς εἰσῆγον θεῖον δόμον, *they led them into the godlike hall*, where εἰς makes the second accusative possible (or at any rate more definite, for without it δόμον would mean *towards* or *to the hall*). Then the preposition was repeated with the case, in order to make the expression more definite still.

Exercise 47.

Vocabulary.—*accused*, *defendant*, ὁ ἀπολογούμενος (= *the answerer*). *accuser*, κατήγορος. *acropolis*, ἀκρόπολις, ἡ. *ambition*, φιλοτιμία. *animal*, ζῶον. *child*, παιδίον. *to cling to*, ἔχεσθαι, with gen. *contrary to*, παρά, with acc. *cowardice*, δειλία. *to deprive* = *to rob*, ἀποστερεῖν. *to desire*, ὀρέγεσθαι, ἐφίεσθαι. *to despise*, καταφρονεῖν. *foolish*, μάταιος. *to forget*, ἐπιλανθάνεσθαι, with gen. *to set free*, ἐλευθεροῦν. *justice*, τὸ δίκαιον. *labour*, πόνος. *to listen to*, ἀκούειν, κλύειν (poet.), ἀκροᾶσθαι. *to be lord of*, ἀνάσσειν, with gen. (poet.). *to be master of*, κρατεῖν, with gen. *to promise*, ὑπισχνεῖσθαι. *to relieve from* (*set free from*), ἀπαλλάττειν, with gen. *to remember*, μεμνῆσθαι, with gen. *to rule over*, ἄρχειν, with gen. (also, *to begin*). *to seize hold of*, λαμβάνεσθαι, with gen. *to spare*, φείδεσθαι, with gen. *to be superior to*, περιγίγνεσθαι, with gen. *to surpass*, *differ from*, διαφέρειν, with gen.

1. We ought not to desire great things contrary to justice. 2. Why do you desire ambition, (the) worst of diseases? 3. It is shameful for me to listen to a foolish man. 4. I will listen to the accuser and the defendant equally. 5. In seeking to deprive his friends of their[9] money, he was himself deprived of all *that he had* (τὰ ὄντα). 6. I will set this land[10] free from tyrants. 7. I will relieve you from all these labours which (ὧν, § 51 (3)) you now endure (ἔχω). 8. By doing this you would quickly be superior to your enemies. 9. He far surpassed all men in the receipt of revenue (*in receiving*—τῷ, with infin.—*revenues*). 10. You came here as lord of Sparta, not as master of us. 11. Man seems to me to differ from the rest of the animals in desiring honour. 12. I shall accuse you of cowardice. 13. Do not[33] despise the good. 14. I do not remember their long speeches (*I do not remember the many things which*—ὧν by attraction, § 51 (3)—*they said*). 15. He quickly forgot all that (ὧν) he had promised. 16. Seize him, without sparing (μηδέ) even his life. 17. The child clung to the hands of its mother. 18. The enemy, after slaying the guards, became masters of the acropolis. 19. Do not seek to rule over others, when yourself unwilling to be ruled. 20. It is natural to man to rule over the other[5] animals.

EXERCISE 48.

VOCABULARY.—*at all*, τὸ παράπαν. *banishment*, φυγή (*flight*). *boat*, πλοῖον. *to lay to a man's charge* = *to accuse of*, κατηγορεῖν, with gen. *to condemn*, καταγιγνώσκειν. *to be condemned in*, ὀφλισκάνειν (Prim. 167), with acc. *drachma* (*a coin*), δραχμή. *judge*, κριτής. *mind*, φρένες, αἱ. *murderer*, φονεύς. *to fix the penalty at*, τιμᾶσθαι, with gen. *prudent*, φρόνιμος. *subtlety*, λεπτότης. *thousand*, χίλιος.

1. They accuse the judge himself of injustice. 2. They condemned them all to death. 3. Socrates was condemned to death (*infin.*). 4. They have condemned Sophroniscus to banishment. 5. Had you done this, I should have accused you of folly. 6. I never went out of the boat at all. 7. Do not [33] listen to the things falsely (*the falsehoods*) laid to my charge. 8. The accuser was condemned in a thousand drachmae. 9. They fled away out of the country. 10. O Zeus! what subtlety [58] of mind! 11. These things happened in the time of our forefathers (Voc. 40). 12. The murderer cannot escape the (sentence of) death pronounced (*condemned*) upon him. 13. He said that, if any man did this, the prudent would accuse him of folly. 14. My (μοι) accuser fixes the punishment at death.

§ 44. *The Genitive continued.*

(1) Verbs and adjectives signifying *abundance* and *want*, *fulness* and *emptiness*, take a genitive.[a]

> μεστόν ἐστι τὸ ζῆν φροντίδων, *life is full of cares.*
> δεῖσθαι χρημάτων, *to be in want of money.*
> δασὺς δένδρων, *thick with trees.*

(2) The *price* or *value* is put in the genitive, and all verbs or adjectives relating to *price* or *value* can therefore take a genitive, as ἀγοράζειν, *to buy* (τι τινος); τιμᾶσθαι, *to value*; ὠνεῖσθαι, *to buy*; ἄξιος, *worth*, &c.; ἄξιον πολλῶν χρημάτων, *worth much money.* In the same way, after

---

[a] Lists of such verbs and adjectives will be found in Madvig, §§ 57 (*a*), 63 (*a*).

verbs that express or imply exchange, the thing for which we exchange another is put in the genitive, as —

τρεῖς μνᾶς κατέθηκε τοῦ ἵππου, *he laid down three minæ for the horse.*

χρήματα τούτων πράττεται, *he exacts money for this.*

(3) The genitive expresses the part *by which* a person *leads, takes,* or *gets hold of* a thing (cp. § 43 (2)).

τὸν λύκον τῶν ὤτων κρατῶ, *I get hold of the wolf by the ears.*

So ἄγειν χειρός, *to lead by the hand,* &c.

(4) With verbs of *deeming happy, pitying,* and the like, the genitive can be used of that *on account of which* we deem a person happy or the reverse.

ζηλῶ σε τοῦ νοῦ, τῆς δὲ δειλίας στυγῶ,
I envy you for your intelligence, but I hate you for your cowardice.

EXERCISE 49.

VOCABULARY.—*Adeimantus,* Ἀδείμαντος. *to admire,* ἄγασθαι, θαυμάζειν. *affliction,* πάθος. *bravery,* ἀνδρεία. *destitute of,* ἔρημος, with gen. *disposition,* τρόπος. *to drag out,* ἐξέλκειν. *to envy,* φθονεῖν. *to exchange,* ἀλλάττειν. *to fill,* πιμπλάναι. *foot,* πούς. *full,* ἐμπλεής, μεστός. *glory,* δόξα. *to think happy,* εὐδαιμονίζειν. *hollow,* κοῖλος. *to introduce, bring forward,* εἰσάγειν. *to live, pass time,* διαιτᾶσθαι. *merchant,* ἔμπορος. *milk,* γάλα, τό. *misery,* δυσπραξία. *to pledge,* ὑποτιθέναι. *present (gift),* δώρημα. *to punish,* κολάζειν. *to purchase,* ὠνεῖσθαι, for the aorist use πρίασθαι. *purchasable, to-be-purchased,* ὠνητός. *service,* λατρεία. *stranger,* ξένος. *toil,* μόχθος. *traitor,* προδότης. *vessel,* ἀγγεῖον. *water,* ὕδωρ. *to be well off for,* εὐπορεῖν, with gen. *worthy of,* ἄξιος, with gen.

1. Adeimantus took me by the hand. 2. They dragged him out of the house by his[9] feet. 3. They filled the vessel with water and milk. 4. When he was well off for money, he lived in the city. 5. The hollows of the earth are full of water. 6. The whole city is full of merchants and strangers, but destitute of good allies. 7. This I would purchase at the price of my

life. 8. He pledged his house for five minæ. 9. Glory is not
to be purchased with money. 10. This person is worthy of
praise because [46] he has rendered his country many benefits. 11.
Timocrates introduces laws for money. 12. I think you happy
in your disposition. 13. I pity you on account of your
affliction. 14. They deem the citizens happy on account of
their virtue. 15. Do you not admire those who [11] are willing to
serve the city for their bravery? 16. *It is just that I* (Ex. 36,
Obs.) should be set free from this charge. 17. I do not envy
you this [10] present. 18. When he heard this, Cyrus pitied him
for his misfortune. 19. The whole land was full of traitors.
20. I would not exchange my [7] misery for your [7] service. 21.
She came into my hands (at the price) of much toil. 22. Let
them be punished as their fault deserves (*worthily of their
fault*).

§ 45. *The Genitive continued.*

(1) Verbal adjectives with a transitive meaning (Prim.
176, 2) take the genitive, i.e. the *object* of the *verb*
stands in the genitive after the adjective derived from
the verb.

> πρακτικὸς τῶν καλῶν, *able to perform* (*capable of*) *honourable
> actions* (πράττειν καλά); ἐπιθυμητικὸς τῶν καλῶν, *eager for honour-
> able actions* (ἐπιθυμεῖν τῶν καλῶν).

> *Obs.*—Whether the *verb* takes a genitive or an accusative makes
> no difference in the government of the adjective.

(2) Any adjective or adverb which expresses a *privative
notion* (being without) may take a genitive. Such
adjectives are often compounded with ἀ- (*privativum*):
ἄπαις ἀρρένων παίδων, *without male children*; ἄγευστος
τῆς ἐλευθερίας, *without a taste of liberty*; ἄνευ τούτων,
without these; χωρὶς τούτων, *apart from these.*[a]

(3) A noun of time is put in the genitive, in answer to
the question *when?* and *since*, or *within what time?*

---

[a] When expressing a privative notion, the Greeks often express the
thing lost twice over—once in the compound adjective, and again in
the substantive in the genitive, e.g. ἄπαις ἀρρένων παίδων, where παῖς
is repeated; ἄτιμος πάσης τιμῆς, where τιμή is repeated. This is
common in the poets; it is more graphic than the simple adverbs,
ἄνευ, χωρίς, &c.

νυκτός, *by night, in the night;* ἡμέρας, *by day, in the day;* χρόνου συχνοῦ, *in* or *for a long time;* πολλῶν ἡμερῶν οὐ μεμελέτηκα, *I have not practised for many days* (Syntax, § 18 (*a*)).

VOCABULARY.—*without accomplishing,* ἄπρακτος. *to be archon,* ἄρχειν. *besides,* χωρίς. *capable of (doing),* πρακτικός. *deprived of,* ἄτιμος (lit. *without honour in*). *evening,* δειλή. *experienced in,* ἔμπειρος, with gen. *forgetful,* ἐπιλήσμων. *to do harm to,* κακοῦργος εἶναι, with gen. *inexperienced in,* ἄπειρος, with gen. *by land,* κατὰ γῆν. *month,* μήν. *robe,* ἱμάτιον. *sea,* θάλαττα. *seven hundred,* ἑπτακόσιοι. *summer,* θέρος. *village,* κώμη. *to wear,* use passive of ἀμφιεννύναι. *winter,* χειμών. *without (the consent of),* ἄνευ.

1. The soldiers arrived at the villages in the evening (Ex. 2). 2. He wore the same robe in summer and winter. 3. This took place in the same month, in the archonship of Theophilus (Ex. 40). 4. For many years he has not come to the city. 5. He said that for many years he had not gone out of the city. 6. He died without male children. 7. These things were done *without the consent of* the rest of [5] the allies. 8. No one who is capable of honourable actions would go away when the city is in danger [55]. 9. I am not experienced in dangers of this sort. 10. Are you so forgetful of the labours which I underwent? 11. He did harm to the rest, but much greater harm (*comparative*) to himself. 12. There were seven hundred hoplites, besides those that came [11] from Sparta. 13. He was experienced in many great dangers by land and sea. 14. May I perish [36] deprived of all honour, if I did this. 15. The ambassadors went away without accomplishing what they desired (§ 51 (3)).

§ 46. *Comparison.*

(1) In Greek the thing with which another is compared is put in the genitive.

μείζων ἐμοῦ, *greater than I.*[a]

---

[a] The Greek *genitive* is here equivalent to the Latin *ablative*. *Starting from, beginning from (greater — beginning from me = greater — then I,* i.e. *greater than I),* appears to be the idea at the base of comparison, so that the ablative is the proper case for expressing this relation.

(2) When this construction cannot conveniently be used, i. e. when the first member of the comparison is in the genitive case, e. g. λαβέσθαι μείζονος ἐμοῦ, ἤ is employed, and the case is the same after ἤ as before.

λαβέσθαι μείζονος ἢ ἐμοῦ, *to take hold of one greater than I.*

Obs.—If ἤ introduces a clause requiring a *second verb* (other than εἰμί), it is followed by the nominative, e. g. τοῖς νεωτέροις καὶ μᾶλλον ἀκμάζουσιν, ἢ ἐγώ, παραινῶ ταῦτα ποιεῖν. Here ἀκμάζω must be supplied to ἐγώ. But if the words καὶ μᾶλλον ἀκμά- ζουσιν were omitted, we might say ἐμοί, because in this case only εἰμί need be supplied.

(3) *Too great for,* &c., is expressed by a comparative with ἢ κατά (with accusative) before a *substantive;* with ἢ ὥστε before a verb in the *infinitive.*

μείζω ἢ κατὰ δάκρυα πεπονθέναι,
     to have suffered afflictions too great for tears.

νεκρὸς μείζων ἢ κατ' ἄνθρωπον,
     a corpse of superhuman size.

ὅπλα πλέω ἢ κατὰ τοὺς νεκρούς,
     more arms than could have been expected from the number of the dead.

νεώτεροί εἰσιν ἢ ὥστε εἰδέναι,
     they were too young to know.

Obs.—ὥστε may be omitted.

Exercise 51.

Vocabulary.—*to advise,* παραινεῖν. *arms,* ὅπλα. *better (more sweetly, pleasantly),* ἥδιον. *brave,* ἀνδρεῖος. *dead (corpse),* νεκρός. *to deceive,* ἀπατᾶν. *desire,* ἐπιθυμία. *eager,* πρόθυμος. *to go on an expedition,* στρατείαν ἐξελθεῖν. *greater, taller,* μείζων. *justice,* δικαιοσύνη. *means,* οὐσία. *rich,* πλούσιος. *to be sensible,* σωφρονεῖν. *to sing,* ἀείδειν. *tear,* δάκρυ. *to trust to,* πιστεύειν, with dat. *to be wise,* σωφρονεῖν.

1. The boy is taller than his[7] father. 2. The daughter sings better than her mother. 3. He suffered afflictions too great for tears. 4. More arms were taken than could have been expected

from the number of the dead. 5. He told me that [35] the corpse
was of superhuman size. 6. He is too wise to be deceived by
his slave. 7. To whom could I trust more than to you? 8.
You have got a house much larger than ours. 9. I advise those
who have more money than I have to purchase such things.
10. He went away far wiser than he came. 11. I advise those
younger than myself to go on this [10] expedition. 12. He had
desires too great for his means. 13. You desire things too great
for a man. 14. He was too brave to go away when the city
was in danger [55]. 15. Had you been wise, you would have
given the horse to one richer than myself. 16. You offer a
house far too large for my means. 17. The son was taller than
his father. 18. The daughter, at twelve years of age, was
taller than her mother. 19. Justice [8] is far more profitable than
injustice. 20. You will not persuade men that justice is far
more profitable than injustice. 21. If justice were profitable [40],
men would be more eager *in pursuing* it (*part.*).

§ 47. *Comparison continued.*

(1) *Greater, &c., than ever, than at any other time,* is
expressed by using αὐτός before the genitive of the
reflexive pronoun.

> δυνατώτεροι αὐτοὶ ἑαυτῶν ἐγένοντο,
> *they became more powerful than ever* (lit. *more powerful them-
> selves than themselves,* i. e. *than they were at any other time*).

(2) When two adjectives or adverbs expressing a
quality belonging to the same subject are compared,
both are put in the comparative degree.[a]

> ἡγοῦνται αὐτὸν βελτίονα εἶναι ἢ πλουσιώτερον,
> *they consider that he is more honest than rich.*

(3) Instead of saying μείζω οἰκίαν τῆς ἐμῆς (οἰκίας)
ἔχεις, the Greeks often say, μείζω οἰκίαν ἔχεις ἐμοῦ, and

---

[a] The double comparative is not otiose. Not only are the two
qualities compared with each other, but in respect of each of them the
possessor is compared with other men, i. e. they consider him to be
better than others, rather than richer than others—distinguished for
honesty rather than wealth.

even οὐδ' ἐσίδον (= εἰσεῖδον) μοίρᾳ τοῦδ' ἐχθίονι συντυχόντα θνατῶν, *I never saw any mortal meeting with a worse fate than this man,* where τοῦδε is = τῆς τοῦδε μοίρας.[a]

(4) πλέον (πλεῖον, πλεῖν) and ἔλαττον (μεῖον) are used, with or without ἤ, in expressing numbers, without influence on the case.

οἱ ἱππεῖς ἀποκτείνουσι τῶν ἀνδρῶν οὐ μεῖον πεντακοσίους, *the cavalry slay no less than 500 of the men.*

πέμψω ὄρνις (acc. plur.) ἐπ' αὐτὸν πλεῖν ἑξακοσίους τὸν ἀριθμόν, *I will send more than 600 birds against him.*

EXERCISE 52.

VOCABULARY.—*to build,* οἰκοδομεῖν. *confident,* θαρραλέος. *beyond all expectation,* κρεῖττον ἐλπίδος. *beyond all expression,* κρεῖττον λόγου. *five hundred,* πεντακόσιοι. *more than the occasion requires,* πλεῖον τοῦ καιροῦ. *piece of good luck,* εὐτύχημα. *to possess,* κεκτῆσθαι (perf. of κτᾶσθαι). *powerful,* δυνατός. *property* (= *means*), οὐσία. *spirit,* φρόνημα. *to surpass themselves* (= *to be better than themselves*), βελτίονες ἑαυτῶν γίγνεσθαι. *twenty-five,* πέντε καὶ εἴκοσι, or εἴκοσι πέντε (cp. Prim. § 89).

1. The Athenians have become more powerful than ever. 2. If you do this[40], you will become more powerful than ever. 3. He said that if they had done this[40], they would have become more powerful than ever. 4. If they were to do this, they would become more powerful than ever. 5. He possessed more than thirty plethra of land. 6. He said that the king possessed more than five hundred plethra of land. 7. The house was sold for not less than five-and-twenty minæ. 8. When they heard this, they became more confident than ever. 9. This king built a city far less than his father's. 10. They desire to become wise rather than rich. 11. He possessed a property far larger than his father's. 12. Do not seek to be rich rather

---

[a] That is, instead of carrying out the comparison between similar things belonging to (affecting, &c.) different persons, the Greeks briefly compare the *thing* possessed by one person with another *person* possessing the same or a similar thing.

than good. 13. Deeds were done *beyond all expression.* 14. Do not think that more are being put to death *than the occasion requires.* 15. This piece-of-good-luck has happened *beyond all expectation.* 16. On this[10] day they far surpassed themselves. 17. I possess a house far larger than yours. 18. He has a spirit too great for a man.

§ 48. *Idioms of the Superlative, &c.*

(1) The words αὐτός, ἑαυτοῦ, &c., can be used with the superlative as well as the comparative (§ 47 (1)).

νέος ὢν πᾶς ἄνθρωπος τὰ τοιαῦτα ἀμβλύτατα αὐτὸς ἑαυτοῦ ὁρᾷ,
when young, every man sees such things most dimly, i. e. *more dimly than at any other period of his life.*

(2) ὡς and ὅτι (like the Latin *quam*) are used to strengthen superlatives.

ὡς τάχιστα, *as quickly as possible;* σιγῇ ὡς ἀνυστὸν προσῄεσαν, *they came up as silently as possible;* ὅτι μέγιστος, *as great as possible.*

In a similar manner ὅσος is used, with δύναμαι, &c.

ὅσους ἠδύνατο πλείστους ἀθροίσας, *having collected as many men as he possibly could.*

Also ὅσον τάχος, ὅσον σθένος, *as quickly, as strongly, as possible.*

(3) εἷς ἀνήρ, and εἴ τις καὶ ἄλλος, are sometimes added to superlatives.

τοὺς ἀγωνιζομένους πλεῖστα εἷς ἀνὴρ δυνάμενος ὠφελεῖν,
being able to be of more service to the contending parties than any other individual.

νυμφείων ὄκνον ἄλγιστον ἔσχον, εἴ τις Αἰτωλὶς γυνή,
I had most painful dread of marriage of any Ætolian woman.

εἴ τις καὶ ἄλλος can also be added to adjectives in the positive degree, thereby giving the force of a superlative to the expression.

καίτοι, εἴ τις καὶ ἄλλος πρὸς τὰ ἔτη, μέλαιναν τὴν τρίχα ἔχεις,
and yet, if any one, you have black hair for your years, i. e. *you have remarkably black hair for your years.*

Obs. i.—The Greeks often prefer to use οὐ and a *negative* adverb in the superlative instead of a positive adverb, e. g. οὐχ ἥκιστα for μάλιστα.

Obs. ii.—The Greeks sometimes use an *inclusive* superlative instead of an *exclusive* comparative, e. g. κάλλιστον τῶν προτέρων φάος = *a light fairer than any previous lights;* lit. *fairest of the previous.*[a]

Obs. iii.—περιττός (*exceeding, over and above*) and adjectives in -πλάσιος (*-fold*) take a genitive from their comparative meaning, e. g. περιττὰ τῶν ἀρκούντων, *more than enough (of money,* &c.); πολλαπλάσιοι ἡμῶν αὐτῶν, *many times as numerous as ourselves.*

Exercise 53.

Vocabulary.—*alone among,* μόνος, with gen. *to associate with,* συγγίγνεσθαι, with dat. *to Athens,* Ἀθήραζε. *to collect,* ἀθροίζειν. *to be enough, to suffice,* ἀρκεῖν. *enough,* τὰ ἀρκοῦντα. *famous,* ἀξιόλογος. *freedom of speech,* παρρησία. *hair,* θρίξ (Prim. 173 (*a*)), ἡ. *more than,* περιττός. *to practise,* ἀσκεῖν. *slowly,* βραδέως (how is the superlative of adverbs formed? Prim. § 86). *to be superior to,* περιγίγνεσθαι, with gen. *temperance,* σωφροσύνη. *wide,* εὐρύς.

1. If any man practises temperance, it is he. 2. He received more gifts than any other one man. 3. I shall collect as many men as possible. 4. The Persians came on as slowly as possible. 5. He has injured the state more than any other single man. 6. If any man has been of great service to the state, it is he. 7. He crossed the river *at its widest point (where it was widest,* add ἑαυτοῦ). 8. At this time the Athenians were most powerful. 9. This war was more famous than any preceding war. 10. When you have collected as many men as possible, march against Cyrus. 11. If you have more than enough, give (some) to your[9] friends. 12. I wish that I had associated[36] with him when he was at his best. 13. When at his best, he was far superior to the rest of the Athenians. 14. He alone, among the soldiers, went away. 15. Desire to become as good as possible. 16. You have come to Athens, where in all Hellas (*gen.*) there is the greatest freedom-of-speech. 17. He caused more trouble to his friends than any other man. 18. I do not know any one who has blacker hair than yours[63].

---

* So Milton:

'Adam, the goodliest man of men,
Since born, and fairest of her daughters Eve.'

§ 49. *The Dative.*

In the Greek dative three cases are combined,—

(*a*) The dative proper, or case of the ' remoter object,' of the person or thing in regard or reference to which something is done.

(*b*) The case of the cause, instrument, &c. This use of the dative in Greek corresponds to the Latin ablative.

(*c*) An old case, expressing the place where, *locative.*

(1) In regard to the dative of reference, we may distinguish the use—

(*a*) With transitive verbs, which can also take an accusative of the more direct object. Such are not only verbs of *giving, promising*, &c., but in general any verb which denotes an action done in reference to another person or thing.[a]

(*b*) With intransitive verbs, which do not take an accusative of the direct object, but appear with the dative only. Such are verbs of *obeying, blaming, aiding, meeting, following,* &c.

φθονῶ, *I envy;* πείθομαι, *I obey;* ἐγκαλῶ, *I accuse;* ἀπειλῶ, *I threaten;* ἐναντιοῦμαι, *I oppose;* χαρίζομαι, *I gratify;* ἀπιστῶ, *I disobey;* ἕπομαι, *I follow;* εὔχομαι, *I pray,* and others.[b]

(2) The dative is used with words denoting *likeness* or *unlikeness, friendship* or *enmity.*

τὰ αἰτὰ πάσχω σοί,
I suffer the same as you.
Θησεὺς κατὰ τὸν αὐτὸν χρόνον Ἡρακλεῖ ἐγένετο,
Theseus lived about the same time as Heracles.

---

[a] Notice, as being distinct from Latin, the compounds of ἀντί, ἐν, ἐπί, περί, πρός, σύν, ὑπό, e. g. περιτιθέναι στέφανον τῷ στρατηγῷ, *to put a crown on the general,* &c.

[b] Here, again, observe that intransitive verbs compounded with ἀντί, ἐν, παρά, πρός, σύν, ὑπό, are used with a dative of reference.

(3) (*a*) The dative is used with ἐστί, ὑπάρχει, γίγνεται, as in Latin with *est*, &c., to denote the *possessor*.

οὐκ ἐστὶν ἡμῖν ὅπλα,
we have no weapons.
νῆες οὐκ εἰσὶν ἡμῖν,
we have no ships.

Obs.—οὐδὲν ἐμοὶ καὶ σοί, *I have nothing to do with you;* τι ἐμοὶ καὶ σοί; *what have I to do with you?*

(*b*) The dative of the personal pronouns is often added to sentences to express an interest on the part of the person in what is said or done.

τούτῳ πάνυ μοι προσέχετε τὸν νοῦν,
I would have you give particular attention to this.

This, the so-called *Ethic dative*, is more common in Greek than in Latin. It may be distinguished from other uses of the dative by the fact that it can be omitted in the sentence without materially affecting the meaning.[a]

---

[a] It is a distinctive feature of Latin as opposed to Greek that the genitive and dative are not used with prepositions. The reason is, probably, that in Latin the genitives and datives were for the most part real genitives and datives, whereas in Greek the ablative has become confused with the genitive, and the locative with the dative (see *supra*). Another cause which greatly favoured the use of prepositions with cases in Greek is the existence of the augment. This, coming as it did between the preposition and the verb in composition, e. g. προσβάλλω, προσέβαλον, tended to keep the two distinct and easily separable, so that the preposition could be easily detached from the verb, and combined with the noun. In Latin, on the other hand, the two became closely connected, so much so that we find a good number of verbs which exist in the compound but not in the simple form, e. g. *inspicio, respicio, induo, condo,* &c.

VOCABULARY.—*to abide by*, ἐμμένειν, with dat. *to be in accord with, to be in harmony with*, συμφωρεῖν, with dat. *to allot*, προστάττειν. *to associate with*, ὁμιλεῖν, with dat. *to be in*, ἐνεῖναι, with dat. *to divide among*, διανέμειν, with dat. *duties*, ἔργα. *everywhere*, πανταχοῦ. *persons of experience*, οἱ ἔμπειροι. *to follow*, ἕπεσθαι, with dat. *four*, τέσσαρες. *friendly to*, εὔνους, with dat. *hostile*, ἐχθρός. *inland-country*, μεσογεία. *to meet with*, συντυγχάνειν, with dat. *neighbour*, ὁ πέλας, ὁ πλησίος. *old age*, γῆρας. *to owe*, ὀφείλειν. *I receive from*, γίγνεται ἐμοὶ ἀπό. *I have on my side*, ὑπάρχει μοι. *treaty*, συνθῆκαι, αἱ.

1. He gave the soldiers pay for four months[61]. 2. He said that he had divided a large sum of money (*much money*) among the soldiers. 3. He entrusted the affairs of the city to persons of the greatest experience. 4. He owed a large sum of money to many (persons). 5. The general sent an ambassador *to announce*[43] to the citizens *what had been done* (perf. pass. part.). 6. He allotted to the slaves their duties. 7. Seek everywhere to associate with the good. 8. When going through the inland-country he met with the ambassadors returning from the king[18]. 9. This[17] (is what) he says; but[19] his deeds do not accord with his words. 10. Philip is doing wrong in not abiding by the treaty. 11. Most men follow their neighbours. 12. He went from Sparta, because[45] he was friendly to the Athenians. 13. I agree with you in my judgment (*I have my judgment the same with you*). 14. Many miseries are in old age. 15. I receive from my slaves an income (of) ten minæ. 16. Do not, *I entreat you*, send this message. 17. *I would not have you* associate with the bad. 18. *You have this on your side*, that no one knows you. 19. He said that he was friendly to the Athenians, but[19] hostile to the Lacedæmonians. 20. What have we to do with them?

§ 50. *The Dative continued.*

(1) The *instrument*, the *manner*, and the *cause* are put in the dative, as τύπτειν ῥάβδῳ, *to beat with a stick;* δρόμῳ παρῆλθεν, *he went past at a run, running;* μεγάλῃ

σπουδῇ, *in great haste;* φόβῳ, *through fear;* ἀλγεῖν τινί, *to be distressed at a thing.*

(2) The dative is sometimes used to express the agent, especially after the perfect passive of a verb, and verbals in -τέος, -τός.

> ταῦτα ἡμῖν λέλεκται, *these things have been said by us;* τὰ τούτοις λελεγμένα, *what these men have said;* τοῦτο ἡμῖν ποιητέον (ἐστί), *we must do this.*

> *Obs.*—With other tenses than the perfect passive, and with quasi-passive verbs (κακῶς πάσχειν, *to be badly treated,* &c.), the genitive with ὑπό is used of the agent.

(3) The definite time *at* which a thing is done, is put in the dative.

> τῇ τρίτῃ ἡμέρᾳ, *on the third day;* τῷ τρίτῳ ἔτει οἴκαδε ἀπέπλευσα, *in the third year I sailed home.*

> *Obs.*—This use of the dative is only to be employed with words expressing time, ἔτος, ἡμέρα, νύξ, &c. With other words, ἐν is added: ἐν τῷ παρόντι, *at the present,* &c. But the Greeks say, ταῖς πομπαῖς, *at the procession;* τοῖς τραγῳδοῖς, *at the tragedians;* τοῖς Διονυσίοις, *at the Dionysia,* where the occasion and the time are coincident.

(4) The place where is sometimes put in the dative, as, Μαραθῶνι, *at Marathon;* Δωδῶνι, *at Dodona.*

EXERCISE 55.

VOCABULARY.—*to agree with,* ὁμολογεῖν, with dat. *to answer,* ἀποκρίνεσθαι. *army,* στρατός. *at the hands of,* ὑπό, with gen. *to attempt,* πειρᾶσθαι. *to burst into,* εἰσπίπτειν εἰς. *hoplite =* *heavy-armed soldier,* ὁπλίτης. *horseman,* ἱππεύς. *I am inclined to,* βουλομένῳ ἐμοί ἐστιν (e. g. τοῦτο ποιεῖν, *to do this).*[a] *I object to,* οὐ βουλομένῳ ἐμοί ἐστιν. *order,* κόσμος. *to promise,* ὑπισχνεῖσθαι. *to ravage, lay waste,* δῃοῦν. *to remain behind, to be left behind,* ὑπολείπεσθαι. *the remainder,* i. e. *those who were left behind,* οἱ λειπόμενοι. *run,* δρόμος. *shouting,* κραυγή. *to suffer hardships,* κακὰ πάσχειν. *two hundred,* διακόσιοι. *two thousand,* δισχίλιοι. *way, manner,* τρόπος.[a]

---

[a] This idiom can be used with other participles, e. g. οὐ προσδεχομένῳ, οὐκ ἐλπομένῳ ἐμοί ἐστιν, *I do not expect.*

1. He attempted in every way to go out of the city. 2. The soldiers burst into the city without any order (*in no order*). 3. The enemy advanced with loud shouts (*with much shouting*). 4. The Athenians marched against the Chalcidians with two thousand hoplites *of their own* (ἑαυτῶν), and two hundred horse. 5. What you promised, you have already accomplished (use *passive*). 6. The Athenians advanced at a run against the barbarians. 7. On this day I am freed from (*rid of*) fear. 8. He suffered many hardships [27] at the hands of the enemy. 9. Demosthenes remained behind, *because he feared* (*part.*) the Athenians on account of what had been done [11]. 10. This happened on the same day on which the Athenians conquered at Marathon. 11. He invaded Eleusis in Attica (*gen.*, § **41** (3)) with an army of Lacedaemonians. 12. With the remainder [29] of his soldiers he ravaged the country, and on the same day he escaped into Euboea. 13. When I said this, he did not agree with me. 14. Answer, Socrates, if you are inclined to do so. 15. They said that they should object to their going through the country.

§ **51.** *The Relative.*

(1) As in Latin, so in Greek, the relative is used more widely than in English. It often introduces the *cause*, *ground*, *motive*, or *design* of what is stated; and in these cases it cannot be translated merely by *who*, *what*, &c.

(*a*) θαυμαστὸν ποιεῖς, ὃς ἡμῖν οὐδὲν δίδως,
   you act strangely in giving us nothing.

(*b*) ἐμακάριζον τὴν μητέρα, οἵων τέκνων ἐκύρησε,
   they pronounced the mother happy in having such children
   (here οἵων = ὅτι τοιούτων).

(*c*) ὅπλα κτῶνται, οἷς ἀμυνοῦνται τοὺς ἀδικοῦντας,
   they are procuring arms to defend themselves with against those who injure them (or, *with which to repel, or punish, those who injure them*).[a]

---

[a] The rules for the gender of the relative are much the same in Greek and Latin.

(1) A relative referring to a number of *persons*, masculine and feminine, is put in the masculine, e. g. ἄνδρες καὶ γυναῖκες οἱ πάρεστε, *ladies and gentlemen present.*

(2) A relative referring to a number of things of different genders, whether masculine or feminine, may be put in the neuter.

(2) *Attraction and omission of the Antecedent.*

(*a*) When the relative clause defines the antecedent, the latter is often expressed in the relative clause, and omitted in the principal clause.

> οὗτός ἐστιν, ὃν εἶδες ἄνδρα, (or,
> ὃν εἶδες ἄνδρα οὗτός ἐστιν,)
> *this is the man you saw.*

(*b*) When the antecedent to a relative is a demonstrative pronoun standing alone, it is often omitted.

> οὐ πάρεστιν, ὃν ἥκειν ἐχρῆν,
> *he who ought to have come is not here.*

(3) *Attraction of the Relative.*

(*a*) The relative is often made to agree in *case* with the antecedent in the principal clause.

> μεταδίδως αὐτῷ τοῦ σίτου, οὗπερ αὐτὸς ἔχεις,
> *you give him a portion of the food which you have yourself.*[a]

(*b*) When the relative is thus *attracted*, the antecedent is often placed in the relative clause, as in 2 (*a*), but in the case in which it would stand in the principal clause.

> ἀπολαύω ὧν ἔχω ἀγαθῶν,
> *I enjoy the good things I possess* = ἀγαθῶν ἃ ἔχω.

Obs.—Here also, as in 2 (*b*), the antecedent, when a demonstrative pronoun standing alone, may be omitted: μεμνημένος ὧν ἔπραξε, *remembering what he had done*; and we even find a preposition transferred from the omitted antecedent to the descriptive relative, e. g. μετεπέμπετο ἄλλο στράτευμα, πρὸς ᾧ πρόσθεν εἶχε = πρὸς ἐκείνῳ ὃ πρόσθεν εἶχε, *he sent for another army in addition to that which he had before.*

---

[a] This seldom takes place except where the relative should regularly stand in the *accusative*, the antecedent being in the *genitive* or *dative* and without a demonstrative pronoun (as οὗτος, ἐκεῖνος).

Exercise 56.

Vocabulary.—*at daybreak*, ἅμ᾽ ἕῳ. *to drink*, πίνειν. *to enact*, θεῖναι. *to enjoy*, ἀπολαύειν, with gen. *to give a share to*, μεταδιδόναι, with dat. *the goods of others*, τὰ ἀλλότρια. *hare*, λαγώς. *helper*, βοηθός. *to neglect*, ἀμελεῖν, with gen. *previously*, πρότερον. *to speak at length*, διεξιέναι. *strange*, θαυμαστός. *every year*, *year by year*, ἀνὰ πᾶν ἔτος.

1. I pity the mother for having been deprived of such a daughter (*of what* (οἵας) *a daughter has she been deprived*, 1 (*b*)). 2. I will give him some of the wine which I have. 3. He sent for more wine in addition to what he had drunk already. 4. This is the hare you saw. 5. You act strangely in speaking ill even of your friends. 6. He knew that I should enjoy the good things I possess. 7. Receive the good things you desire. 8. Our [9] father, who was the only helper we had, was absent. 9. Those who are most satisfied with what they have got (*to whom the (things) present are mostly sufficient*), least desire the goods of others. 10. Not one of those persons who ought to have come is here. 11. I have given to all a share of what I have received. 12. I neglect what I ought to do. 13. I have no need of the gifts which I receive from you. 14. The other laws I will pass over, but I will speak at length about the law which Timocrates previously enacted himself. 15. You act unjustly in breaking the conditions of peace (use *relative construction* [66]). 16. They have carried out none of the commands I gave them. 17. Do not send away [33] the only helper we have. 18. The man, whom you saw, went away into the city to announce [43] what had happened. 19. Every year he passed four months in the country. 20. He went away at daybreak. 21. He paid them (for) wages a drachma a [3] day (*gen.*).

§ 52. *The Relative continued.*

(1) *The Relative in apposition* (*as complement of the Predicate*).

When the relative, with such a verb as *to be*, *call*, *believe*, &c., stands in apposition to a noun, it generally agrees in gender with *it*, rather than with the antecedent.

φύβος, ἣν αἰδῶ καλοῦμεν,
fear which we call modesty.
φίλος, ὃ μέγιστον ἀγαθὸν εἶναί φασιν,
a friend, which they say is the greatest blessing.

(2) ἔστιν *with the Relative.*

(*a*) ἔστιν — οἵ is = ἔνιοι, *some,* and may be declined throughout, as,—

    N. ἔστιν οἵ, ἔστιν αἵ, ἔστιν ἅ.
    G. ἔστιν ὧν.
    D. ἔστιν οἷς, ἔστιν αἷς, ἔστιν οἷς.

(*b*) In the same way ἔστιν ὅτε is = *sometimes;* ἔστιν ὅπου is = *somewhere,* &c.

These phrases can be used interrogatively: *is there a time when? a place where?*

(*c*) ἔστιν ὅστις (with ἔστιν indeclinable) is found as an interrogative.

(*a*) ἀπὸ τῶν ἐν Σικελίᾳ πόλεων ἔστιν ὧν,
    from some of the cities in Sicily.
    Πελοποννήσιοι ᾤκισαν τῆς ἄλλης Ἑλλάδος ἔστιν ἃ χωρία,
    the Peloponnesians colonised some places in the rest of Hellas = ἔνια χωρία.
(*b*) οὕσπερ εἶδον ἔστιν ὅπου,
    whom I saw somewhere.
(*c*) ἔστιν οὕστινας ἀνθρώπους τεθαύμακας ἐπὶ σοφίᾳ;
    are there any persons whom you have admired for their wisdom?
    Obs.—For the difference of ὅς and ὅστις, cp. § 13, 2 (*c*).

Phrases.

Similar phrases into which ἔστιν and a relative adverb enters are—ἔστιν ἵνα, *sometimes, in some cases* = ἔστιν ὅπου; ἔστιν οὗ, *somewhere;* ἔστιν ὅπη, *in some way, to some place;* ἔστιν ἔνθα, *in many places;* ἔστιν ᾗ, *in a certain degree;* ἔστιν ὅπως, *it is possible.* These phrases may also be used as interrogatives, or with negatives.

    ἔστ' οὖν ὅπως Ἄλκηστις ἐς γῆρας μόλοι; *is it possible for Alcestis to reach old age?* οὐκ ἔσθ' ὅπως οὐ τοῦτο γενήσεται, *this will certainly happen,* &c.

(3) (*a*) ἐφ' ᾧ, or, more commonly, ἐφ' ᾧτε, is, *on condition that,* with the *future indicative* or the *infinitive.*

    λέξω σοι ἐφ' ᾧ σιγήσει.
    I will tell you on condition that you will hold your tongue.
    ᾑρέθησαν ἐφ' ᾧτε συγγράψαι νόμους,
    they were chosen on the condition that they should draw up laws,
    i. e. to draw up laws.

(*b*) ἀνθ' ὧν is often = *because, for*.

χάριν σοι οἶδα ἀνθ' ὧν ἦλθες,
I feel thankful to you for coming.

(*c*) εἴ τις is used as equivalent to ὅστις, *whosoever, whatsoever* (= *all that*), without expressing a condition.

Exercise 57.

VOCABULARY.—*to attack*, ἐπιτίθεσθαι, with dat. *to blame*, μέμφεσθαι. *to capture*, καταλαμβάνειν. *disease*, νόσημα. *except*, πλήν. *faction*, στάσις. *to put to flight*, ἀποτρέπειν. *gate*, πύλη. *guide*, ἡγεμών. *in heaven's name*, πρὸς θεῶν. *hill*, ἄκρα. *key*, κλείς, κλῆς (Prim. § 173 (*b*)). *to be mad*, μαίνεσθαι. *money*, ἀργύριον (κέρδος in such phrases as *love of money*, &c.). *nation*, ἔθνος, τό. *to be naturally*, πεφυκέναι, e. g. *to be naturally bad*, πεφυκέναι κακός. *to withhold from*, ἀπέχεσθαι, with gen. *to write out*, ἀναγράφειν.

1. Is there any one who is wiser than he? 2. They put the soldiers to flight, and *some* they capture. 3. The city is stricken with (Voc. 43) a disease *which* we call faction. 4. It is impossible that you should escape these [10] evils. 5. They seized the hill, which *is called* the keys of Cyprus. 6. The Lacedæmonians bade *any one who wished* (τὸν βουλόμενον) of the rest of the Greeks to follow, except the Ionians and Achæans, and *some other* nations. 7. There is no one who would not blame you. 8. The soldiers retired on condition that the citizens should open the gates. 9. Ten men were elected to write out the laws. 10. There is no one so foolish *that he* (*rel.*) [71] desires death. 11. I wonder at the extent of your wisdom (*I wonder at you, what wisdom you have*). 12. Tell me, in heaven's name, is there any one naturally so foolish *as to* (ὥστε) desire death? 13. Is there any one to whom you entrust more than your wife? 14. Who is so mad *that he does not* [71] wish to be your friend (ὅστις οὐ)? 15. I gave him (some) money on condition that he should go away at once. 16. There is nothing he will not do *for* money (*for the sake of*). 17. We will ask Cyrus for a guide *to* [43] lead us away. 18. It is impossible that the enemy should not attack us. 19. Is there any place in the world to which I can fly? 20. He withheld from the sources of gain which [67] he formerly pursued, thinking (them) disgraceful.

§ 53. *The Relative continued.*

In some phrases the relative and antecedent are combined together, as it were, and put under the immediate government of the verb. This may lead to the entire suppression of the verb in the antecedent clause, or in the relative clause (εἰμί in both cases). Such phrases are—

(1) οὐδεὶς ὅστις οὐ (ἐστίν omitted in the antecedent clause).

N. οὐδεὶς ὅστις οὐκ ἂν ταῦτα ποιήσειεν,
there is no one who would not do this.

G. οὐδενὸς ὅτου οὐ κατεγέλασεν
= οὐδεὶς ἦν ὅτου, κ.τ.λ.,
there is no one whom he did not laugh at.

D. οὐδενὶ ὅτῳ οὐκ ἀπεκρίνατο
= οὐδεὶς ἦν ὅτῳ, κ.τ.λ.,
there was no one whom he did not answer.

A. οὐδένα ὅντινα οὐ κατέκλαυσε
= οὐδεὶς ἦν ὅντινα, κ.τ.λ.,
there was no one whom he did not weep for.

So οὐδὲν ὅ τι οὐκ ἀπώλετο, *everything was lost.*

(2) ὁ οἷος σὺ ἀνήρ, or οἷος σὺ ἀνήρ (εἰ omitted in the relative clause).

N. ὁ οἷος σὺ (ἀνήρ), *such a man as you.*

G. τοῦ οἵου σοῦ (ἀνδρός), *of such a man as you,* &c.

G. ἔραμαι οἵου σοῦ ἀνδρός, *I love such a man as you.*

D. χαρίζομαι οἵῳ σοὶ ἀνδρί, *I gratify such a man as you.*

A. ἐπαινῶ οἷον σὲ ἄνδρα, *I praise such a man as you.*[a]

(3) θαυμαστὸν ὅσον προὐχώρησε, *he made astonishing progress;* θαυμαστῶς ὡς ἄθλιος γέγονε, *he has become surprisingly miserable.*

Here, as in 1, the antecedent clause is sacrificed to

---

[a] In this idiom the substantive (ἀνήρ) is attracted into the relative clause (§ 51 (3)), and the whole relative clause is then deprived of its verb, and put under the government of the verb in the antecedent clause. For ἔραμαι οἵου σοῦ ἀνδρός is = ἔραμαι ἀνδρὸς τοιούτου, οἷος σὺ εἶ.

the relative; the complete expression is, θαυμαστὸν ἔστιν, ὅσον προὐχώρησε.

Obs.—In this construction ὅσος follows such words as θαυμαστός, πλεῖστος, ἄφθονος; and ὡς the adverbs in -ως, θαυμασίως, θαυμαστῶς, &c.

EXERCISE 58.

VOCABULARY.—*to accomplish*, ἐκτελέσαι. *in age*, κατὰ ἡλικίαν. *of (my) age*, ἥλικος (ἐμοί). *extraordinary*, θαυμαστὸς ὅσος. *form of constitution*, πολιτεία. *gladly*, ἡδέως. *hard, difficult*, χαλεπός. *impossible*, ἀδύνατος. *infantry*, ὁ πεζός. *nothing like hearing*, οὐδὲν οἷον ἀκοῦσαι. *to plot against*, ἐπιβουλεύειν, with dat. *to praise*, ἐπαινεῖν. *pretext*, πρόφασις. *slight*, βραχύς. *to weep for*, κατακλαίειν, with acc.

1. Men gladly gratify such a man as you are. 2. I would gladly gratify such men as you. 3. This is hard, and for men like us impossible. 4. He said that [35] he would gladly gratify a man like you. 5. Men like you always speak well of the good. 6. No one speaks well of men like us. 7. A man like you is praised by everybody. 8. There is no one who would not weep for such men as you. 9. There is no one whom he does not despise. 10. There was none of those present whom he had not plotted against. 11. There is nothing like hearing the ambassadors themselves. 12. He acted strangely in [66] speaking evil of a man like you. 13. The infantry, and ships, and everything was lost. 14. There is not one among all (of) you whose father I might not be in age. 15. To persons of our age such things are naturally difficult. 16. To persons like ourselves and you, democracy is a difficult form of constitution. 17. Of all the men whom I ever saw, this man is by far the most handsome. 18. This achievement cost him extraordinary labour (*he accomplished this work with (dat.)*, &c.). 19. He answered every one of those who questioned him about virtue. 20. Who do you think that there is who would not revolt on a slight pretext?

§ 54. *Adverbs of Time, &c.*

(1) *Until* and *as long as* are expressed by ἄχρι or μέχρι (ἄχρις, μέχρις before vowels, also ἄχρις οὗ, μέχρις οὗ), and ἕως, ἔστε. When the limitation of time is un-

certain, these adverbs take the subjunctive or optative with *ἄν*.

πεμμενῶ ἕως ἄν (μέχρις ἄν) ἐλθῇ, *I will wait till he comes (when-ever that may be)*; οὔποτε λήγουσιν ἔστ' ἄν ἄρχωσιν αὐτῶν, *they never leave off till they rule over them*; ἠξίουν αὐτοὺς μαστιγοῦν τὸν ἐκδοθέντα, ἕως ἄν τἀληθῆ δόξειεν αὐτοῖς λέγειν, *I requested them to scourge the person given up to them till he should seem to them to speak the truth.*

With the optative *ἄν* is frequently omitted.

When there is no uncertainty in the limitation of time the indicative is used.

ποίησον τοῦτο ἕως ἔτι ἔξεστι, *do this while it is in your power*; ἔστε αἱ σπονδαὶ ἦσαν, οὔποτε ἐπαυόμην ἡμᾶς οἰκτείρων, *as long as the treaty lasted, I never ceased to think upon ourselves with pity.*

Of course, in *oratio obliqua* the *optative* will appear without *ἄν*, even when there is no uncertainty.

ἐκέλευε ποιῆσαι τοῦτο ἕως ἔτι ἐξείη.[a]

(2) (a) *πρίν, before, until*, generally takes the infinitive.

ἀπῆλθε πρὶν ἐλθεῖν ἐμέ,
he went away before I came.

(b) But if the main clause is *negative*, and the event referred to is *future*, *πρὶν ἄν* with the subjunctive is used.[b]

In *oratio obliqua* this construction becomes the optative without *ἄν*.

ἔδοξέ μοι μὴ σῖγα, πρὶν φράσαιμί σοι, τὸν πλοῦν ποιεῖσθαι,
I resolved not to make my voyage in silence, before I told you.

(c) *πρίν* can also be used with an aorist *indicative* of a definite point in past time.

οὐκ ἀπῆλθε πρὶν εἶπε, *he did not go away till he said.*

---

[a] Hence, when a thing is spoken of as an object or purpose con-templated, the subjunctive with *ἄν* will be used in connexion with present or future time; the optative in connexion with past tenses, and *oratio obliqua*.

[b] "The infinitive instead of *πρὶν ἄν* with the subjunctive is very rare." Madvig, § 167, Rem.

EXERCISE 59.

VOCABULARY.—*to damage*, κακοῖν. *immediately*, εὐθύς.[a]
near, ἐγγύς, with gen. *leisure, to be at*, σχολὴν ἔχειν. *near
the city*, ἐγγὺς τῆς πόλεως. *we ought to set about*, ἡμῖν ἐπιχειρητέον ἐστί (with dative of the thing). *out of, outside*,
ἔξω, with gen. *straight to*, εὐθύ, with gen. *to subjugate
to (put in the power of)*, ποιεῖν ὑπό, with dat. *to take the
initiative, and*, φθάνοντες, with verb. *to*, ὡς, with acc. (of
persons only).[b] *together with*, ἅμα, ὁμοῦ, with dat.[b] *up to
this point, till*, μέχρι τούτου ἕως. *worthily of, in a manner
worthy of*, ἀξίως, with gen.[c]

1. Do not go away [33] till I come. 2. I will not cease fighting
till I have conquered the enemy. 3. It is not possible for you
(*plur.*) to conquer your enemies outside the city till you have
punished those in the city itself. 4. I was banished myself
before you returned from banishment. 5. Whilst you are at
leisure, speak. 6. We were afraid till the Greeks sailed away.
7. We used-to-wait till the gates were opened. 8. He said
that he would come to us whilst he still might. 9. He said
that he feared the gods most whenever he was most prosperous
(*was doing best*). 10. The general went in to the king. 11.
They march straight to the city. 12. Immediately on our
arrival he told us that we ought to set about the task. 13.
From our very birth we want many things. 14. He died as
soon as he was born. 15. They were called the friends of
Philip up to this point—till they subjugated their city to
Philip. 16. If I seem to be doing wrong, I ought not to go
away from this place till I have paid the penalty. 17. We do
not wait till our country is damaged, but we take the initiative,
and are already laying waste the land of our enemies. 18.
Many men die before their character is known (*before it
becomes clear* [54] *what sort of persons they are*). 19. I will not
stop till I am master of the city. 20. He said that he would
not stop making war till he was master of the city.

---

[a] εὐθύς and εὐθύ are the same word, but εὐθύς is used of *time*, εὐθύ
of *space: immediately on his arrival*, εὐθὺς ἥκων; *from our very
birth, as soon as we are born*, εὐθὺς γενόμενοι.

[b] As adverbs and prepositions were originally one and the same
class of words, we find some adverbs which are used as prepositions.

[c] Adverbs take a substantive in the same case as the substantives
from which they are derived. Hence comparative and superlative
adverbs take a genitive in the same way as comparative and superlative
adjectives.

§ 55. *Interrogative Particles, &c.*

Besides the interrogative adverbs and pronouns, the following particles are used in questions, and by this means the Greeks often express on paper what we express by the tone of the voice, &c.

ἆρα is mostly used in questions which imply something of *surprise, uncertainty,* or *doubt.*

> ἆρ οὐ ; expects the answer, *yes.*
> ἆρα μή ; expects the answer, *no.*
> ἆρα εὐτυχεῖς ; *are you prosperous, then ?*
> ἆρ' οὐκ ἔστιν ἀσθενής ; *he is ill, then, is he not ?*
> ἆρα μὴ ἔστιν ἀσθενής ; *he is not ill, then, is he ?*

Questions expecting the answer *yes* are also asked by ἦ γάρ ; *why, is it ?* οὐ ; *is it not ?* οὔκουν ; ἄλλο τι ἤ ; &c.

Obs. Distinguish οὔκουν with the interrogative = *is it not ?* from οὐκοῦν without the interrogative = *therefore.*

Questions expecting the answer *no* are asked by ἦ που (*num forte ?*) ; μή or μῶν ;

εἶτα, ἔπειτα (*then — and yet — and nevertheless*) express *astonishment* and *displeasure,* implying that what the speaker supposes has been done is inconsistent with something before mentioned, or the impression previously made on the mind.

ἄλλο τι ἤ ; is strictly, *is it anything else than ?* i. e. *is it not the case that ?* From frequent use it came to be regarded merely as an *interrogative particle,* and the ἤ was often dropped.

τί παθών ; (*having suffered what ?*) *what possesses you to ?* &c. (cf. Voc. 41) ; τί μαθών ; (*having learnt what ?*) *what induces you to ?* &c., are also found.

These phrases are used in *indignant, reproachful* questions ; the former obviously relates to the *feelings,* the latter to the *understanding.*

EXAMPLES.

(1) ἦ που τετόλμηκας ταῦτα ;
surely you have not dared to do this ? [*No.*]

(2) ἦ γὰρ, ἐάν τι ἐρωτᾷ σε Σωκράτης, ἀποκρινεῖ ;
*why, you will answer, will you not, if Socrates puts a question
to you ?* [*Yes.*]

(3) οὔ τί που ἐγὼ ἀγροικίζομαι ;
surely, I am not behaving rudely, am I ? [*No.*]

(4) μῶν τί σε ἀδικεῖ ;
he is not injuring you in any respect, is he ? [*No.*]

(5) εἶτ' ἐσίγας Πλοῦτος ὤν ;
and yet you held your tongue, you Plutus ?

(6) ἔπειτ' οὐκ οἴει θεοὺς ἀνθρώπων τι φροντίζειν ;
do you then really think that the gods do not regard mankind ?

(7) ἄλλο τι ἢ περὶ πλείστου ποιεῖ, ὅπως ὡς βέλτιστοι οἱ νεώτεροι
ἔσονται ;
*do you not regard it as a thing of the first importance that
the rising generation should turn out as well as possible ?*

(8) ἄλλο τι οὖν οἵ γε φιλοκερδεῖς φιλοῦσι τὸ κέρδος ;
what ! do not the covetous love gain ?

(9) τί παθὼν οὕτω ταχὺς ἀπῆλθε ;
what induced him to go away so quickly ?

EXERCISE 60.

VOCABULARY.—*to bring bad news*, νεώτερόν τι ἀγγέλλειν. *to
insult*, ὑβρίζειν, with acc., or ὑβρίζειν εἰς. *to be for a person's
interest*, εἶναι πρός τινος. *to lose one's labour*, πονεῖν μάτην.
pleasure, ἡδονή. *to be punished for* = *to pay the penalty for*,
δίκην διδόναι, with gen. *release*, ἀπαλλαγή. *to remain*, μένειν.

1. Are not these things for our interest rather than for that
of our[9] enemies? (Yes.) 2. You are not come to bring us any
bad news, I hope, are you? (No.) 3. And do you *then* think
that you will not be punished for what you have done (*p. pass.*)
against the laws of the gods? 4. What possesses you that you
will not cease to insult your friends? 5. These things are not
more for the interest of our enemies than of us, are they? 6.
Surely you don't think, do you, that such men[17] do not pay the
penalty? 7. What am I to say (§ 20 (3))? Is it (he), or
is it not? 8. Are we to consider death to be anything but the
release of the soul from the body? (No.) 9. And do you
still tell us that you never went into the house at all? 10.
He does not say, does he, that those who pursue[11] pleasure are
good men? 11. Why! did you ever go to Athens? 12. What

possessed you to go into the city, when you might have remained at home in the country ? 13. Does such a man[17] do anything else than lose his labour (= does he not simply lose his labour) ?

§ 56. *Indirect Single Questions.*

(1) As has been already stated (p. 82, note), the proper forms for indirect questions are those pronouns and adverbs which are formed from the direct interrogatives by the prefixed *relative* syllable ὁ-, which connects them with what precedes. Thus from—

πόσος; ποῖος; ποῖ; πόθεν; πῶς; &c.,
we have ὁπόσος, ὁποῖος, ὅπου, ὁπόθεν, ὅπως, &c.;
and from τίς; we have ὅστις.

So that ποῖ τράπωμαι; *whither am I to turn?* becomes οὐκ οἶδα (or οὐκ ἔχω), ὅποι τράπωμαι, *I don't know whither to turn.* Similarly, οὐκ οἶδα ὅστις ἐστί, *I don't know who he is;* οὐκ οἶδα ὅπως τὸ πρᾶγμα ἔπραξεν *I don't know how he did the thing;* ἀπόκριναι ἀνδρείως ὁπότερά σοι φαίνεται, *answer boldly which of the two is your opinion.*

The Greeks, however, do not adhere strictly to the distinction between the direct and indirect interrogatives ; they often use the direct forms in indirect questions, and sometimes intermix the two.

ἴσμεν πόσα τέ ἐστι καὶ ὁποῖα, *we know how many there are, and of what kind.*[a]

---

[a] ὅστις is both the indirect form of τίς; *who?* and a relative, *whosoever* (§ **13** (2)). As the former τίς; can be used for it, just as πῶς can be used for ὅπως, ποῖ for ὅποι, &c. But it is very doubtful whether τίς can be used for ὅστις *as a relative = whosoever.* There are a few passages in the Greek tragedians and elsewhere, in which τίς (τί) seems to be so used, but the precise construction of such passages is contested by scholars. (Cf. Soph. El. 316, with the commentators.) In English and in Latin the interrogative and the relative spring from the same root, and therefore the difficulties and distinctions which are found in Greek do not occur in those languages. In English, however, the distinction between relative and interrogative is not wholly lost; we cannot say, *tell me which he says,* for *what he says.* Originally it was marked more strongly than now, *that* being the relative, and *what* the interrogative. (Cf. Abbott's "Grammar of Shakespeare," §§ 258, 259.)

(2) Sometimes, though rarely, the relative forms are used in dependent questions.

ὁρᾷς οὖν ἡμᾶς, ἐφη, ὅσοι ἐσμέν; *do you see, said he, how many we are!*

(3) When the person *of whom a question is asked* repeats it, he uses the forms beginning with ὁ- : οὗτος, τί ποιεῖς; ὅ τι ποιῶ; *You there, what are you doing? What am I doing?* σὺ δ' εἰ τίς ἀνδρῶν; ὅστις εἴμ' ἐγώ; Μέτων. *Who in the world are you? Who am I? Meton.*

Exercise 61.

VOCABULARY.—*by compulsion*, ὑπ' ἀνάγκης. *to enter secretly* (say : *to escape notice when entering* (§ **35** (2)), λανθάνειν εἰσελθών. *to learn many lessons*, διδάσκεσθαι πολλά. *master*, δεσπότης. *about nightfall*, ὑπὸ νύκτα. *to provide with*, παρασκευάζειν. *weapons, arms*, ὅπλα. *what?* τί δή; *to wound*, τραυματίζειν.

Obs.—The Greeks are very partial to interrogatives, and short interrogative sentences are often used by them where in English we should not employ that mode of speech : thus, τί μήν; (properly, *what else!*) is = *certainly.* Similarly, πῶς γὰρ οὔ; = *of course;* τί οὔ = *πᾶν,* τί ἄλλο ἤ = *merely.* e. g. ἄνθρωπε, τί ποιεῖς; ὅ τι ποιῶ; τί δ' ἄλλο γ' ἢ διαλεπτολογοῦμαι ; *You fellow, what are you doing! What am I doing! I am merely chopping logic;* and many others. Also, the habit of connecting every sentence with what precedes, leads the Greeks to unite various particles with the interrogatives, e. g. τί γάρ; τί δέ; τί οὖν; τί δαί; &c.

1. The women asked them who they were, and whence they came. 2. I do not know what language I shall use in my answer (*what words using I shall speak*). 3. Do you see, said he, how many men are wounded by how few? 4. Who are you! Do you ask, we replied, who we are? We are Athenians. 5. I asked him whither the enemy had retired. He answered, that he did not know whither they had retired, nor how many they were. 6. What! will you go away when the city is in such danger? 7. He asked with what kind of weapons the citizens had been provided. 8. Who is this person? This person! Indeed, I do not know who he is; ask him yourself. 9. Do you see how many there are of the enemy, and how few we are! 10. The slave died at the hands

of his master. 11. These things happened about the same
time. 12. He learned many hard[27] lessons by compulsion. 13.
After suffering many grievous[27] hardships at the hands of the
enemy, he returned to the city in the tenth year. 14. He
praised all whom he saw marching in good order. 15. He
entered the city secretly[50], about nightfall.

§ **57.** *Double Questions, εἰ, &c.*

(1) Direct double questions, *whether — or*, are asked
by πότερον (or πότερα) — ἤ (less commonly by ἆρα — ἤ).

> πότερον ἔψονται Κύρῳ, ἤ οὔ; *will they follow Cyrus, or not?*

(2) Indirect double questions are asked by εἴτε — εἴτε,
εἰ — ἤ, or πότερον — ἤ.

> σκοπῶμεν εἴτε εἰκὸς οὕτως ἔχειν, εἴτε μή,
> *let us consider whether it is likely to be so or not.*
>
> τούτῳ τὸν νοῦν πρόσεχε, εἰ δίκαια λεγω, ἤ μή,
> *attend to this, whether what I speak is just or not.*
>
> πρὶν δῆλον εἶναι πότερον ἔψονται Κύρῳ ἤ οὔ,
> *before it was known whether they would follow Cyrus or not.*

Obs.—For πότερον, πότερα is found, and sometimes the word is
omitted altogether in direct double questions.

(3) After verbs of *seeing, knowing, considering, asking,
saying, trying*, &c., *whether* is to be translated by εἰ;
and when the question relates to an expected case that
remains to be proved, ἐάν with the subjunctive may be
used.

> σκέψαι, εἰ ὁ Ἑλλήνων νόμος κάλλιον ἔχει,
> *consider whether the Grecian law is the better.*
>
> σκέψαι, ἐὰν τόδε σοὶ μᾶλλον ἀρέσκῃ,
> *consider whether this pleases you better.*

(4) After θαυμάζω, *I wonder*, and some other verbs
expressive of *feelings*, the Greeks use εἰ where we use
that, i. e. they treat these verbs as belonging to the
class mentioned in (3).

θαυμάζω εἰ μηδεὶς ὑμῶν ὀργίζεται,
I am astonished, that not one amongst you is angry.

ἀγανακτῶ εἰ οὑτωσὶ, ἃ νοῶ, μὴ οἷός τ᾽ εἰμὶ εἰπεῖν,
I am indignant at being so unable to express my meaning.

οὐκ ἀγαπᾷ, εἰ μὴ δίκην ἔδωκεν,
he is not contented with escaping punishment.

EXERCISE 62.

VOCABULARY.—*to allow with impunity,* περιορᾶν (= *to overlook, to stand by and see*). *at once,* αὐτίκα. *in such circumstances,* τούτων οὕτως ἐχόντων. *to be content,* ἀγαπᾶν. *to continue to exist, to exist still,* ἔτι εἶναι. *crown,* στέφανος. *to crown,* στεφανοῦν. *to deliberate,* βουλεύεσθαι. *each party,* ἑκάτεροι. *to ravage,* τέμνειν. *recently,* ἄρτι. *some time since,* πάλαι. *to be vexed at, indignant at,* ἀγανακτεῖν.

1. I do not know whether he is alive or dead. 2. He said that he did not know whether the general had been slain or not. 3. He was deliberating whether he should send a messenger, or go himself to the camp. 4. Whether the soul will still exist when we are dead, does not seem to me to have been proved. 5. Demosthenes is not content that he has not paid the penalty, but he is vexed that he will not be crowned with a golden crown. 6. In such circumstances [55], there is no wonder that the allies revolt. 7. Are you recently from the country [18], or (did you come) some time since? 8. He asked whether he was to go away at once, or wait till the general came. 9. We must consider whether we are telling the truth or not. 10. They made peace on condition [70] that each party should retain (have) their own. 11. He says that more arms were taken than could have been expected [62], from the number of the dead. 12. It is this very thing, O Athenians, that I am indignant at, that you allow half your country [29] *to be ravaged* (*part.*). 13. He went away before I returned from the country.

§ 58. *Condensed Questions.*

In asking questions, the Greeks often use one sentence where in English we should use two; for (1) they can

use the interrogative with a *participle* which, in its turn,
is attached to a finite verb ; and (2) they can use the
interrogative pronouns in the oblique cases.

(1) τί ἂν ποιοῦντες ἀναλάβοιεν τὴν ἀρχαίαν ἀρετήν ;
 what must they do to recover their ancient virtue ?
 (or, *by what conduct could they recover, &c.?*)

 καταμεμάθηκας οὖν, τοὺς τί ποιοῦντας τὸ ὄνομα τοῦτο ἀποκαλοῦσιν ;
 *do you know then (have you learnt) what those persons do, to
 whom men apply this name ?*

(2) τίνας τούσδ' ὁρῶ ξένους ;
 *who are these strangers whom I behold ! Who are the
 strangers whom I see here !*

EXERCISE 63.

VOCABULARY.—*to examine,* ἐξετάζεσθαι. *to laugh at,* καταγελᾶν, *with gen. society,* συνουσία. *to understand,* ἐπίστασθαι.
in what must this wisdom consist (say: *(being) wise in
what* (§ **40** (1)) ?

1. What did you see Critobulus do, that you thus condemn
him ? 2. What must you see them do to be content (*seeing
them do what, will you, &c.*) ? 3. In what must their wisdom
consist, from whose society tyrants [5] will become wise ? 4.
Who are the strangers whom we see coming hither ? 5.
Whither were they going when you saw them ? 6. What
were they doing [55] when you went away ? 7. We must examine
who is guilty, (and) of what. 8. What is wisdom, *and* what
do we learn to govern *by its means* (*relative*) ? 9. What
must happen before you go away ? 10. We must consider
which of the two laws is the better. 11. Do you know of
what kind the laws of the Persians are ? 12. He says that he
is not a man to do anything whatever for the sake of gain.
13. They will not stand by and see us injured. 14. What is
the man doing, I asked, that you thus laugh at him ? 15. I
will not allow our land to have been ravaged with impunity.
16. He says that he has been entrusted with these things
(§ **39** (1)). 17. I asked how many of the men [29] he had seen. 19.
There is nothing he did not do for the sake of gain. 20. What
induced [72] the Athenians to undertake an expedition against so
great (an island) as Sicily (*against Sicily being so great*) ?

§ 59. *Various Uses of the Verb* ἔχω.

(1) *Intransitive uses.*

(*a*) ἔχε, *stop.*

(*b*) καλῶς ἔχει, *it is well;* πῶς ἔχομεν; *how are we?* πῶς ἔχομεν χρημάτων; *how are we off for money?* εὖ ἔχειν χρημάτων, *to be well off for money;* ὡς ὀργῆς ἔχω, *in such a temper am I!*

(2) ἔχειν *with abstract nouns.*

(*a*) ἔχειν αἰσχύνην = αἰσχύνεσθαι, *to be ashamed,* also, *to be shameful.*
ἔχειν ἐπιθυμίαν = ἐπιθυμεῖν, *to desire.*

(*b*) ἔχειν ἀπιστίαν, *to admit of doubt, to be incredible.*
ἔχειν αἰτίαν, *to be blameable, to be blamed.*

(3) οὐκ ἔχω = *I don't understand, I cannot;* οὐκ εἶχον ὅ τι χρὴ λέγειν, *they knew not what they ought to say;* οὐκ ἔχω ποῦ πέσω, *I know not where to fall.*

(4) ἔχω is often used with the aorist participle as a circumlocution for the aorist.

ἀτιμάσας ἔχει, *has dishonoured, dishonoured.*

Compare also ᾤχετο λαβών, *went off with.*

Obs.—The notion of continuance and result is more prominent than in the simple aorist.

(5) (*a*) The participle ἔχων is often used where we use *with.* (Cp. Voc. 1, *Obs.* i.)

ὃς ἂν ἥκῃ στρατὸν ἔχων, *whosoever should come with an army.*

(*b*) The participle ἔχων with the *present,* 'adds a notion of duration to that of present action.'

τί ληρεῖς ἔχων; *why do you go on talking nonsense? why do you continue to talk nonsense?* &c.

Obs.—Others explain this idiom like τί παθών (§ 55); τί ἔχων being = *what makes you . . .!*

I

EXERCISE 64.

VOCABULARY.—*to associate with*, συνεῖναι, with dat. *to be blamed*, αἰτίαν ἔχειν (add πολλήν, πλείστην, *for much, very much*). *body-guard*, δορυφόροι. *to have a doubt, to admit of a doubt*, ἀπιστίαν ἔχειν, with nom. of person or thing. *education*, παιδεία. *as fast as their feet could carry them*, ὡς τάχιστα ποδῶν εἶχον. *to gape about*, κοικύλλειν. *to go off with*, οἴχεσθαι λαβών. *loyally*, εὔνοια. *loyalty to*, εὔνοια πρός, with acc. *to lurk about*, κυπτάζειν περί, with acc. *to be neglectful of*, ἀμελῶς ἔχειν, with gen. *to reduce*, κατατρέπειν (ὑπό, with dat.). *reproach*, κατάμεμψις. *to go to the rescue*, βοηθεῖν πρός. *to run*, θεῖν. *to run away*, ἀποφεύγειν, ἀποδιδράσκειν. *to be shameful*, αἰσχύνην ἔχειν.

1. Why do I continue to stand here, when the city has determined on this (*when these things seem good to the city*)? 2. Why do you go on gaping about? 3. I asked him how he was off for money. 4. The soldiers were thoroughly [a] loyal to their general. 5. The loyalty of the soldiers to their general admits of no reproach. 6. He is blamed for burning down his own house. 7. They ran away as fast as their feet could carry them. 8. I have no place to run to. 9. To associate with tyrants is very blameable *in the eyes of* (dat.) freemen. 10. Creon *has gone off with* the only one of my daughters whom I have (left). 11. He is very much blamed for such conduct (*having done such things*). 12. Is it not shameful to go away when the city is in danger [55]? 13. I have great doubt about what you say. 14. What you say admits of considerable doubt. 15. Has he not married my sister? 16. He came *with* a large body-guard into the city. 17. You, there! stop where you are. 18. The affairs of the city [15] are in a good condition. 19. I do not know how I am to tell you what I think. 20. He was neglectful of the business entrusted to him. 21. I do not know how he stands *in regard to* (gen.) education and justice. 22. The Athenians went to the rescue of the citadel as quickly as they could. 23. Crœsus had reduced all the rest under his power (*under himself*). 24. Why do you go on lurking about the door?

---

[a] *To be thoroughly* = εὖ ἔχειν, with gen. of the substantive.

§ 60. *Various Uses of* ποιῶ, ποιοῦμαι, &c.

(1) Instead of a verb active, ποιεῖσθαι, with the sub-stantive derived from the verb, can be used.

τὴν μάθησιν ποιεῖσθαι = μανθάνειν.

The substantive which forms the object of this circum-locution is either in the genitive case, πολλῶν τὴν μάθησιν ποιεῖσθαι = πολλὰ μανθάνειν, or in the accusa-tive, the circumlocution taking the government of the verb which it represents.

More frequently, this circumlocution is used in the place of verbs which do not take a direct accusative, as λήθην ποιεῖσθαι for λανθάνεσθαι, βουλὴν ποιεῖσθαι for βουλεύεσθαι, &c.

(2) In the middle, ποιεῖσθαι is *to estimate, to deem.*

περὶ πολλοῦ ποιεῖσθαι, *to make much of, to rate highly.*

(3) εὖ ποιεῖν, κακῶς ποιεῖν, are, *to do good to, to do harm to;* when followed by an accusative, εὖ ποιεῖν τινα, *to do good to a person, to benefit him,* &c. Used absolutely they are = *to be kind, to be unkind.*

εὖ ἐποίησας ἀφικόμενος, *it was kind of you to come.*

καλῶς ποιῶν is also used in an adverbial sense = *deservedly,* as καλῶς ποιοῦντες εὖ πράττετε, *you are prosperous, and well you deserve it.*

(4) (a) εὖ πράττειν, κακῶς πράττειν, are *to be prosperous,* or *in misery;* πράττειν πολλά is *to be over busy, to be a busybody.*

(b) πράττειν with two accusatives is *to exact money from.*

πράττει με τὸ ἀργύριον τὸ ὀφειλόμενον, *he exacts from me the money due to him.*

I 2

So also in the middle voice, if the meaning is *to exact for one's self*.

(*e*) πράττειν used absolutely is *to negotiate, to take measures that*, &c.

> πράττειν ὅπως πόλεμος γενήσεται, *to take measures for bringing about war;* ὅπως τιμωρήσονται, *for exacting vengeance,* &c.

Exercise 65.

Vocabulary. — *to damage*, κακῶς ποιεῖν. *debt*, χρέος. *desolation*, ἐρημία. *to find refuge*, καταφυγὴν ποιεῖσθαι. *flight*, φυγή. *to grieve*, λύπην ποιεῖσθαι. *interest*, τόκος. *to make of no account*, παρ' οὐδὲν ποιεῖσθαι. *to regard with wonder*, θαῦμα ποιεῖσθαι, with acc. *to be treated well, ill*, εὖ, κακῶς πάσχειν.

1. I regard with wonder the folly of the general. 2. When he has been treated thus [47] by his dearest friends, where else will he find refuge than with you? 3. They gathered together the bones of the dead *in grief* (*grieving*). 4. They made their flight by night, that (§ **31** (3), *a*) none of the enemy might see them. 5. They made of no account the tears of the mother, or the desolation of the house. 6. They considered it of the highest importance to get away as soon as possible [64]. 7. It is kind of you to have carried this message into the city. 8. We ought to damage his country by triremes and hoplites, and in every manner. 9. You possess much, and well you deserve it. 10. He demands from me the interest of the debt. 11. He has been badly off [32] for many years now (§ **40** (2)). 12. He is endeavouring (*taking measures*) to bring the affairs of the city into the best condition [32]. 13. Do not go away till you have learnt whether the affairs of the city are in a good condition. 14. When he learnt how matters stood, he went to the aid of the city with two hundred hoplites.

§ **61.** *The Middle Voice.*

The middle voice denotes:

(1) That the agent does the action *upon himself*; or,

(2) That the agent does the action *for his own advantage*; or,

(3) That the agent *gets* the action *done* for his own advantage.

The strictly reflexive meaning (1) is found in but few verbs, principally those that describe some simple action done *to our own persons*, as, *to clothe, crown, wash,* &c.

The middle voice is often equivalent to a new meaning, which may be either transitive or intransitive.

μισθόω, *I let out for hire;* μισθοῦμαι, *I hire.*

The tenses that have the middle meaning, when the verb has it at all, are—

(1) Present and imperfect ⎱
(2) Perfect and pluperfect ⎰ of the *passive form.*
(3) Future and aorist middle.

And in some verbs—

(4) The aor. 1 of the *passive form.*

LIST OF VERBS WITH DIFFERENT SIGNIFICATION IN ACTIVE AND MIDDLE.

λούω, *I wash.*	λούομαι (λοῦμαι), *I bathe (wash myself).*
ἀπάγχω, *I strangle.*	ἀπάγχομαι, *I hang myself.*
στέλλω, *I send.*	στέλλομαι, *I journey* (also, *I send for).*
παύω, *I make to cease.*	παύομαι, *I cease.*
περαιῶ, *I make to cross.*	περαιοῦμαι, *I cross,* with acc.
εἰρήνην ποιῶ, *I make peace.*	εἰρήνην ποιοῦμαι, *I make peace for my own advantage.*
πόλεμον ποιῶ, *I make war.*	πόλεμον ποιοῦμαι, *I carry on war.*

Similarly, σύμμαχον ποιεῖσθαί τινα is *to make a man an ally* (for one's own advantage); καταστήσασθαι φύλακας is *to place guards* (over one's own property, or for one's own advantage in some way or other).

εὑρίσκω, *I find.*	εὑρίσκομαι, *I get,* i.e. *find for myself.*
διδάσκω, *I teach.*	διδάσκομαι, *I get a person taught.* διδάσκομαι (pass.) is, *I learn, am taught.*

αἴρω, *I take.*	αἴρομαι, *I choose.*
λαμβάνω, *I take.*	λαμβάνομαι, *I take hold of.*
βουλεύω, *I consult, devise.*	βουλεύομαι, *I deliberate* (rather of persons deliberating together, or of a man deliberating with himself).
δανείζω, *I lend.*	δανείζομαι, *I borrow.*

So θεῖναι νόμους, *to enact laws*, of an *absolute* prince, who does not make them for himself, but for others only. θέσθαι νόμους, of the legislator in a *free* state, who makes laws for himself as well as other people.

Hence, in general, any reference to the agent is expressed by the middle voice of the verb.

Exercise 66.

Vocabulary.—*to advance*, ἐπιέναι. *arm*, βραχίων, ὁ. *coming from*, πρός, with gen. *to convey*, κομίζεσθαι. *to be a different thing from*, διαφέρειν, with gen. *to do in return*, ἀντιδρᾶν. *to enact laws*, θεῖναι, θέσθαι νόμους. *to grow old*, γηράσκειν. *guard*, φύλαξ. *to put before them*, προβάλλεσθαι. *as quickly as possible*, ὡς τάχος. *shield*, ἀσπίς, ἡ. *slaves*, ἀνδράποδα. *subjects*, ὑπήκοοι. *to have taught*, διδάσκεσθαι.

1. Solon enacted laws for the Athenians. 2. The tyrant laid down laws for his subjects such as he would not himself obey. 3. They washed their own hands and feet. 4. Whereas he ought (*acc. abs.*, § 37 (2)) to have let the house, he hired another, and twenty slaves. 5. I borrowed twenty minæ from (παρά) him. 6. To deliberate quickly is a different thing from deliberating wisely. 7. He caught hold of his arm, *and* (§ 34 (2), *b*) dragged him out of the house. 8. Let us deliberate how the affairs of the city shall be in the best condition [32]. 9. He had his son taught (to be) a horseman. 10. He grew old, learning many things. 11. The citizens *in alarm* (*part.*) placed guards. 12. Though he had suffered [47] many hardships [57] from the citizens, he did them no evil in return. 13. Let us guard against the evils coming from our enemies. 14. The Platæans conveyed their wives and children to Athens. 15. They chose themselves a general out of the three hundred who were present. 16. If you do this, you will get something good. 17. Seeing the enemy advancing, they put their shields before them. 18. I crossed the river as quickly as I could.

§ 62. *Additional Remarks on some of the Moods and Tenses.*

(1) The *perfect future* expresses a future action continuing in its effects (§ 18 (1)), a *state* continuing in the future.

Hence the perfect future in Greek is not used where the perfect future is used in Latin. The Latins, having lost the distinction between the aorist and the perfect, use the future perfect where the Greeks use the aorist: ἐὰν τοῦτο λέξῃς = *si hoc dixeris*. But in Greek, the idea of a continuing or completed *state* is always more or less prominent, in the tense.

> ἡ πολιτεία τελέως κεκοσμήσεται, ἐὰν ὁ τοιοῦτος αὐτὴν ἐπισκοπῇ φύλαξ, *the constitution will be in perfect order* (that will be its *state*) *if such a person superintends it.*

(2) But the perfect future is sometimes used to denote the *speedy* or *certain completion* of an action, as, φράξε καὶ πεπράξεται, *speak, and it shall be done* (*a completed thing*).

With those perfects which, from their marking a continued state, are equivalent to a present with a new meaning, as, μέμνημαι, *I bear in mind*; κέκτημαι, *I possess*, the future perfect is, of course, the common future in use. So also the imperative, e. g. μέμνησο, *remember, bear in mind.*

(3) In the active voice, a continued future state, or a future action continuing in its effects, is expressed by ἔσομαι with the perfect participle; and the same circumlocution can be used in the passive (cp. §§ 35 (2), 59 (4)).

> τὰ δέοντα ἐσόμεθα ἐγνωκότες, καὶ λόγων ματαίων ἀπηλλαγμένοι, *we shall have passed the necessary measures, and be rid of futile speeches.*

(4) The perfect of the subjunctive and optative is rarely used; we can, indeed, say, εἴθε ὁ υἱὸς νενικήκοι,

would that my son might be the victor, but the perfect participle with εἴην or ὦ is generally preferred to the simple tense.

The optative of the *future* is perhaps only found in *oratio obliqua*.

εἶπεν ὅτι ἥξοι ἡμέρᾳ τρίτῃ, *he said that he should come on the third day*.

(5) A wish can be expressed by the use of εἴθε with the optative, or if the wish has not and cannot now be realized, by εἴθε with the indicative aorist or imperfect, according as the time to which the wish refers is past or present.

Similarly, ὤφελον, εἴθ᾽ ὤφελον, ὡς ὤφελον can be used of a wish which cannot be realized.

(1) ὡς ὤφελε τοῦτο ποιεῖν, *would that he were doing this (but he is not)*.

(2) ὡς ὤφελε τοῦτο ποιῆσαι, *would that he had done this*.

Exercise 67.

VOCABULARY.—*if it is agreeable to you*, εἴ σοι βουλομένῳ ἐστί. *and that too*, καὶ ταῦτα. *constitution*, πολιτεία. *as far as they are concerned*, τὸ ἐπὶ τούτοις εἶναι. *for the present, at any rate*, τό γε νῦν εἶναι. *to superintend, overlook*, ἐπισκοπεῖν. *what we ought*, τὰ δέοντα. *would that*, εἴθ᾽, εἴθ᾽ ὤφελον, ἐς, ἐ, &c.

1. For thus we shall have done what we ought. 2. For thus what we ought to do will have been done. 3. I will remember my former[14] folly. 4. He told me that they had forgotten their former virtue. 5. Let us place the wise and good as guardians of this[10] most excellent constitution. 6. If it is agreeable to you, these things shall be done (*at once*). 7. The general said that he would come on the fourth day. 8. Would that the wise superintended the state. 9. Would that the prudent managed the affairs of the state. 10. Would that the Greeks had conquered. 11. They condemned him to death, and that though he was your citizen. 12. For the present, at any rate, we will make use of him. 13. So far as

they are concerned, I am undone. 14. He refused to go away *without* (μή) receiving the money. 15. The Athenians were not pleased with this *arrangement* (ταῦτα), but wished to be generals themselves [24].

§ 63. *Verbals in -τέος.*

(1) These verbals are *passive*, and take the *agent* in the *dative*, but they also take the *object* in the same case as the verb from which they are derived. When used in the neuter, as is generally the case, they are equivalent to the Latin gerund in *-dum* (or gerundive), and express *we must, ought,* &c.

G. ἐπιθυμητέον ἐστὶ τῆς ἀρετῆς, *we* (you, &c.) *should desire virtue.*

D. ἐπιχειρητέον ἐστὶ τῷ ἔργῳ, *we* (you, &c.) *should set about the work.*

A. κολαστέον ἐστὶ τὸν παῖδα, *we* (you, &c.) *should punish the boy.*

(2) When formed from transitive verbs, these adjectives may be used in agreement, like the Latin participle in *-dus,* in Latin.

ἀσκητέα ἐστί σοι ἡ ἀρετή, *you should practise virtue* (as well as ἀσκητέον ἐστί σοι τὴν ἀρετήν).

(3) Verbals may include the meaning of the active and the middle voices of verbs, and thus retain the difference of meaning which prevails between active and middle, and the difference of government in respect to cases, &c.

πειστέον ἐστὶν αὐτόν, *we must persuade him* (πείθω).
πειστέον ἐστὶν αὐτῷ, *we must obey him* (πείθομαι).

Obs. i.—The neuter plural of these verbals is used as well as the neuter singular, ἀσκητέα, πειστέα, &c.

Obs. ii.—Verbals are formed from *aor.* 1 *pass.* by rejecting the *augment,* turning *-θην* into *-τέος,* and the preceding *aspirate* (if there is one) into its corresponding *mute.*

ἐπείσθην	πειστέον.
ἠσκήθην	ἀσκητέον.
ἐγράφθην	γραπτέον.

Exercise 68.

VOCABULARY.—*to run to the assistance of, assist in the defence of,* βοηθεῖν, with dat. *to help, confer benefits on,* ὠφελεῖν, with acc. *it is necessary,* ἀνάγκη (ἐστί). *to practise, exercise, cultivate,* ἀσκεῖν. *to restrain by punishment, punish, chastise,* κολάζειν. *to set about, take in hand,* ἐπιχειρεῖν, with dat. *work, task, production,* ἔργον. *to shun,* φεύγειν.

1. The great work must be set about. 2. We must not shun the labour. 3. All the citizens should confer benefits on the state. 4. He said that all the citizens ought to confer benefits on their country, when there is any occasion (δεῖ). 5. We must go to the assistance of our [9] country. 6. If the slave had done this, it would be necessary to punish him. 7. If the boy were to do this, it would be necessary to punish him. 8. He told us that if this were [75] so, we ought to set about the task. 9. We must punish not only my slave, but also my brother's [15]. 10. He said that virtue should be cultivated by all. 11. He said that we ought to obey Solon, when he had laid down such a law. 12. We ought to persuade those who do wrong, rather than punish them. 13. We must guard against the dangers coming from the enemy. 14. We must go to the help of our city, when it is in danger. 15. Who, that is a good citizen, would not be willing to obey the laws of his city? 16. He [11] who will not obey the laws should go away into another land.

TABLE OF IDIOMS.

1. The beauty of virtue. — The beauty of *the* virtue (§ 5 (2)); (or) The of the virtue beauty (§ 9 (2) *b*).

2. The road leading into the city. — The into the city leading road.

3. *A* slave. — *A certain* slave (δοῦλός τις) (§ 1 2.).
   A Phenician. — *A man* a Phenician.
   Thrice a day. — Thrice *the* day.

4. The dog has a long tail. — The dog has *the* tail long (§ 2).
   He rejoiced that the citizens were rich. — He rejoiced *at rich the citizens.*

5. Beautiful women. — *The* beautiful women (§ 3).
   The rest. — οἱ ἄλλοι.
   Others. — ἄλλοι.
   The multitude. — οἱ πολλοί.
   Many. — πολλοί.
   The whole city. — ἡ πᾶσα πόλις.
   Every city. — πᾶσα πόλις.
   Beautiful things. }
   What is beautiful. } — τὰ καλά.

6. Socrates. — *The* Socrates (§ 4).
   The river Euphrates. — The Euphrates river, (or) The river the Euphrates.

   The city Mende. — The Mende city; (or) The city the Mende.

7. *My* slave. — *The* my slave (§ 6 (1)).
   Your slave, &c. — *The* your slave.

8. Virtue, justice. — *The* virtue, *the* justice (§ 5 (2)).
   Gold, silver. — *The* gold, *the* silver.

9. I have a pain in my head. — I have a pain in *the* head (§ 5).
   He lost his dog. — He lost *the* dog.

10. This city. — This *the* city (ἥδε ἡ πόλις) (§ 6 (2)).
    This great city. — This *the* great city.

11. He who does. — ὁ πράττων (§ 7).
    Those who do. — οἱ πράττοντες.

He who does *not* do.	ὁ μὴ πράττων, &c.
12. Talking.	The *to talk* (*infinitive*).
Doing good to everybody.	The *to-do good* to all (τὸ πάντας εὖ ποιεῖν).
13. Beauty.	*The beautiful* (τὸ καλόν) (§ 8).
Honour.	*The honourable* (τὸ καλόν).
14. The people in the city.	*The in city* (οἱ ἐν ἄστει).
The disciples of Plato.	*The round* Plato (οἱ περὶ Πλάτωνα).
The men of old.	οἱ πάλαι.
The interval (of time).	ὁ μεταξὺ χρόνος.
The facts.	τὰ πεπραγμένα.
	τὰ γενόμενα.
15. The affairs of the city.	*The* (*neut. pl.*) of the city.
What comes from the gods.	τὰ ἐκ θεῶν.
Alexander, the son of Philip.	Alexander *the of Philip* (§ 9).
His dog and his brother's.	The dog of him, and the of the brother.
16. The good man.	The good man ; (or)
	The man the good.
17. Doing this.	The this (these things) to do.
(Such conduct.)	τὰ ταῦτα πράττειν.
Such a person.	ὁ τοιοῦτος.
18. *The* city.	City (§ 10).
The king.	King.
The largest and *the* smallest.	The largest and smallest.
19. The one — the other.	ὁ μὲν — ὁ δέ (§ 11).
Some — others.	οἱ μὲν — οἱ δέ.
But he.	ὁ δέ.
And he.	καὶ ὅς.
20. He came of his own accord.	αὐτὸς ἦλθεν (§ 12).
We are alone.	αὐτοί ἐσμεν.
21. I saw him.	εἶδον αὐτόν.
I saw the man himself.	αὐτὸν εἶδον.
22. The ships and their crews.	αἱ νῆες αὐταῖς τοῖς ἀνδράσιν.
Pericles with nine others.	Περικλῆς δέκατος αὐτός.
23. I did it myself.	αὐτὸς ἐποίησα.
I pricked myself.	ἔνυξα ἐμαυτόν (§ 14).
I pricked *myself*.	αὐτὸν ἐμὲ ἔνυξα.
24. He said that he did it himself.	ἔφη αὐτὸς ποιῆσαι.
He said that another did it, not himself.	ἔφη ἄλλον τινά, καὶ οὐκ αὐτὸς ποιῆσαι.
25. The opposite party.	οἱ ἕτεροι (§ 15).
A different cup.	ἕτερον ποτήριον.
One cup more.	ἄλλο ποτήριον.
No grass, nor yet any tree.	No grass nor *any other* tree.
26. You say right, true, &c.	You say *right, true* (*things*) (δίκαια, ἀληθῆ) (§ 16).

What comes from the gods.	τὰ ἐκ θεῶν.
Fortune.	τὰ τῆς τύχης.
27. To render many services.	πολλὰ ὑπηρετεῖν.
To render many great services.	πολλὰ καὶ μεγάλα ὑπηρετεῖν.
28. Virtue is praiseworthy.	The virtue is a praiseworthy thing (*neut. sing.*).
29. Half the land.	The half (*adj.*) of the land (§ 16 (5)).
Half the time.	The half (*adj.*) of the time (§ 16 (5)).
Most men.	οἱ πολλοὶ τῶν ἀνθρώπων.
Sensible men.	οἱ φρόνιμοι τῶν ἀνθρώπων.
30. Animals run.	The animals runs (τὰ ζῷα τρέχει).
31. So to say.	ὡς εἰπεῖν.
	ὡς ἔπος εἰπεῖν.
32. To be well off.	εὖ πράττειν.
To be in a good state.	εὖ διακεῖσθαι.
33. Do not steal.	μὴ κλέψῃς (*of a single act*).
Do not be a thief.	μὴ κλέπτε (*of a habit*).
34. On his arrival he saw.	Having come he saw (§ 18).
It was kind of you to come.	You did well having come (§ 18).
35. To say that.	φάναι, followed by acc. and inf.
	λέγειν, followed by acc. and inf. or ὅτι (ὡς).
	εἰπεῖν, followed by ὅτι (ὡς).
36. *Modes of expressing a wish* (§ 62 (5)).	
Would I were one of them.	τούτων ἐγὼ εἴην.
O that you might wish it.	ἀλλὰ βουληθείης.
Heaven forbid.	μὴ γένοιτο.
O that I were there.	ἐκεῖ γενοίμην.
Would that you were our friend.	εἴθε σὺ φίλος ἡμῖν γένοιο.
O that I might perish.	πῶς ἂν ὀλοίμην;
Would I had been with you then.	εἴθε σοι τότε συνεγενόμην.
Would that they were able.	εἰ γὰρ ὤφελον οἷοί τε εἶναι.
Would I had never left Scyrus.	μήποτ' ὤφελον λιπεῖν τὴν Σκῖρον.
37. What am I to say?	τί φῶ; (§ 20 (3)).
Shall we stay?	βούλει μένωμεν;
38. *Sequence—Sentences of purpose* (§ 21).	
I am here to see.	πάρειμι ἵνα (ὡς, ὅπως) ἴδω.
I was there to see.	παρῆν ἵνα ἴδοιμι.
39. *Indirect questions* (§ 21).	
Whence am I come, do you ask?	πόθεν ἥκω, ἔρει;
He asked whence he was come.	πόθεν ἥκοι, ἤρετο.
I am at a loss what to say.	τί φῶ, ἀπορῶ.

He was at a loss what to do.   τί δρῴη, ἠπύρει.

He asked if (whether) this was true.   ἤρετο εἰ τοῦτ᾽ ἀληθὲς εἴη.

40. *Conditional Sentences* (§ 22 ff.).

If it thunders, it also lightens.   εἰ βροντεῖ, καὶ ἀστράπτει.

If it thundered, it also lightened.   εἰ ἐβρόντησε, καὶ ἤστραψε.

If we have anything, we will give it.   ἐάν τι ἔχωμεν, δώσομεν.

If we should have anything, we would give it.   εἴ τι ἔχοιμεν, διδοίημεν ἄν.

If he had anything, he would give it.   εἴ τι εἶχον, ἐδίδου ἄν.

If he had had anything, he would have given it.   εἴ τι ἔσχεν, ἔδωκεν ἄν.

He said that if he had anything, he would give it.   ἔφη εἴ τι ἔχοι διδόναι ἄν.

He said that if he had had anything, he would have given it.   ἔφη εἴ τι ἔσχεν δοῦναι ἄν.

41. Every one denied.   No one said.

No one either saw or heard.   οὐδεὶς οὔτ᾽ εἶδεν, οὔτ᾽ ἤκουσεν (§ 26).

He went away that no one might either hear or see.   ἀπῆλθεν ἵνα μηδεὶς μήτε ἴδοι μήτε ἀκούσαι.

No one ever saw him anywhere.   No one *never* saw him *nowhere*.

He who does *not* do.   ὁ μὴ ποιῶν.

What is *not* honourable.   τὰ μὴ καλά.

42. This will not happen.   οὐ μὴ γένηται τοῦτο (§ 28).

Don't talk.   οὐ μὴ λαλήσεις;

43. Vereor *ne* morior.   φοβοῦμαι μὴ θάνω.

Vereor *ut* morior.   φοβοῦμαι μὴ οὐ θάνω.

44. Clever at finding.   Clever *to find*.

I offer myself *to be questioned*.   I offer myself *to question* (act.).

45. Alexander said that he was the son of Zeus.   Ἀλέξανδρος ἔφασκεν εἶναι Διὸς υἱός (§ 31).

They besought him to be zealous.   ἐδέοντο αὐτοῦ εἶναι προθύμου.

It is possible for me to become happy.   ἔξεστί μοι γενέσθαι εὐδαίμονι.

46. Nothing was done because he was not present.   Nothing was done owing to the him not being present (διὰ τὸ μὴ παρεῖναι ἐκεῖνον).

They live with a view to self-interest, because they are lovers of themselves.   They live towards the advantageous, owing to the being self-lovers (διὰ τὸ φίλαυτοι εἶναι).

47. He went off *with*.   Having taken, he went off (λαβὼν ἀπῴχετο).

After doing this, he went away.	ταῦτα πράξας ἀπῴχετο (§ **34**).	

He who did this, went away. | }
The guilty person went away. | } ὁ ταῦτα πράξας, ἀπῴχετο.

48. I am here to help you. — πάρειμι ἐπικουρήσων (§ **35**).
He sends men to do this. — πέμπει ἄνδρας τοῦτο ποιήσοντας.
49. He continues *to do* this. — He continues *doing* this.
He happened *to be* present. — He happened *being* present.
50. I do it unconsciously. }
I do it secretly. } λανθάνω ποιῶν.
I arrived before them. — I was before them in arriving (ἔφθην ἀφικόμενος) (§ **35** (2)).

You cannot do it too soon. — οὐκ ἂν φθάνοις ποιήσας.
Do it, and be quick. — πράττε ἀνύσας τι.
51. I forgot that I had done this. — I forgot having done this (ἐλαθό-μην τοῦτο ποιήσας).

I knew that he was dead. — I knew of him being dead (ᾔδειν αὐτὸν τεθνηκότα).

They announced that he was dead. — They announced him having died (ἤγγειλαν αὐτὸν τεθνηκότα).
52. He was convicted of crime. — He was convicted having done wrong (ἀδικήσας).

He perceived that he had fallen into the ditch. — He perceived having fallen into the ditch (ᾔσθετο εἰς τὴν τάφρον πεσών, sensit medius delapsus in hostes).

53. I am ashamed *while I speak*. — αἰσχύνομαι λέγων (§ **35** (3)).
I am ashamed *to speak*. — αἰσχύνομαι λέγειν.
I obviously do. — φαίνομαι ποιῶν.
I seem to do. — φαίνομαι ποιεῖν.
54. It was clear that he did. — δῆλος ἦν ποιῶν.
— φανερὸς ἦν ποιῶν.
55. This being the case. — τούτων οὕτως ἐχόντων (§ **37**).
Without your orders. — ὑμῶν μὴ κελευσάντων.
When you ought —. — δέον.
When you can —. — ἐξόν.
56. I have a little difficulty. — I am at a loss in a little degree (σμικρόν τι ἀπορῶ).

I make a moderate request of you. — δέομαι μέτρια ὑμῶν.
57. Many great sights. — Many *and* great sights.
58. What impudence! — *The* impudence (*gen.*) (§ **41**).
No Greek. — No one of (the) Greeks.
I gave you some money. — I gave you of money.
My property, unhappy me! — τἀμὰ τοῦ κακοδαίμονος.
59. It is not like an honest man to do such things. — It is not of an honest (man) to do such things.
In favour of the rich. — πρὸς τῶν ἐχόντων.

60. To indict a person for cowardice.   γράφεσθαί τινα δειλίας (§ 43 (4)).

    To be indicted for cowardice.

    To be on one's trial for cowardice. }   To fly of cowardice.

    To charge a person with folly.   κατηγορεῖν μωρίαν τινός.

61. I have not practised for many days.   I have not practised *of* many days (*gen.*).

62. Too great for tears.   μεῖζον ἢ κατὰ δάκρυα (§ 46 (3)).

    Of superhuman size.   μείζων ἢ κατ' ἄνθρωπον.

    Too young to know.   νεώτεροι ἢ ὥστε εἰδέναι.

63. Greater than ever.   Greater *themselves* than themselves (αὐτοὶ ἑαυτῶν) (§ 47).

    More honest than rich.   More honest than *more* rich.

    He has a larger house than mine.   He has a house larger *than me.*

64. As — as possible.   ὡς, ὅσος, with superlative; ὡς τάχιστα, ὅσοι πλεῖστοι.

    More painful than any other.   *Most* painful *if* any other (§ 48).

    You have *remarkably black* hair.   You have *the* hair black, if any other person (has).

    Fairer than any before.   Fairest of all before.

65. We have no ships.   There are not ships to us.

    What have I to do with you?   What (is there) to me and to you?

66. You act strangely in giving us nothing.   You do a strange (thing), who give us nothing (§ 51).

    They pitied the mother for being deprived of such children.   They pitied the mother, of what children she had been deprived.

67. I enjoy the goods I have.   I enjoy of what goods I have (ἀπολαύω ὧν ἔχω ἀγαθῶν).

68. Some say.   ἔστιν οἳ λέγουσι (§ 52).

    Sometimes.   ἔστιν ὅτε.

    Somewhere.   ἔστιν ὅπου.

    Is there any one who?   ἔστιν ὅστις;

69. All who do not say.   ὅσοι μὴ λέγουσι.

    All who deny.   ὅσοι οὐ φασί.

70. I will tell you on condition that you will hold your tongue.   λέξω σοι ἐφ' ᾧ σιγήσει; (or) ἐφ' ᾧ σιγῆσαι (*infinitive*).

71. No one who.   οὐδεὶς ὅστις.

    No one whom.   οὐδένα ὅντινα (§ 53).

    Such a man as you.   οἷος σὺ ἀνήρ.

    Of such a man as you.   οἵου σοῦ ἀνδρός.

    He made astonishing progress.   θαυμαστὸν ὅσον προὐχώρησε.

72. What induced you to do this?   Having suffered what (τί παθών) — Having learnt what (τί μαθών) — did you do this? (§ 55).

73. I wonder that.   I wonder *if* (εἰ).

74. What must they do to recover?   By doing what would they recover?

Who are these strangers whom I behold ?

75. It is well.

How are we off for money ?

76. To be ashamed. }
To be shameful. }
To be blameable.

77. Why do you go on talking nonsense ?
To come *with*.

78. To make much of.

To grieve.
You are deservedly prosperous.

79. It is not agreeable to me. }
I am not pleased with. }

80. We ought to desire virtue.
We must persuade him.
We must obey him.
We ought to set about the work.

What strangers do I behold here ?
(τίνας τοίσδ' ὁρῶ ξένους ;)
It *has* well.
How have we of money ? (πῶς ἔχομεν χρημάτων ;)

To *have* shame (§ 59).

To *have* blame.

τί ληρεῖς ἔχων ;

To come *having*.

To make (ποιεῖσθαι) about much (§ 60).

To make grief (λύπην ποιεῖσθαι).
καλῶς ποιοῦντες εὖ πράττετε.

It is not *to me wishing*.

ἐπιθυμητέον ἐστὶ τῆς ἀρετῆς (§ 63).
πειστέον ἐστὶν αὐτόν.
πειστέον ἐστὶν αὐτῷ.
The work must be set about.

VOCABULARY.

The Numbers refer to the Vocabularies at the commencement of each Exercise.

Abandon, προίεσθαι, 27.
Abide by, ἐμμέ·ειν, *with dat.*, 54.
Able, to be, οἷός τε εἶναι, 17.
About (= *Lat. de*), περί, *with gen.*, 10, 39.
Absent, to be, ἀπεῖναι, 20.
Accept, παραλαμβάνειν, 21.
Accomplish, ἐκτελέσαι, 58.
Accomplishing, without, ἄπρακτος, 50.
Accord with, to be in, to be in harmony with, συμφωνεῖν, *with dat.*, 54.
Accuse, κατηγορεῖν, 46.
Accused, defendant, ὁ ἀπολογούμενος (= the answerer), 47.
Accuser, κατήγορος, 18, 47.
Accustom, ἐθίζειν (*aug.* εἴθιζον, εἴθισμαι. *For the pass.* = to be accustomed, εἴωθα *is often used*), 14.
Ache, κάμνειν, 44.
Acquit, ἀφιέναι, 20.
Acropolis, ἀκρόπολις, ἡ, 47.
Adeimantus, 'Αδείμαντος, 49.
Admirable, θαυμαστός, 10.
Admire, θαυμάζειν, 11, ἄγασθαι, 49.
Advance, ἐπιέναι, 27, 66.
Advanced in years (age), to be, πόρρω τῆς ἡλικίας εἶναι, 45.
Advantage for, to be a great, πολλῷ προσέχειν πρός, *with acc.*, 34.
Advantage to, it will be our, ἄμεινον ἔσται ἡμῖν, *with particip.*, 38.
Advantageous, λυσιτελής, ὁ, συμφέρων, 9.
Advice, to give, συμβουλεύειν, *with dat.*, 33.

Advise, παραινεῖν, 51.
Æschines, Αἰσχίνης, 7.
Affairs, πράγματα, τά, 4.
Affliction, πάθος, τό, 49.
After, μετά, *with acc.*, 10.
Against, ἐπί, *with acc.*, 10.
Age, in, κατὰ ἡλικίαν, 58.
Age, of (my), ἧλικος (ἐμοί), 58.
Agree with, ὁμολογεῖν, 55, ὁμολογεῖσθαι, 43.
Agreeable to you, if it is, εἴ σοι βουλομένῳ ἐστί, 67.
Agreed, it is, δοκεῖ, 29.
Alcibiades, 'Αλκιβιάδης, 5.
Alike (*adv.*), ὁμοίως, 44.
All, πᾶς, 4.
All of you, ὑμεῖς πάντες, 18.
Allot, προστάττειν, 54.
Allow with impunity, stand by and see, περιορᾶν, 39, 62.
Ally, σύμμαχος, ὁ, 25.
Alone among, μόνος, *with gen.*, 53.
Already, ἤδη, 43.
Also, καί, 2.
Always, ἀεί, 4.
Ambassador, πρεσβευτής, πρέσβυς (*for pl.* πρέσβεις *is used*), 12.
Ambition, φιλοτιμία, ἡ, 47.
Ambitious, φιλότιμος, 35.
Amusement, παιδιά, ἡ, 27.
Ancient, παλαιός, 45.
And that too, καὶ ταῦτα, 67.
Andocides, 'Ανδοκίδης, 19.
Animal, ζῷον, τό, 47.
Announce, bring news, ἀπαγγέλλειν, 21.
Answer, ἀποκρίνεσθαι, 18, 55.

Anticipate, φθάνειν, 39.
Anything = everything, πᾶν, 18.
Aphobus, 'Άφοβος, 21.
Aphrodite, 'Αφροδίτη, 10.
Arbitration, δίαιτα, ἡ, 43.
Archon, to be, ἄρχειν, 50.
Argument, λόγος, ὁ, 30.
Arguments, false, οἱ λόγοι οἱ ἐψευσ-μένοι (for their, my false arguments, *add* ὑπ' ἐκείνων, ὑπ' ἐμοῦ, &c., *with the part.*), 41.
Arm, βραχίων, ὁ, 66.
Arms, ὅπλα, τά, 51.
Army, στράτευμα, τό, 10, 30, στρα-τός, ὁ, 55.
Arrange, equip, furnish, κατασκευά-ζειν, 23.
Art, τέχνη, ἡ, 2.
As — as possible, *use the super. adj.* with ὡς, e. g. as good as possible, ὡς βέλτιστος, 30.
As good as, ἀντί, *with gen.*, 6.
Ascend, ἀναβαίνειν, 9.
Ashamed, to be, αἰσχύνεσθαι, 33, 39.
Ask, ἔρεσθαι, ἐρωτᾶν, 15, 21.
Assinarus, 'Ασσίναρος, 5.
Assistance of, run to the, assist in the defence of, βοηθεῖν, 68.
Associate with, συγγίγνεσθαι, 53, ὁμιλεῖν, *with dat.*, 54, συνεῖναι, *with dat.*, 64.
At all, τὸ παράπαν, 48.
At home, οἴκοι, ἔνδον, I.
At once, αὐτίκα, 62.
At the hands of, ὑπό, *with gen.*, 55.
Athenian, 'Αθηναῖος, 5.
Athens, to, 'Αθήναζε, 53.
Attack, ἐπικεῖσθαι, 27, ἐπιτίθεσθαι, 57, προσβάλλειν, 31, ἐπιέναι, ἐπελθεῖν, 35.
Attempt, πειρᾶσθαι, 55.
Attica, ἡ 'Αττική, 16.
Autocratic, αὐτοκράτωρ, 34.
Avoid, φεύγειν, 9.

Babylon, Βαβυλών, ἡ, 5.
Bad, κακός, 4.
Badly off, to be, κακῶς πράττειν, 9.
Banishment, φυγή (flight), ἡ, 48.
Barbarian, βάρβαρος, 42.
Base, αἰσχρός, 46.
Basely, κακῶς, 36.

Battle, μάχη, ἡ, 5, 43.
Be, εἶναι, γίγνεσθαι, 13.
Be so, οὕτως ἔχειν, 22.
Bear, φέρειν, 16.
Bear in mind, μεμνῆσθαι, 7.
Beat, παίειν, τύπτειν, 13.
Beat off, ἀμύνεσθαι, 35.
Beautiful, καλός, I.
Bee, μέλισσα, ἡ, 42.
Beggar, to be a, πτωχεύειν, 33.
Beginning of, to be the, ἄρχειν, 35.
Belong to, be becoming to, or for, προσήκειν, *with dat.*, 29.
Beloved, φίλος, 9.
Benefit, ὠφέλεια, ἡ, 7.
Benefit, do a service, ὠφελεῖν, *with acc.*, 22.
Benefit, for his own, ἑαυτοῦ ἕνεκα, 38.
Besides, χωρίς, 50.
Besiege, πολιορκεῖν, 5.
Best, ἄριστος, 8.
Better, κρεῖττον, 19.
Better (more sweetly, pleasantly), ἥδιον, 51.
Better than, to think oneself (= to despise), καταφρονεῖν, 9.
Beyond all expectation, κρεῖττον ἐλπίδος, 52.
Beyond all expression, κρεῖττον λόγου, 52.
Bird, ὄρνεον, τό, 43.
Black, μέλας, 7.
Blame, μέμφεσθαι, 46, 57.
Blamed, to be, αἰτίαν ἔχειν (*add* πολλήν, πλείστην, for much, very much), 64.
Blessings (goods), ἀγαθά, τά, 23.
Boat, πλοῖον, τό, 48.
Body-guard, δορυφόροι, 64.
Born, to be, πεφυκέναι, 33.
Bowman, τοξότης, ὁ, 15.
Brasidas, Βρασίδας, 9.
Brave, ἀγαθός, 9, ἀνδρεῖος, 29, 51.
Bravery, ἀνδρεία, ἡ, 49.
Breadth, εὖρος, τό, 46.
Bring, ἄγειν, I.
Bring bad news, νεώτερόν τι ἀγγέλ-λειν, 60.
Bring down, κατάγειν, 3.
Bring in (apply), προσφέρειν, 30.
Brother, ἀδελφός, 15.
Brown, ξουθός, 3.

Build, οἰκοδομεῖν, 52.
Building, οἴκημα, τό, 21.
Burn, κατακαίειν, 21, καίειν, 33.
Burst into, εἰσπίπτειν εἰς, 55.
But, ἀλλά, 7.
Buy up, συνωνεῖσθαι, 17.
By, ὑπό, *with gen. (of agent)*, 10.

Calamity, συμφορά, ἡ, 39.
Call, καλεῖν, 40.
Camp, στρατόπεδον, τό, 1.
Capable of (doing), πρακτικός, 50.
Captive (prisoner), αἰχμάλωτος, 20.
Capture (seize), καταλαμβάνειν, 21, 54.
Cease, παύεσθαι, 39.
Charge, to lay to a man's = to accuse of, κατηγορεῖν, *with gen.*, 48.
Child, τέκνον, τό, 42, παιδίον, τό, 49.
Choose, αἱρεῖσθαι, 12, καταλέγειν, 46.
Circumstances, in such, τούτων οὕτως ἐχόντων, 62.
Citizen, πολίτης, ὁ, 2, 8.
City, state, πόλις, ἡ, 4.
Clearly, σαφῶς, 25.
Cling to, ἀντέχειν, *with gen.*, 6, ἔχεσθαι, *with gen.*, 47.
Clothe, ἀμφιεννύναι, 42.
Clothing, clothes, ἐσθής, ἡ, ἱμάτια, τά, 12.
Cold, to be, ῥιγοῦν, 43.
Collect, ἀθροίζειν, 53.
Come, ἰέναι (*for aor. use ἐλθεῖν*), 2.
Come, arrive, ἀφικνεῖσθαι, 46.
Come, has (= is present), πάρεστι, 7.
Come in (of money), προσιέναι, 23.
Come into, εἰσιέναι, 14.
Come, to have, ἥκειν, 44.
Coming from, πρός, *with gen.*, 66.
Command, give a command, ἐπιστέλλειν τινί τι (*the pass. = to receive commands*), 43.
Compassion, to have, συγγνώμην ἔχειν, *with dat.*, 33.
Compel, ἀναγκάζειν, 38.
Competent, ἱκανός, 33.
Compulsion, ὑπ' ἀνάγκης, 61.
Conceal, κρύπτειν, 42.
Concerned, as far as they are, τὸ ἐπὶ τούτοις εἶναι, 67.

Condemn, καταγιγνώσκειν, 48.
Condemned in, to be, ὑφλισκάνειν, *with acc.* of the penalty, 48.
Condition, to be in good, bad, εὖ, κακῶς ἔχειν, 44.
Confer benefits on, εὖ ποιεῖν, *with acc.*, 14.
Confess, ὁμολογεῖν, 19.
Confident, θαρραλέος, 52.
Confirm, βεβαιοῦν, 41.
Conjecture, ἐπεικάζειν, 35.
Conquer, overthrow, νικᾶν, 3.
Conquered, to be, ἡττᾶσθαι, 18.
Conscious of, I am, σύνοιδ' ἐμαυτῷ, *with particip.*, 38.
Consider, οἴεσθαι, 11, νομίζειν, 18, φράζεσθαι, φροντίζειν, 30, λογίζεσθαι, 33.
Consideration, ἀξίωμα, τό, 45.
Constitution, form of, πολιτεία, 58, 67.
Content, to be, ἀγαπᾶν, 62.
Contented with, to be, love, ἀγαπᾶν, *with acc.*, 14.
Continue, διατελεῖν, 39.
Continue to exist, to exist still, ἔτι εἶναι, 62.
Contrary, ἐναντίος, 43.
Contrary to, παρά, *with acc.*, 47.
Contribute money, εἰσφέρειν χρήματα, 25.
Converse with, διαλέγεσθαι, *with dat.*, 21.
Convey, κομίζεσθαι, 66.
Convict, ἐξελέγχειν, 38.
Corinthian, Κορίνθιος, 11.
Corn, σῖτος, ὁ, 17.
Corn-seller, σιτοπώλης, ὁ, 17.
Country, χώρα, ἡ, 13.
Country (as opposed to the town), ἀγρός, ὁ, 6.
Country, one's, ἡ πατρίς, 31.
Court, αὐλή, ἡ, 40.
Cow, βοῦς, ἡ, 1.
Cowardice, δειλία, ἡ, 47.
Cowardly, δειλός, 30.
Crew, ἄνδρες, οἱ, 12.
Criticise, find fault with, ἐπιτιμᾶν, *with dat.*, 34.
Crocodile, κροκόδειλος, ὁ, 3.
Cross, διαβαίνειν, 30.
Crown, στέφανος, ὁ, 42, 62.
Crown, στεφανοῦν, 62.

Cut, τέμνειν, 33.
Cyrus, Κῦρος, 5.

Damage, κακοῦν, 59, κακῶς ποιεῖν, 65.
Dance away, ἀπορχεῖσθαι, 42.
Danger, to be in, κινδυνεύειν, 28.
Dangerous, σφαλερός, 29.
Daughter, θυγάτηρ, 11.
Day, towards, πρὸς ἡμέραν, 19.
Day, what time of? πηνίκα τῆς ἡμέρας; 46.
Daybreak, at, ἅμ' ἔῳ, 56.
Dead (corpse), νεκρός, ὁ, 51.
Death, θάνατος, ὁ, 17, 33.
Death, to be put to (=to die), ἀποθνήσκειν, 10.
Debt, χρέος, τό, 65.
Deceive, ἐξαπατᾶν, 11, ἀπατᾶν, 51.
Declare = to say, φάναι, λέγειν, 18.
Deed, πρᾶγμα, τό, 7.
Defeat, conquer, νικᾶν, 18.
Defend, ἀμύνειν, *with dat.*, 5.
Delay, μέλλειν, 13.
Deliberate, βουλεύεσθαι, 20, 21, 62.
Delight, ἡδονή, ἡ, 9.
Delight in doing, χαίρειν ποιῶν, 38.
Delighted at, to be, ἥδεσθαι ἐπί, *with dat.*, 3.
Demand, πράττεσθαι (*lit.* to get for oneself), 19.
Democracy, δημοκρατία (during the democracy = when the democracy was, δημοκρατίας οὔσης, *gen. absol.*), 19.
Demosthenes, Δημοσθένης, 5.
Denies, every one, οὐδείς φησι, 17.
Deny, ἀπαρνεῖσθαι, 31.
Depart, ἀποίχεσθαι, 9.
Deposed, to be, ἐκπίπτειν τῆς ἀρχῆς (*lit.* to fall out of the government), 37.
Depositions (evidence), μαρτυρία, ἡ, 20.
Deprive, στερεῖν, *ful. in passive sense*, στερήσεσθαι, 23, 47.
Deprived of, ἄτιμος (*lit.* without honour in), 50.
Desert, abandon, προδιδόναι, 46.
Deserter, αὐτόμολος, 42.
Desire (wish), βούλεσθαι, 33.
Desire, ἐπιθυμία, ἡ, 51.
Desire, ἐπιθυμεῖν, *with gen.*, 8, ἐρᾶν,

with gen. (*lit.* to love), 33, ὀρέγεσθαι, ἐφίεσθαι, 47.
Desolation, ἐρημία, ἡ, 65.
Despise, καταφρονεῖν, *with gen.*, 9, 38, 47.
Destitute of, ἔρημος, *with gen.*, 49.
Detect, ἐξελέγχειν, 28.
Determine, γνῶναι, 33.
Die, ἀποθνήσκειν, 8.
Different thing from, to be a, διαφέρειν, *with gen*, 66.
Dilatoriness, τὸ μέλλον, 46.
Disease, νόσημα, τό, 57.
Disease, to be afflicted with, νόσον νοσεῖν, 43.
Disgraceful, αἰσχρός, 9.
Dishonourable in one's office, to be, οὐ καλῶς ἄρχειν, 17.
Disobedient, to be, ἀπιστεῖν, 28.
Disposition, τρόπος, ὁ, 49.
Distant from, to be, ἀπέχειν, διέχειν, 44.
Distressed at, to be, ἄχθεσθαι ἐπί, *with dat.*, 3.
Divide, διανέμειν, 54.
Do, ποιεῖν, 13.
Do in return, ἀντιδρᾶν, 66.
Do something with, χρῆσθαί τι, *with dat.*, 21.
Do — to, ἐργάζεσθαι, *with double acc.*, 38.
Dog, κύων, ὁ, 11.
Door, θύρα, ἡ, 19.
Dorian (woman), Δωρίς, 11.
Doubt, to have a, to admit of a, ἀπιστίαν ἔχειν, *with nom. of person or thing*, 64.
Drachma (a coin), δραχμή, ἡ, 48.
Drag out, ἐξέλκειν, 49.
Drink, πίνν. *v.* 56.
Duties, ἔργα, τά, 54.

Each party, ἑκάτεροι, 62.
Eager, πρόθυμος, 51.
Eagle, ἀετός, ὁ, 3.
Earth, γῆ, ἡ, 12.
Education, παιδεία, 64.
Either — or, ἤ — ἤ; *in questions* was it either — or? πότερον — ἤ; 19.
Elatea, Ἐλάτεια, 21.
Enact, θεῖναι, 56.

134

Enact laws, θεῖναι, θέσθαι νόμους, 66.
Encamp, αὐλίζεσθαι, 27.
Enemy, hostile, ἐχθρός, 11.
Enemy, πολέμιος, 3.
Enemy, the affairs of the, τὰ ἐκ τῶν πολεμίων, 42.
Engaged in serious business, to be, σπουδαῖόν τι πράττειν, 27.
Enjoy, ἀπολαύειν, 56.
Enough, to be, to suffice, ἀρκεῖν, 53.
Enough, τὰ ἀρκοῦντα, 53.
Enter secretly (say: to escape the notice when entering), 61.
Entreat, beseech, ἱκετεύειν, 19.
Entreat, δεῖσθαι, 33.
Entrust to, ἐπιτρέπειν, πιστεύειν τινί (pers.) τι, 43.
Envy, φθονεῖν, 49.
Epidamnus, Ἐπίδαμνος, 10.
Equal, ὅμοιος, 35.
Escape (run away), ἀποδρᾶν, 20.
Escape, ἐκφυγεῖν, 8.
Escape notice, λανθάνειν, 39.
Especially, μάλιστα, 46.
Estate, χωρίον, τό, 19.
Euthycles, Εὐθυκλῆς, 12.
Evening, δειλή, ἡ, 50.
Evening, in the, ἑσπέριος, 2.
Ever, ἀεί, 9.
Every one, πᾶς, 8.
Everywhere, πανταχοῦ, 54.
Examine, ἐξετάζεσθαι, 63.
Exceedingly, use sup. of adj., e. g. exceedingly beautiful, κάλλιστος, 3.
Excel, προέχειν, 35.
Excessive pity, favour, to show, κατελεεῖν, with acc., καταχαρίζεσθαι, with dat., 19.
Exchange, ἀλλάττειν, 49.
Exile, to share, συμφεύγειν, 43.
Expedition, to go on an, στρατεύειν, στρατεύεσθαι, 16, στρατείαν ἐξελθεῖν, 51.
Experience, persons of, οἱ ἔμπειροι, 54.
Experienced in, ἔμπειρος, with gen., 50.
Extraordinary, θαυμαστὸς ὅσος, 58.
Eye, ὀφθαλμός, ὁ, 3.

Fact that, the, use τό with the infin., e. g. τὸ ἐλθεῖν αὐτόν, the fact that

he came, the fact of his coming, 34.
Faction, στάσις, ἡ, 57.
Facts, the, τὰ γενόμενα, 37.
Fall, πίπτειν, 12.
False, ψευδής, 7.
Famous, ἀξιόλογος, 53.
Fast, as fast as their feet could carry them, ὡς τάχιστα ποδῶν εἶχον, 64.
Fasten—to, δεῖν — ἐκ (lit. to bind from), 19.
Fear, δεῖσαι, of rational apprehension, 37.
Fear, φοβεῖσθαι, 7, 20.
Feather, πτερόν, τό, 3.
Few, ὀλίγοι, 2.
Fifth, πέμπτος, 12.
Fight, μάχεσθαι, 5.
Figure, σχῆμα, τό, 45.
Fill, πιμπλάναι, 49.
Find, εὑρίσκειν, 25.
Find refuge, καταφυγὴν ποιεῖσθαι, 65.
Finished, to be, πεπρᾶχθαι, 40.
Fire, to set fire to, ἐμπιπράναι, 21.
First, πρῶτος, 6.
Five, πέντε, 12.
Five hundred, πεντακόσιοι, 52.
Flatter, θωπεύειν, 42.
Fleeting (short), βραχύς, 2.
Flight, φυγή, ἡ, 65.
Flight, to put to, ἀποτρέπειν, 57.
Fly for refuge, καταφεύγειν, 11.
Follow, ἕπεσθαι, with dat., 54.
Folly, μωρία, ἡ, 46.
Food, σῖτος, ὁ, 12, σιτία, τά, 50.
Foolish, μωρός, 29, ἀνόητος, 34, μάταιος, 47.
Foolish, to be, κακῶς φρονεῖν, 34.
Foolishness, ἀβουλία, ἡ, 45.
Foot, πούς, ὁ, 49.
Force, στρατιά, ἡ, 9.
Forefathers, πρόγονοι, 16.
Foresee, προορᾶν, 41.
Forget, ἐπιλανθάνεσθαι, with gen., 47.
Forgetful, ἐπιλήσμων, 50.
Fortify, τειχίζειν, 34.
Foundation, κρηπίς, ἡ, 46.
Four, τέσσαρες, 54.
Freedom, ἐλευθερία, ἡ, 6, 30.
Freedom of speech, παρρησία, ἡ, 53.
Friend, φίλος, 3.

Friendly to, εὔνους, *with dat.*, 54.
From, ἀπό, *with gen.*, 10, παρά, *with gen.*, 37, 45.
Full, πλήρης, 4, ἐμπλεής, μεστός, 49.
Furnish (find), provide, παρέχειν. 17.
Future, τὸ μέλλον, 41.

Gain, benefit, ὠφέλεια, ἡ, 7.
Gape about, κοικύλλειν, 64.
Gate, πύλη, ἡ, 57.
General, στρατηγός, ὁ, 3.
General, to be, στρατηγεῖν, 5.
Give, διδόναι, 11.
Give a share, μεταδιδόναι, 56.
Give orders, προαγορεύειν, 41.
Give up, παραδιδόναι, 21, 33.
Gladly, ἡδέως, 58.
Glory, δόξα, ἡ, 49.
Go away, ἀπιέναι (*for aor. use* ἀπελθεῖν), 2.
Go off with, οἴχεσθαι λαβών, 64.
Go out from, ἐξέρχεσθαι ἐκ, 30.
God, θεός, ὁ, 12, 20.
Gold, χρυσός, ὁ, 6.
Gold (of money), χρυσίον, τό, 14.
Golden, χρύσεος, 3, 45.
Good, ἀγαθός, 2. As good as, ἀντί, *with gen.*, 6.
Goods of others, τὰ ἀλλότρια, 56.
Goodwill, from, ἐπ’ εὐνοίᾳ, 17.
Govern, ἄρχειν, 4.
Government, ἀρχή, ἡ, 43.
Greater, larger, taller, μείζων, 51.
Greek, Ἕλλην, 41.
Grieve, λύπην ποιεῖσθαι, 65.
Grow old, γηράσκειν, 66.
Guard, φύλαξ, ὁ, 27, 66.
Guard, φυλάττειν, 33
Guards, to set, φύλακας καθιστάναι, 27.
Guide, ἡγεμών, ὁ, 57.
Guilty, αἴτιος, 38.
Guilty of a breach of the law, to be, παρανομεῖν τι, 17.
Guilty of, to be found, ἁλίσκεσθαι, *with gen.*, 22.
Gulf, κόλπος, ὁ, 10.
Gylippus, Γύλιππος, 5.

Hair, θρίξ, ἡ, 53.

Handle, ῥόπτρον, τό, 19.
Happen to be, τυγχάνειν ὤν, 1.
Happen to know, τυγχάνειν εἰδώς, 23.
Happily, εὐδαιμόνως, 25.
Happy, to think, εὐδαιμονίζειν, 49.
Hard, difficult, χαλεπός, 58.
Hare, λαγώς, ὁ, 56.
Harm, βλάβη, ἡ, 8, συμφορά, ἡ, 38.
Harm to, to do, κακοῦργος εἶναι, *with gen.*, 50.
Haste, σπουδή, ἡ. 44.
Hate, μισεῖν, 34.
Have, ἔχειν, 1.
Have one’s head broken, συντρίβεσθαι τῆς κεφαλῆς, 6.
Head, κεφαλή, ἡ, 3, 44.
Hear, ἀκούειν, 11.
Heaven’s name, in, πρὸς θεῶν, 57.
Heavy, βαρύς, 6.
Hellas, Ἑλλάς, ἡ, 40.
Help, ἀρκεῖν, *fut.* ἀρκέσειν, 27. ἐπικουρεῖν, *with dat.*, 38, ὠφελεῖν, 68.
Help, to come to, βοηθεῖν, 40.
Helper, σύνεργος, 21, βοηθός, 56.
Here, ἐνθάδε, 9.
Here, I am, πάρειμι, 38.
Hill, ἄκρα, ἡ, 57.
Hollow, κοῖλος, 49.
Home, at, οἴκοι, ἔνδον, 1.
Honeycomb, κηρίον, τό, 46.
Honour, τιμάν, 4.
Honour, τιμή, ἡ, 4.
Honourable = beautiful, καλός, 1.
Hope, ἐλπίζειν, 36
Hope, ἐλπίς, ἡ, 36.
Hoplite = heavy-armed soldier, ὁπλίτης, ὁ, 55.
Horse, ἵππος, ὁ, 1.
Horseman, ἱππεύς, ὁ, 55.
Hostile, ἐχθρός, 54.
House, οἰκία, ἡ, 1.
Housekeeper, οἰκονόμος, ὁ, ἡ, 33.
How? πῶς; (*indirect question*), ὅπως, 20.
How, ὡς, 2.
How many? πόσοι; ὁπόσοι, ὅσοι, 20.
Human affairs, τὰ ἀνθρώπινα, 29.
Hungry, to be, πεινῆν, *with irreg. contr. into* -ῆν *for* -ᾶν, 43.
Hunt after, θηρᾶν, *with acc.*, 46.

Hurt, injure, βλάπτειν, *with acc.*, 22.

Husband, ἀνήρ, 42.

If, εἰ, 21.

Imitate, ἀπομιμεῖσθαι, 15, μιμεῖσθαι, *with acc.*, 45.

Immediately, εὐθύς, 10, 59.

Impious, ἀνόσιος, 44.

Impossible, ἀδύνατος, 19, 58.

Impossible things, ἀμήχανα, 46.

In, ἐν, *with dat.*, 1, 6.

In, to be, ἐνεῖναι, *with dat.*, 54.

Incentive, ἀφορμή, ἡ, 34.

Inclined to, I am, βουλομένῳ ἐμοί ἐστιν (e. g. τοῦτο ποιεῖν, to do this), 55.

Income, πρόσοδος, ἡ, 46.

Indict, γράφεσθαι, 42.

Induced; what has induced you? τί μαθών, μαθόντες; *or* τί παθών, παθόντες; 41.

Indulge (in an amusement), χρῆσθαι, *with dat.*, 27.

Inexperienced in, ἄπειρος, *with gen.*, 50.

Infantry, ὁ πεζός, 58.

Inflict, suffer injury, ποιεῖν, πάσχειν κακῶς, 23.

Inhabit, οἰκεῖν, *with acc.*, 23, 36.

Injuries to, to do many grievous, πολλὰ καὶ μεγάλα ἀδικεῖν τινα, 43.

Injustice, ἀδικία, ἡ, 45, 48.

Inland-country, μεσογεία, 54.

Innumerable, ἄπειρος, 44.

Inquire, ἐρωτᾶν, 10.

Insult, ὑβρίζειν, *with acc.*, ὑβρίζειν εἰς, 60.

Intend, be about to do, μέλλειν, *with infin.*, 7, 36.

Interest, τόκος, ὁ, 65.

Interest, to be for a person's, εἶναι πρός τινος, 60.

Into, εἰς, *with acc.*, 1.

Introduce, bring forward, εἰσάγειν. 49.

Invade, εἰσβάλλειν, 7.

Invasion, εἰσβολή, ἡ, 10.

Ionian, Ἰόνιος, 10.

Iron, σίδηρος, ὁ, 6.

Irremediable, ἀνήκεστον, 31.

Island, νῆσος, ἡ, 5.

Join (as an ally), προστίθεσθαι, 26.

Journey, ὁδός, ἡ, 44.

Judge, δικάζειν, 27, γνῶναι, 33.

Judge, κριτής, ὁ, 48.

Judges, *say:* the judging (*particip. and article*), 27.

Judgment, γνώμη, ἡ, 44.

Just, δίκαιος, 2, 4.

Justice, δικαιοσύνη, 6, 57, τὸ δίκαιον, 27, 47.

Justly, δικαίως, 25.

Keep (a peace), ἄγειν, 30.

Key, κλείς, κλῇς, ἡ, 57.

Kill, ἀποκτείνειν, 19.

King, βασιλεύς, ὁ, 3.

Know, εἰδέναι, 15, ἐπίστασθαι, 28.

Labour, πόνος, ὁ, 47.

Labour with, συμπονεῖν, *with dat.*, 31.

Lacedæmonian, Λακεδαιμόνιος, 7.

Land, γῆ, ἡ, 7.

Land, by, κατὰ γῆν, 50.

Large, μέγας, πολύς, 3, 9.

Last, τελευταῖος, 43.

Lasting, βέβαιος, 29.

Late, ὀψέ, 46.

Late in the day, till, μέχρι πόρρω τῆς ἡμέρας, 45.

Laugh at, καταγελᾶν, *with gen.*, 63.

Law, νόμος, ὁ, 20.

Law, according to, κατὰ νόμον, 17.

Lay waste, τέμνειν (*lit.* to cut), 13.

Lead, μόλυβδος, ὁ, 6.

Lead past (of a road), φέρειν παρά, *with acc.*, 10.

Learn many lessons, διδάσκεσθαι πολλά, 61.

Leave, καταλείπειν, 33.

Leg, σκέλος, τό, 44.

Leisure, to be at, σχολὴν ἔχειν, 59.

Let be, leave alone, ἐᾶν, 28.

Let go, ἀφίεσθαι, 19.

Letter, ἐπιστολή, ἡ, 12.

Liberty, to set at, i e. to ransom, λύεσθαι, 20.

Life, ψυχή, ἡ, 42.

Like to, I should —, ἡδέως ἄν, *with opt. of the verb*, 24.

Lily, κρίνον, τό, 45.

Listen to, ἀκούειν, κλύειν (*poet.*), ἀκροᾶσθαι, 47.

Live a life, βιοῦν βίον, 43.
Live, pass time, διαιτᾶσθαι, 49.
Live, pass life, διατελεῖν, 16, ζῆν, 25.
Living, not worth, ἀβίωτος, 43.
Long, μακρός, 2.
Long for, ἐπιθυμεῖν, *with gen.*, 34.
Loose, λύειν, 11.
Lord, κύριος, ὁ, 34.
Lord of, to be, ἀνάσσειν, *with gen.* (*poet.*), 47.
Lose, ἀπολλύναι (*perdere*), 34.
Lose one's labour, πονεῖν μάτην, 60.
Loss, ζημία, ἡ, 7.
Loss, to be at a, ἀπορεῖν, 20.
Lovers of self, φίλαυτοι, 35.
Loyalty, εὔνοια, ἡ, 64.
Loyalty to, εὔνοια πρός, *with acc.*, 64.
Luck, a piece of good, εὐτύχημα, τό, 43.
Lucky, to be, to have good luck, εὐτυχεῖν, 43.
Lurk about, κυπτάζειν περί, *with acc.*, 64.
Lydian, Λυδός, 1.

Mad, to be, μαίνεσθαι, 57.
Make (king), καθιστάναι, 42.
Make a good use of, εὖ χρῆσθαι, *with dat.*, 8.
Make mention of, μιμνήσκεσθαι, *with gen.*, 19.
Make money, κερδαίνειν, 17.
Make of no account, παρ' οὐδὲν ποιεῖσθαι, 65.
Man, ἀνήρ, ἄνθρωπος, ὁ, 1.
Manage, πράττειν, 4.
Manage (a house), οἰκεῖν, *with acc.*, 33.
Manage the affairs of the city, τὰ τῆς πόλεως (πράγματα) πράττειν, 8.
Manage well (of a form of political constitution), καλῶς πολιτεύειν, 35.
Many, πολύς. *pl.* πολλοί, αἱ, ά, 1.
Marathon, Μαραθών, ῶνος, 43.
March (of a general), ἐλαύνειν, 16. (of an army), πορεύεσθαι, 10.
March against, στρατεύεσθαι ἐπί, *with acc.*, 5, ἐπιστρατεύειν, 46.
March into, στρατεύεσθαι εἰς, *with acc.*, 7.

Market-place, ἀγορά, ἡ, 26.
Master, δεσπότης, ὁ, 61.
Master of, to be, ἄρχειν, *with gen.*, 23, κρατεῖν, *with gen*, 47.
Matter, πρᾶγμα, τό, 15.
May, you may go away, *say:* it is possible for you, &c., ἔξεστί σοι, 26.
Meadow, λειμών, ὁ, 11.
Mean, λέγειν, 15.
Means, οὐσία, ἡ, 61.
Meanwhile, ἐν τούτῳ, 9.
Meet, ἀπαντᾶν, *with dat.*, 37.
Meet with, τυγχάνειν, *τὸ τά gen.*, 37, συντυγχάνειν, 54.
Memory, μνήμη, ἡ, 2.
Mention, to make, of, μιμνήσκεσθαι, *with gen.*, 19.
Merchant, ἔμπορος, ὁ, 49.
Mercy, ἔλεος, τό, 37.
Messenger, ἄγγελος, ὁ, 24, 39.
Middle, μέσος, 44.
Mile, reckon eight stades for a mile, e.g. 10 miles = 80 stades, 44.
Milk, γάλα, τό, 49.
Mina, μνᾶ, ἡ, 22.
Mind, διάνοια, ἡ, 44, φρένες, αἱ, 48.
Mines, μέταλλα, τά, 23.
Mischief to, to do great, μέγα κακὸν ποιεῖν, *with acc.*, 39.
Miserable, ἄθλιος, 42.
Misery, δυσπραξία, ἡ, 49.
Misfortune, δυστυχία, ἡ, 19, συμφορά, ἡ, 20.
Misfortunes, τὰ κακά, 28.
Mistake, to acknowledge a, μεταγιγνώσκειν, 17.
Moment, for the, εἰς τὸ παραυτίκα, 41.
Money, χρήματα, τά, 11, 18, ἀργύριον, τό (κέρδος, τό, *in such phrases as* love of money, &c.), 57.
Money, a large sum of, χρήματα πάμπολλα, 23.
Money, to contribute, εἰσφέρειν χρήματα, 25.
Money, to get, χρήματα λαβεῖν, 24.
Money, to make, κερδαίνειν, 17.
Month, μήν, ὁ, 50.
More than, περιττός, 53.
More than the occasion requires, πλεῖον τοῦ καιροῦ, 52.
Mortal, θνητός, 39, βροτός, 42.

Mother, μήτηρ, 11.
Mount, ἀναβαίνειν, 1.
Mountainous, ὀρεινός, 10.
Multitude, πλῆθος, τό, 15.
Murder, φόνος, ὁ, 22.
Murderer, φονεύς, ὁ, 48.

Nation, ἔθνος, τό, 16, 57.
Naturally, to be, πεφυκέναι, e.g.
to be naturally bad, πεφυκέναι
κακός, 57.
Near, ἐγγύς, *with gen.*, near the
city, ἐγγὺς τῆς πόλεως, 59.
Necessaries, τὰ ἐπιτήδεια, 17.
Necessary, it is, ἀνάγκη ἐστί, 19,
68.
Necessary, to make, ἀναγκάζειν, 26.
Necessity, ἀνάγκη, 36.
Need, to have need of, δεῖσθαι,
with gen., 21.
Neglect, ἀμελεῖν, 56.
Neglect, ἀμέλεια, ἡ, 34.
Neglectful of, to be, ἀμελῶς ἔχειν,
with gen., 64.
Neighbour, ὁ πέλας, ὁ πλησίος, 54.
Neighbours, οἱ πέλας, 9.
Neither (of two), οὐδέτερος, 15.
Neither — nor, οὔτε — οὔτε, 7.
Never, οὔποτε, 15.
Nicias, Νικίας, 5.
Night, the next, ἡ ἐπιοῦσα νύξ, 19.
Nightfall, about, ὑπὸ νύκτα, 61.
Nightingale, ἀηδών, ἡ, 3.
No one, οὐδείς, 13.
No other person, οὐδεὶς ἄλλος, 14.
None of the citizens, οὐδεὶς τῶν
πολιτῶν, 18.
Not, οὐ, *with indic.*; μή, *with im-
perat.*, 12 ; *with the infin.*, μή, 19.
Not only — but also, οὐχ ὅτι — ἀλλὰ
καί, 22.
Not — yet, οὐ — πω, 44.
Not to know a thing, ἀγνοεῖν τι, 25.
Nothing, οὐδέν, 11.
Nothing like hearing, οὐδὲν οἷον
ἀκοῦσαι, 58.
Now, νῦν, 12.
Now (*conj.*), δέ (*this word is used
in Greek to connect sentences where
in English no connecting word is
required*), 5.
Number, multitude, πλῆθος, τό, 44.

Numbers, in great (= many), πολύς,
πολλοί, 2.

Oath, to exact an, ὅρκον ὁρκοῦν (*lit.*
to cause a person to swear an
oath), 43.
Obedient-to-law, νόμιμος, 4.
Obey, πείθεσθαι, *with dat.*, 20.
Object to, I, οὐ βουλομένῳ ἐμοί ἐστιν,
55.
Obtain, διαπράττεσθαι, 27, φέρεσθαι
(*lit.* to carry off for oneself),
41.
Obvious, clear, φανερός, 38.
Of = about, περί, *with gen.*, 19.
Offensive, δυσχερής, 18.
Offer, παρέχειν, 33.
Old, of, πάλαι, 9.
Old, to be — old, εἶναι — γεγονώς
(*lit.* to be — born), 44.
Old, old man, γέρων, ὁ, 4.
Old age, γῆρας, τό, 54.
Olive-tree (enclosed in a fence),
σηκός, ὁ, 19.
On, ἐν, 19.
On, ἐπί, *with gen.*, 9.
On the third day, τριταῖος, 2.
Once, at, αὐτίκα, 40.
One, εἷς, 12.
Open, ἀνοιγνύναι, 19.
Opinion, to give an, γνώμην εἰπεῖν,
37.
Opinion, in my, — ought, δοκεῖ μοι,
followed by acc. and infin. (*lit.* it
seems good to me that), 17.
Or, ἤ, 6.
Orator, ῥήτωρ, ὁ, 17.
Order, κελεύειν, 14.
Order, κόσμος, ὁ, 55.
Order — not, to forbid, ἀπαγορεύειν,
28.
Orders, to give, προστάττειν, *with
dat.*, 18, προαγορεύειν, 41.
Other, ἄλλος, § 14.
Ought, δεῖ, *impers.* (e.g. τί δεῖ ποιεῖν
(sc. ἐμέ); what must I, ought I to
do ?), 15.
Ought, you ought to hear, προσήκει
ὑμῖν ἀκοῦσαι, 19.
Ought to set about, we, ἡμῖν ἐπι-
χειρητέον ἐστί (*with dat. of the
thing*), 59.

Out of, outside, ἔξω, *with gen.*, 59.
Owe, ὀφείλειν, 54.

Pactolus, Πακτωλός, 3.
Pain, to have a, ἀλγεῖν, 44.
Painful, ἀλγεινός, 28.
Parent, γονεύς, ὁ, 20.
Parents, οἱ τεκόντες, 42.
Pass over, ἐᾶν, 19.
Pasture, νέμεσθαι, 1.
Pay (give), ἀποδιδόναι, *with dat. of pers.*, 21.
Peace, εἰρήνη, ἡ, 30.
Pelasgians, Πελασγοί, 40.
Peloponnesian, Πελοποννήσιος, 10.
Pelt, βάλλειν, 13.
Peltast, πελταστής, ὁ, 15.
Penalty, to fix the penalty at, τιμᾶσθαι, *with gen.*, 48.
Perceive, αἰσθάνεσθαι, 39.
Perhaps, ἴσως, 17.
Perish, ἀπόλλυσθαι, 2.
Permitted to me, it is, ἔξεστί μοι, 18.
Persian, Πέρσης, ὁ, 10.
Persuade, πείθειν, *or better, aorist,* πεῖσαι, 34.
Philip, Φίλιππος, 7.
Phliasians, Φλιάσιοι, 33.
Piece of good luck, εὐτύχημα, 52.
Pity, αἰδώς, ἡ, 37.
Pity, ἐλεεῖν, 23, οἰκτίζειν, 30, οἰκτείρειν, 37.
Plant, φυτεύειν, 16.
Platæan, Πλαταιεύς, 18.
Play, παίζειν, 40.
Please, ἀρέσκειν (i. e. to satisfy), *with dat.*, 24.
Pleasure, ἡδονή, ἡ, 60.
Pledge, ὑποτιθέναι, 49.
Plethron (100 feet), πλέθρον, 46.
Plot against, ἐπιβουλεύειν, *with dat.*, 20, 58.
Plough, ἀροῦν, 16.
Plunder, διαρπάζειν, 45.
Poet, ποιητής, ὁ, 10.
Polished, ξεστός, 46.
Pool, λίμνη, ἡ, 12.
Poor, πτωχός, 3, 42.
Poor, the, οἱ ἀπόρως διακείμενοι, 17.
Portion (give a dowry to), ἐκδιδόναι, 20.

Possess, κεκτῆσθαι (*perf. of* κτᾶσθαι), 52.
Possession, κτῆμα, τό, 8.
Power, in my, ἐπ' ἐμοί, 16.
Power, to be in a person's, ἐπί τινι εἶναι, 41.
Power, to have in my, ὑπάρχειν ἐμοί (ὑπάρχειν *is used impersonally*), 23.
Power, with full, autocratic, αὐτοκράτωρ, 34.
Powerful, δυνατός, 52.
Practise, ἀσκεῖν, 53, 68.
Praise, ἐπαινεῖν, 23, 58.
Praiseworthy, ἐπαίνετος, 16.
Prefer, βούλεσθαι μᾶλλον, 35.
Preference to, in, ἀντί, *with gen.*, 35.
Prepared (ready), ἕτοιμος, 33.
Present (gift), δώρημα, τό, 49.
Present, for the, at any rate, τό γε νῦν εἶναι, 67.
Present oneself, be present, παρεῖναι, 1.
Present, to be, παρεῖναι, 20.
Pretext, πρόφασις, ἡ, 58.
Prevent, ἀπείργειν, κωλύειν (κωλύειν *as a rule is* not *followed by* μή), 8, 31.
Previously, πρότερον, 56.
Prison, δεσμωτήριον, τό, 27.
Prized by, to be highly, τίμιος εἶναι, *with dat.*, 35.
Proclamation of death, to publish, κηρύττειν θάνατον, 27.
Produce, παρέχεσθαι, 19.
Promise, ὑπισχνεῖσθαι, 47, 55.
Prone to fall, οὐκ ἀσφαλής (*lit.* not secure), 2.
Properly, ὡς δεῖ, 23.
Property (= means), οὐσία, ἡ, 52.
Prosperity (= to prosper), τὸ εὖ πράττειν, 8.
Prosperous, to be, εὐτυχεῖν, 3.
Prove, ἐπιδεικνύναι, 25.
Proved to be, to be, ἐπιδειχθῆναι ὤν, 23.
Provide with, παρασκευάζειν, 61.
Prudent, φρόνιμος, 48.
Prytany (public officer at Athens), πρυτανεύς, 21.
Punish, ζημιοῦν, 17, 26, κολάζειν, 49.

Punished for, to be = to pay the penalty for, δίκην διδόναι, *with gen.*, 60.

Punishment, ζημία, ή, 29, τιμωρία, ή, 37.

Punishment, to suffer, δίκην διδόναι, 35.

Purchasable, to be purchased, ὠνητός, 49.

Purchase, ὠνεῖσθαι ; *for the aor. use* πρίασθαι, 49.

Pursue, διώκειν, 4.

Put before them, προβάλλεσθαι, 66.

Put down to, τιθέναι, *with gen.* (e. g. τιθέναι μωρίας, to put down to folly), 34.

Put in rapid execution, to execute rapidly, τὸ ταχὺ πράττειν, 34.

Put on (of clothes), ἐνδύειν, 42.

Quick (swift), ταχύς, 2.

Quickly, as quickly as possible, ὡς τάχος, 66.

Rack, put on the rack, στρεβλοῦν, 41.

Rain, ὔμβρος, ὁ, 7.

Ransom, λύεσθαι, 20.

Rather — than, ἥδιον — ἤ, 25.

Ravage, lay waste, δῃοῦν, 16, 55, τέμνειν, 13, 62.

Receive, δέχεσθαι, 15, λαμβάνειν, 18.

Receive from, 1, γίγνεταί ἐμοὶ ἀπό, 54.

Recently, ἄρτι, 62.

Recess, μυχός, ὁ, 12.

Reduce, κατατρέπειν (ὑπό, *with dat.*), 64.

Refrain from, ἀπέχεσθαι, *with gen.*, 40.

Refuge with, to take, καταφεύγειν ἐπί, *with acc.*, 38.

Refuse, οὐκ ἐθέλειν (to be not willing), 5.

Regard with wonder, θαῦμα ποιεῖσθαι, *with acc.*, 65.

Reign, βασιλεύειν, 40.

Reign of Cyrus, in the, ἐπὶ Κύρου βασιλεύοντος, 40.

Release, ἀπαλλαγή, 60.

Relieve from (set free from), ἀπαλλάττειν, *with gen.*, 47.

Remain, μένειν, 60.

Remain behind, to be left behind, ὑπολείπεσθαι, 55.

Remainder, i. e. those who were left behind, οἱ λειπόμενοι, 55.

Remember, μεμνῆσθαι, *with gen.*, 47.

Remind, ἀναμιμνήσκειν, 42.

Render services = to serve, ὑπηρετεῖν, *with dat.*, 16.

Repent, μεταμέλειν (*impers.*, μεταμέλει μοι, I repent), 29, 38.

Report, to make a, ἀπαγγέλλειν (N.B. to make a false report = ψευδῆ ἀπαγγέλλειν), 7.

Reproach, κατάμεμψις, ή, 64.

Reproach, ὀνειδίζειν, *with acc. of thing, dat. of person*, 11, 20.

Request, to make a just, δίκαια δεῖσθαι, 43.

Rescue, to go to the, βοηθεῖν πρός, 64.

Restrain by punishment, punish, chastise, κολάζειν, 68.

Retire, ἀποχωρεῖν, 3, ὑποχωρεῖν, ἀναχωρεῖν (*the first in sense of* making room for one), 27.

Retreat, ἀναχωρεῖν, 5.

Return, κατιέναι, 12.

Return, to do in, ἀντιδρᾶν, 66.

Revolt from, ἀποστῆναι ἀπό, 10, 58.

Rich, πλούσιος, 4, 51.

Rich, the, οἱ ἔχοντες, 17.

Riches, πλοῦτος, ὁ, 6.

Rid of, to be, ἀπηλλάχθαι, *with gen.* (*the perf. denotes a state*), 41.

Ride, ἐλαύνειν, 11.

Ride away, ἀπελαύνειν, 1.

Right, it is, it is a duty, προσήκει, 33.

Right, more than is, καιροῦ πέρα, 42.

Right, what is, τὰ δίκαια, 36.

Right hand, on the, ἐκ δεξιᾶς, 10.

River, ποταμός, ὁ, 5, 44.

Road, ὁδός, ή, 10.

Rob, ἀποστερεῖν, *with double acc.*, 45.

Robe, ἱμάτιον, τό, 50.

Rule over, ἄρχειν, *with gen.* (*also* to begin), 15, 47.

Ruler, ἄρχων, ὁ, 34.

Run, δρόμος, ὁ, 55.

Run, θεῖν, ἀποδιδράσκειν, 42, 64.

Run away, ἀποφεύγειν, 64.
Run down, κατατρέχειν, 9.
Rustic, ἀγροῖκος, ὁ, 9.

Said, he, ἔφη, he said that, ἔφη *with infin.*. 14.
Sail, πλεῖν, 46.
Sail away, ἐκπλεῖν, 17.
Sail-into, εἰσπλεῖν, 10.
Sake of, for the, χάριν, ἕνεκα, *with gen.*, 42.
Sand, ψάμμος, ἡ, 3.
Save, σώζειν, 36.
Save, keep safe, preserve, διασώζειν, 30.
Say, φάναι, 7, λέγειν, 15.
Scythian, Σκύθης, 10.
Sea, θάλαττα, ἡ, 23, 50.
See, ὁρᾶν, 7.
Seek, ζητεῖν, 9.
Seems good, δοκεῖ, 28.
Seize hold of, λαμβάνεσθαι, *with gen.*, 47.
Send, πέμπειν, 6, 12.
Send for, μεταπέμπεσθαι, 1.
Senses, to lose one's, ἄφρων γενέσθαι, 46.
Sensible, φρόνιμος, 45.
Sensible, to be, σωφρονεῖν, 51.
Servant, παῖς, ὁ, 1, οἰκέτης, ὁ, 29.
Serve, ὑπηρετεῖν, *with dat.*, 14.
Service, λατρεία, ἡ, 49.
Set about, to take in hand, ἐπιχειρεῖν, 68.
Set free, ἐλευθεροῦν, 47.
Set out, πορεύεσθαι (to a person, ὡς, *with acc.*), 37.
Set sail, ἐκπλεῖν, 29.
Seven hundred, ἑπτακόσιοι, 50.
Shameful, to be, αἰσχύνην ἔχειν, 64.
Shameless, ἀναίσχυντος, 46.
Sheep, ὕïς, ἡ, 11.
Shepherd, ποιμήν, ὁ, 30.
Shield, ἀσπίς, ἡ, 66.
Ship, ναῦς, ἡ, 11.
Shouting, κραυγή, ἡ, 55.
Show (prove), ἀποδεικνύναι, 17.
Show (display), ἐπιδεικνύναι, 19.
Show (or prove) false, ψευδῆ καθιστάναι, 14.
Shrine, τὸ ἱερόν, 19.

Shuffle, εἰς τριβὰς ἐλαύνειν, 13.
Shun, φεύγειν, 68.
Sicily, Σικελία, 5.
Side, I have on my, ὑπάρχει μοι, 54.
Silent, to be, σιγᾶν, 20, 40.
Silver, ἄργυρος, ὁ, 6.
Sing, ἐπᾴδειν, 43, ἀείδειν, 51.
Sister, ἀδελφή, 20.
Situated, to be (in a certain condition), καθεστάναι, 33.
Six hundred, ἑξακόσιοι, 44.
Slain, to be (to perish), ἀπόλλυσθαι, 3.
Slave, οἰκέτης, ὁ, παῖς, ὁ, ἡ, δοῦλος, ὁ, 7.
Slave, to be a, δουλεύειν, 33.
Slaves, ἀνδράποδα, τά, 66.
Slavish, ἀνδραποδώδης, 25.
Sleep, καθεύδειν, 45.
Slight, βραχύς, 58.
Slowly, βραδέως, 53.
Small, μικρός, 3, ὀλίγος, 10.
Snow, χιών, ἡ, 7.
So long as, ἕως, *with indic.*, 23.
Society, συνουσία, ἡ, 63.
Soldier, στρατιώτης, 3.
Some time since, πάλαι, 62.
Sources of gain, κέρδη, τά, 40.
Spare, φείδεσθαι, 47.
Sparta, Σπάρτη, 12.
Speak, εἰπεῖν, 11.
Speak at length, διεξιέναι, 56.
Speak well of, εὖ λέγειν, *with acc.*, 39.
Speed, at full, κατὰ κράτος, 11.
Spend, ἀναλίσκειν, 40.
Spend in horse-breeding, καθιπποτροφεῖν, 42.
Spirit, φρόνημα, τό, 52.
Stade, στάδιον, *pl.* -ιοι, -α, 44.
Standing, ἑστώς, 12.
State (city), πόλις, ἡ, 14.
Statue, ἀνδριάς, ὁ, 3, εἰκών, ἡ, 40.
Stay, i. e. to pass time, διατρίβειν, 26.
Step down, παραβαίνειν, 37.
Step into, εἰσβαίνειν εἰς, 12.
Stone, λίθος, ὁ, 6.
Straight to, εὐθύ, *with gen.*, 50.
Strange, θαυμαστός, 56.
Stranger, ξένος, 49.
Street, ὁδός, ἡ, 6.

Strength, ἰσχύς, ἡ, 25.
Strip, ἐκδύειν, 42.
Strong, ἰσχυρός, 29.
Subjects, ὑπήκοοι, 66.
Subjugate to (put in the power of), ποιεῖν ὑπό, *with dat.*, 59.
Subtlety, λεπτότης, ἡ, 48.
Succeed, success, τὸ εὖ πράττειν, 34.
Suffer, πάσχειν, 15.
Suffer hardships, κακὰ πάσχειν, 55.
Suffer pain, be in pain, λύπην λυπεῖσθαι, 43.
Suffer punishment, δίκην διδόναι, 35.
Sum of money, ἀργύριον, τό, 19.
Summer, θέρος, τό, 50.
Summon, παρακαλεῖν, 29.
Superintend, overlook, ἐπισκοπεῖν, 67.
Superior to, to be, περιγίγνεσθαι, *with gen.*, 47, 53.
Support, τρέφειν, 44.
Surpass, differ from, διαφέρειν, *with gen.*, 47.
Surpass themselves (= to be better than themselves), 52.
Swan, κύκνος, ὁ, 7.
Sweet, ἡδύς, 3.
Syracuse, Συράκουσαι (*nom. plur.*), 5.

Take, αἱρεῖν, 12.
Take = bring, ἄγειν, 27.
Take away, ἀφαιρεῖσθαι, 19.
Take down, καθαιρεῖν, 12.
Take measures, προθυμεῖσθαι (*lit.* to be anxious or zealous), ἐπιμελεῖσθαι (*lit.* to take care, be careful), παρασκευάζειν (*lit.* to make preparations), πράττειν, 30.
Take place, γίγνεσθαι, 6.
Take the initiative, φθάνοντες, *with verb*, 59.
Taken, to be, ἀλῶναι (ἁλίσκεσθαι), 11.
Talent, τάλαντον, τό, 15.
Tall, μέγας, 42.
Tantalus, Τάνταλος, 12.
Tasted, to have never, ἄγευστος εἶναι, *with gen.*, 35.
Taught, to have, διδάσκεσθαι, 66.
Teacher, διδάσκαλος, ὁ, 10.

Tear, δάκρυ, τό, 51.
Tell, announce, ἀγγέλλειν, 12.
Temperance, σωφροσύνη, ἡ, 53.
Temple, ναός, ὁ, 11.
Ten, δέκα, 15.
Ten times, δεκάκις, 25.
Tenth, δέκατος, 12.
Theatre, θέατρον, τό, 41.
Theban, Θηβαῖος, 7, 21.
Then, τότε, 8.
Theramenes, Θηραμένης, 12.
Think (regard as), φρονεῖν, 8, νομίζειν, 14, ἡγεῖσθαι, 19.
Third, τρίτος, 44. On the third day, τριταῖος, 2.
Thirty, τριάκοντα (in the rule of the thirty (tyrants), ἐπὶ τῶν τριάκοντα), 19.
Thousand, χίλιοι, 15, χίλιος, 48.
Thrace, the parts about, τὰ ἐπὶ Θράκης (*lit.* in the direction of Thrace), 9.
Thrasylus, Θρασύλος, 46.
Three, τρεῖς, τρία, 37.
Three hundred, τριακόσιοι, 18.
Thrice, τρίς, 45.
Through, διά, *with gen.*, 44.
Time, χρόνος, ὁ, 2.
Time, at that = then, τότε, 43.
Time, in my, ἐπ' ἐμοῦ, 16.
To, εἰς, *with acc.*, 6, παρά, *with acc.*, 27, ὡς, *with acc.* (*of persons only*), 59; = after, μετά, *with acc.*, 12.
Together with, ἅμα, ὁμοῦ, *with dat.*, 59.
Toil, μόχθος, ὁ, 49.
Torture, βάσανος, ἡ, 41.
Traitor, προδότης, ὁ, 49.
Transgress, παραβαίνειν, 8.
Transgress the law, παρανομεῖν, 19.
Treated, to be ill-, well-, κακῶς, εὖ πάσχειν, 17, 65.
Treaty, συνθῆκαι, αἱ, 54.
Tree, δένδρον, τό, 7.
Trench, τάφρος, ἡ, 9.
Trierarch, τριήραρχος, ὁ, 46.
Trireme, τριήρης, ἡ, 12.
Troubled with, to be, πράγματα ἔχειν ὑπό, *with gen.*, 24.
Truce, to break a, σπονδὰς λύειν, 38.
Truly, πάνυ, 10.

Trust to, πιστεύειν, 51.
Truth, ἀλήθεια, ἡ, 6, 37.
Truth (true things), τἀληθῆ, 20.
Truth, to tell the, τῇ ἀληθείᾳ χρῆσθαι, τὰ ἀληθῆ λέγειν, 41.
Tumult, θόρυβος, ὁ, 4.
Tunic, χιτών, ὁ, 42.
Twenty-five, πέντε καὶ εἴκοσι, or εἴκοσι πέντε, 52.
Twice, δίς, 12.
Two hundred, διακόσιοι, 55.
Two thousand, δισχίλιοι, 55.
Tyrant, to be a, τυραννεύειν, 37.

Undergo (endure, suffer), ὑπομένειν, 33.
Understand, ἐπίστασθαι, 63.
Understanding, on an understanding that, ἐπὶ τῷ, *with inf.*, 25.
Undertake, ἐπιχειρεῖν, 41.
Undeservedly, παρὰ τὴν ἀξίαν, 34.
Unfortunate, to be, δυστυχεῖν, 3.
Unjustly, ἀδίκως, 11.
Unless, εἰ μή, 28.
Unprepared, ἀπαράσκευος, 29.
Unveil, ἐκκαλύπτειν, 40.
Up to this point, till, μέχρι τούτου ἕως, 59.
Use of, to make, χρῆσθαι, *with dat.*, 29; a good use of, εὖ χρῆσθαι, 8.

Valour, ἀρ, τή, ἡ, 19.
Valuable, τιμήεις, 6.
Venture, τολμᾶν, 24.
Very (person), αὐτός, 13.
Vessel, ἀγγεῖον, τό, 49.
Vexed, to be, ἀγανακτεῖν, 62.
Vice, κακία, ἡ, 6.
Victory, νίκη, ἡ, 9.
Victory (= to conquer), τὸ νικᾶν, 8.
Village, κώμη, ἡ, 1, 50.
Violent, βίαιος, 18.
Violet, ἴον, τό, 45.
Virtue, ἀρετή, ἡ, 6.
Voice, φωνή, ἡ, 3.
Vote, ψηφίζεσθαι, 29.

Wall, τεῖχος, τό, 9.
Wander across, διέρχεσθαι, 42.
Want, δεῖσθαι, 27.

Warlike scheme, plans, τὰ τοῦ πολέμου, 34.
Water, ὕδωρ, τό, 49.
Way, manner, τρόπος, ὁ, 55.
Weapons, arms, ὅπλα, τά, 61.
Wear, *use pass. of* ἀμφιεννύναι, 50.
Weep for, κατακλαίειν, *with acc.*, 58.
Well, εὖ, 8.
Well for, to be, καλῶς ἔχειν (*impers.*), *with dat. of person*, 24.
Well off, to be, εὐπορεῖν, *with gen.*, 49.
What? τί δή; 91.
What we ought, τὰ δέοντα, 67.
When, ἐπειδή, 19, ὅτε, 21.
Whenever, ὁπόταν, ὁπότε, 26.
Whether — or, εἴτε — εἴτε, 21.
Who, which, ὅς, ἥ, ὅ, 1.
Why? τί; 13.
Wicked, κακός, 3.
Wide, εὐρύς, 53.
Willing, to be, ἐθέλειν, 17, 33.
Win, νικᾶν, 9.
Wine, οἶνος, ὁ, 45.
Wing, πτέρυξ, υγος. ἡ, 3.
Winter, χειμών, ὁ, 50.
Wisdom, σοφία, ἡ, 6.
Wisdom, to go far in, πόρρω ἐλαύνειν τῆς σοφίας, 46.
Wise, σοφός, 4.
Wise, to be, σωφρονεῖν, 26, 51.
Wish, ἐθέλειν, 14.
With, μετά, *with gen.*, 10.
Withhold from, ἀπέχεσθαι, *with gen.*, 57.
Without (the consent of), ἄνευ, 50.
Witness, μάρτυς, ὁ, 19.
Wits' end, to be at one's, εἰς πολλὴν ἀπορίαν καθεστηκέναι, 25.
Wolf, λύκος, ὁ, 13.
Wonder at, θαυμάζειν, *with acc.*, 42.
Wont to, to be, to love to, φιλεῖν, 44.
Wood, ξύλον, τό, 6.
Work, task, production, ἔργον, τό, 68.
Worse, χείρων, 34.
Worth while, ἄξιον, 33.
Worthily of, in a manner worthy of, ἀξίως, *with gen.*, 50.
Worthy of, ἄξιος, *with gen.*, 4, 49.
Would that, εἴθ', εἴθ' ὤφελον, ἐς, ἐ, &c., 67.

Would simply say that = would say so much (τοσοῦτον) that, 23.
Wound, τραυματίζειν, 61.
Write out, ἀναγράφειν, 57.
Wrong, to do (to make a mistake, to err), ἐξαμαρτάνειν, 13.
Wrong, to do, πλημμελεῖν (*lit.* to strike a false note), 26.
Wrong, to do, to, ἀδικεῖν, *with acc.*, 21.

Xenoclides, Ξενοκλείδης, 12.

Year, ἔτος, τό, 45.
Year, every, year by year, ἀνὰ πᾶν ἔτος, 56.
Years old, *use gen. of* ἔτος, e. g. τριῶν ἐτῶν εἶναι, to be three years old, 46.
Youth, young man, νεανίσκος, 19.

INDEX.